ROUGH AROUND THE SOUL

Maria Monroe

Visit www.graffitifiction.com for more information about Maria Monroe's books.

Edited by Erica Scott
Cover design © by Sarah Hansen, Okay Creations

ALSO BY MARIA MONROE

The Rescue
Julian & Lia
Love (Literally)
Afterglow

CHAPTER ONE – JAKE

This town? It's a fucking armpit. You wake up in the morning and step outside, expecting a lungful of fresh early air. Instead it smells like a swamp. "God farted and the whole place stinks," is what my uncle says. I wouldn't put it that way, but I've only been here a few weeks and already can't wait to leave. Hell, I would have left already if I wasn't here doing a favor for him. And maybe I'm not quite ready to go back home to Chicago yet.

I lock the door of my lease-by-the-month apartment and shove my hands into the pockets of my jeans, heading to one of the town's two bars. It's farther from the mostly boarded-up main stretch, but the guys at the station said they've occasionally seen women there. I'm in the mood for some company.

It's practically pitch black out, but the moon provides enough light as I walk the mile or so to the battered building. Technically it's called Lucky's, but apparently the "k" in the illuminated sign has been burnt out for so many years that people started referring to it as "Lucy's." The sign is like a tacky orange beacon, and though the place is falling apart, it's bright inside. And there's beer.

The bartender, a grizzled guy in his fifties, nods at me.

"What's on tap?" I ask.

"Bud. Bud Light."

"Anything else?"

"What? Like craft beer? Shit's for pussies." He coughs vigorously for a few seconds.

"Budweiser, then."

A couple of slightly flat beers later, I'm listening to Grizzly's thoughts on politics and thinking my coworkers were fucking with me, because there's not a single girl in sight. A few locals lean against a beat-up pool table in the corner, watching some game on the TV. Some other suckers like me drink at the bar, and a group of young twenty-something guys with construction gear laugh loudly around a table.

And then I see her. It's like a magic trick; she unfurls herself from the back corner where she was hidden, appearing as if out of thin air. And I can't take my eyes off her.

Her legs are long and thin, and over her skin-tight jeans are a pair of knee-high black leather boots. The white sweater she's wearing clings to her chest, which is absolutely perfect. I mean, if you could design a pair of flawless breasts, that's exactly the fuck how they'd look. The sweater is low cut, the swell of her tits visible, her skin creamy and pale. Long black hair frames her face, and her lips are painted dark red.

She's wearing too much makeup, but she's so gorgeous I don't even care. And I no longer know what Grizzly's saying, because all thought has left my mind except one thing: I'm going to fuck this girl tonight. I'm going to take her home and strip off those tight jeans and sweater, and make love to her for hours.

She tosses a few bills on the table, then walks right the fuck past me on her way to the door, without even a glance in my direction, the sultry and dark smell of perfume hovering in her wake.

"Closing out my tab," I say to Grizzly, putting a twenty on the rough and worn bar top and sliding off my stool. I follow the girl over the dingy wood floor and out the door.

Her head's bent, one hand cupping a cigarette she's trying to light in the wind. Her lighter clicks over and over again.

"Let me help." I stride toward her.

She looks up at me, holding my gaze for a few moments before shrugging and handing me the lighter. With both of our hands as a shield, her cigarette catches immediately, the tip glowing orange as she inhales.

"Thanks." She turns her head to exhale as I hand back the lighter, which she shoves in her pocket. I can't help noticing her nipples, underneath that fucking white sweater, are hard.

"Cigarettes will kill you," I say.

"Oh really? I hadn't heard." She raises an eyebrow at me as she inhales again. She's so pretty I feel breathless. Though it's dark out, I can see how expressive her eyes are, harboring what looks like a hint of sadness, which she's trying hard to hide with her tough girl act.

I watch the smoke she breathes out float and dissipate into the chill air. She turns her body away from me so she's facing the abandoned quarry across the road.

She's hot, but I don't like to work too hard, and I don't like to play games. And that vulnerability showing through the crack in her veneer makes me want to run.

"Have a good night." I head away from Lucy's, toward my almost empty apartment.

"Wait." Her voice has a slight rasp to it, like she's getting a cold, but I think it's just her natural sound. And it's really goddamn sexy.

I turn back.

"I don't want to be alone." She flicks her cigarette into the darkness, and when it hits the pavement it bounces, sparks shooting and then disappearing.

"You should go home."

"I said I don't want to be alone." She takes a step closer, the heat in her eyes burning so hot it almost eclipses the sadness I saw before.

"So you want to use me to keep your loneliness at bay?" I joke. I think I'd let her use me for anything she wanted.

She shakes her head. "I misspoke." She walks steadily till she's standing right in front of me, looking up into my eyes.

"What did you mean to say?" She smells like that perfume mixed with cigarettes, and I bend my head down slightly. Not close enough to kiss her, but enough to feel her breath when she speaks.

"It's not *just* that I don't want to be alone." She scratches her cheek and grinds the gravel beneath her feet with the tip of her black boot.

"No?" I bend closer.

Her fingers find my bicep, then run down my arm to my hand, which she grasps, pulling herself nearer to my body. "No. I meant to say I want to be with you tonight."

"What's your name?" I whisper against her lips.

She hesitates for a moment too long before answering. "Aria."

"Is that your real name, Aria?"

She shrugs. "No questions, OK? No strings. That all right with you?"

She reaches up, pulling my neck so she can kiss me. It's light at first, and I taste the smoke on her breath and her sticky fruity lip gloss—I can't remember the last time I've kissed a woman who wore fruity stuff on her mouth—and then her tongue finds mine and I don't care about anything else. I almost always listen to my instincts, but the small voice inside my head saying this is a mistake can go to hell right now.

"That's fine with me, Aria," I growl. "I'm Jake, by the way."

"Whatever," she says. "Take me home with you."

I'm surprised she can keep up with my pace along the dark streets, and I can't get my key into the lock fucking fast enough. Before we're even halfway up the stairs, we have to stop to kiss, our tongues battling one another, our breath coming short and fast. When I kiss her neck and bite it gently she moans. And I can't wait any longer.

She drops her purse right inside the front door, and I grab her hand and pull her into the bedroom. But then she pushes me away.

4

"Stop," she whispers, putting up one dainty hand.

I stand still and watch. In an instant, she pulls her sweater up and over her head, and I'm not surprised to see her bare breasts, no bra, her nipples hard and pink and small. I shift slightly, my cock already hard, as she sits on the bed and unzips one tall leather boot, slipping it off and tossing it aside. She does the same with the other, and I take a step closer.

But she shakes her head.

She stands again, this time her hands finding the zipper of her jeans, and she stares at me as she pulls the zipper down and starts to push the denim down her hips. She wiggles her body to get the tight jeans off, and I bite back a groan. *Fuck.*

Her jeans are on the floor, and she's stepping out of them, and all she's got on are these fucking lacy black panties.

"Your turn," she says in that sultry voice.

I don't waste a second. I've never undressed this fast, my T-shirt and jeans on the floor in an instant, so I'm just in my underwear.

She smiles, then walks up to me, grabbing the elastic of my underwear and pulling me right up against her. Her hand so close to my cock makes me moan, and this time I don't hold it back.

"You're so fucking gorgeous," I whisper into her ear. "You're the most beautiful thing in this entire town."

She laughs. "That's not saying much. But you are too. Gorgeous, I mean." I'm surprised by how shy she sounds. Her hand runs over my chest and abs. "I can tell you work out a lot."

We kiss, her mouth pliant and eager, and I reach behind her, cupping one of her ass cheeks in my hand. *Jesus.* Her body is slim and luscious, soft and eager, and I don't remember ever being this fucking turned on before.

Her hand rubs my cock through my boxer-briefs, and I slip my fingers inside the front of her panties, feeling her already wet pussy.

"God, Aria," I moan as we stumble toward the bed, our hands eager. Saying her fake-name gives me a twinge of doubt. But if she doesn't want me to know her real identity, what does it matter? No strings, like she said. All I care about right now is sinking deep inside her soft, wet body.

• • •

That was the best fucking sex of my entire life. It's not the first time I've said it, but this time it's true. I sit up and switch on the lamp next to the bed.

"You a fucking cop?" Aria sits up too, pulling the comforter around her and staring at my badge on the nightstand. She shakes her head, a bemused smile on her face.

"Yeah. What do you do?" I stretch my neck, rolling my head back, my body more relaxed than it's been in a long time.

She bends over the side of the bed and picks up her sweater. "No strings, right?"

"Right. I'm going to go clean up." I head to the bathroom to throw away the condom. I wipe off with a damp towel and splash cold water on my face. I probably smell like stale beer, so I brush my teeth too, then head back to the bedroom, surprised by how eager I am.

She's gone. Clothes. Purse from by the front door. Everything.

Fuck.

I peer out the window, and even open the door to look around the black night, but she's disappeared. Feeling foolish, I go back inside and get a beer from the fridge.

No strings. I'm cool with that. But for some reason I think I'm going to have a hard time getting "Aria" out of my mind.

CHAPTER TWO – MELANIE

The Drug Ed class meets in a decrepit classroom in the lower level of the public library. The lights are too bright and institutional, like someone thought lightening up the room would make it more cheerful. All it does, though, is give a spotlight to the many flaws: the cracked linoleum floor, the dusty blinds on the windows, the green blackboard covered with faint writing that somebody didn't quite erase all the way.

I pull out my phone to surf the internet before class starts, but there's no reception down here in the library basement, so I stuff it into my backpack and look around me instead, careful not to make eye contact with anybody. I'm not interested in making friends.

It's not really called Drug Ed. It's called Life Choices, or something like that. It's part of a program run by the local police department to get first-time underage offenders off drugs through mentoring and education instead of punishment.

I'm here because the principal of Columbus High, where I go, pulled some strings when a Marlboro box filled with joints was found in my locker during an all-locker search a few weeks ago. "Melanie, you can't throw your future away like this," she said. "You're a good student. You're lucky you're still seventeen so you can get into the program."

I stared at her eyes, which were sympathetic, so I wouldn't have to look at her frown. I wanted to tell her I was disappointed in myself enough for everyone. But instead I looked away.

My eighteenth birthday was literally the day after the drugs were found, but I was still underage when I was caught, so at least I won't get a police record. I'm relieved, of course, because I don't want anything to mess up my chance to get far away from Bells Park. But I'm angry too, and worried, and lately I feel like I'm trying to climb out of a deep hole in my mind, but I keep sliding back down again and again.

I bite my nail idly and check out the other people. There's a blonde in the front row, dressed in a skirt and blazer—what kind of high school student wears a fucking blazer? Her hair is brushed shiny, and I wonder what she's here for. Weed's too pedestrian for someone like her. Must be pills or heroin, which I've heard is a problem in some of the richer suburbs around here. And she's definitely not from this podunk town.

Some guy sits a few desks to my right, his ripped-jeans–clad legs stretched out in front of him. He's wearing ragged flannel, and his hair is long and slightly greasy. He catches my eye and smiles, his teeth yellow and crooked, and I look away quickly.

Nope. Not interested. First, he's gross. And second, the only thing I want is to get through this class—and the next five—as quickly as possible and be done with this. It's stupid because the joints weren't even mine, but whatever. I've known for a while now that life's not fair, and fighting that only makes things worse.

The clock on the wall above the dirty blackboard says it's 7:05. Just because we start late, I hope it doesn't mean we'll end late too.

Suddenly the door opens, and the librarian, a sour-looking man in his fifties in a thread-worn brown suit comes in, frowning. "Apparently," he says, "the officer teaching your class had to *cancel*." He does air quotes when he says *cancel*, but what he means by that I'm not sure. Weirdo. "So we're waiting on a substitute, who should *supposedly* be here in about ten minutes. I'm to instruct you to stay put." More air quotes around *supposedly*. Then he leaves abruptly, sighing.

Ten minutes. I head to the bathroom. Despite the fact that smoking's not allowed anywhere inside, the bathroom reeks of stale cigarettes mixed with oversweet institutional air freshener. I'm feeling rebellious and nervous, though I'm not sure why, so I light up a generic cigarette—if I'm going to kill myself, at least I'll pay as little for the privilege as possible—and inhale.

When I blow the smoke out, it fills the small two-stall bathroom with a haze. I take a few more pulls, then carefully put the cigarette out on the side of the sink to save for later. I wash my hands and clean the ashes off the dingy porcelain.

In the dim hallway I shake my arms around, hoping the smell won't follow me, because when I glance through the window in the classroom door, I catch a glimpse of a man in front of the room. The teacher's already here. *Fuck.*

I put my head down and slip in, heading straight to my seat without looking up.

"There's a $200 fine for smoking inside this building," says the teacher, and I cringe but sit down, letting my hair cover my face and looking down at my desk.

The chalk squeaks on the board, and I glance up to see what he's writing. "Detective Beck" he scribbles, but I only see the words for a moment. Because class suddenly got *way* more interesting.

Instead of a chubby middle-aged balding cop or a pinched-faced woman with something to prove, this guy is young, or looks like it from behind. He's in plainclothes, wearing jeans and a tucked-in black T-shirt. His belt is black leather, a holster holding his gun. For a second I stare at his arms, because they're really muscular and strong, and I can see ink on one of them, disappearing into the sleeve of his shirt. And his ass. Of *course* I check out his ass, which is magazine-worthy. Six sessions staring at that won't be so bad.

"All right," he says. "I'm Detective Jake Beck." He clears his throat and something about the "Jake" and those tattoos on his arm make me sit up straight.

There's no way.

But as he slowly turns around, I gasp. The thick brown hair. The scruffy jaw. Those glinting eyes.

It's him. The guy I went home with the night after getting caught with Stacey's drugs in my locker. The night I wanted to do something stupid and reckless. The night I turned eighteen.

This is the guy I haven't been able to stop thinking about, because even though the "no strings" was my idea, and even though I lied-without-actually-lying about my age, I wanted to see him again.

Except not like this.

"You're here because you've all made a mistake, and this is your…" His voice breaks off as his eyes meet mine.

You know that phrase about the blood draining from someone's face? I finally see it right in front of me. He's pale as a sheet of paper as he stares at me.

My heart hammers, and I can barely breathe.

He recovers quickly and continues talking, but I can't hear him over the pounding in my ears.

What the actual fuck? I take a deep breath and will my body to calm down.

He starts taking roll, and I look up, studying him as he glances at the other students. Part of me hopes I was wrong, that it's not the guy from the other night. But it's definitely him. And even though I'm shaking from this horrible coincidence, I can't help noticing again how sexy he is.

His face is rugged and needs a shave, which conjures up images of bad boys, though "boys" doesn't exactly fit since he's the oldest guy I've ever been with. His jaw's chiseled, the kind of jaw they write about in the romance novels my mom sometimes reads. He has light brown hair that's tousled and messy, and brown eyes that, when

I sneak a glance at them, look half pissed and half scared out of his mind.

"Melanie Cannon."

"Um, here," I say quietly, but I don't look up.

"See me after class, Ms. Cannon."

Fuck.

The kid with the yellow teeth makes a low "oooh," and I shoot him a pissed-off look.

Jake—Detective Beck—clears his throat. "I don't usually teach this class. I'm doing a favor for a friend and taking it over, so I'll be your instructor for the next five weeks."

He's pacing in front of us, but then he sits on the edge of the desk, kind of leaning back so his T-shirt pulls over his chest. I can actually see the outline of his pecs through his shirt, and even though I know I'm in deep shit with him, my heart beats quickly looking at his muscles.

He runs a hand through his hair and continues. "You're all here because you were caught in a drug-related offense. I want to remind you that you're lucky to be here." He gestures around the crappy room like it's a palace. "This class is a slap on the wrist. You'll have no record. You'll have a second chance. Don't fuck that up. I expect you to be here every week. I expect you to pay attention. I expect you to pass all the tests I give you. I expect you to be on time. And I expect you to follow the rules." He glances my way.

My cheeks flush.

He gives each of us a worksheet with blanks to fill in, and we laboriously read each question out loud and discuss the answers, which he instructs us to write down.

Regular use of methamphetamine causes chemical and molecular changes in the brain.

Marijuana affects learning and memory, coordination, and judgment.

Like in school, I begin to doodle at the bottom of the page. First I draw an intricate flower. Then I print the word *fuck*, because I can't help feeling pissed that I have to be here and that this situation is

11

really messed up, and start to draw viney designs around it. It's the fanciest *fuck* I've ever seen, and I get really into it, while a part of my brain listens to the discussion around me and writes down the answers.

I do plan to pass this class. But I don't need 100% focus to do it. School stuff—memorization and all that—has always been easy for me. In *real* school, including AP English and AP Psychology, I have straight A's. I've always known that if I wanted to get away from this crappy town, I'd have to do it myself, so I've been working hard for years.

I spend the two hours of class working on my doodles, writing down facts about drugs, and studiously avoiding all eye contact with Detective Beck. It feels like the longest two hours of my life, and all I want to do is run out of the room so I can breathe again.

"OK," he finally says. "Turn in your work. I'll see you next week."

I look in dismay at my paper, covered in drawings and a dark and prominent *fuck* across the bottom. How the hell did I miss the part about how we'd have to turn them in? I consider crossing it all out, but then decide it's not worth it. That'll make it look worse, and anyway, it's not against the law to write a swear word, is it? Besides, I've got bigger problems when it comes to the teacher.

Slowly, I gather up my things and drop the paper on his desk as I start to leave the room. I'm the last student out.

"Ms. Cannon."

I freeze.

"I thought I asked you to stay after class."

I turn to meet his blazing eyes, which are staring at mine, holding me in place.

"Sit." He gestures with his chin at the desk right in front of his.

I slink into the seat and play with my fingernails. I'm embarrassed to be here. Horrified that he probably thinks I'm some sort of druggie. I even feel a flicker of concern for him; I didn't set out to get anyone in trouble.

Yet despite all that, I can't help the swirling in my belly, the tingle that makes me wish he'd touch me, that makes me hope he's thinking about that night we shared.

For a few moments that seriously seem to stretch on forever he's silent. Outside the classroom the fluorescent lights hum, and one flickers on and off with a buzz.

He picks up a file from the desk and opens it, leafing through the papers. Apparently he finds what he was looking for because he puts it down again. "Eighteen," he says. "You're fucking eighteen years old. *Melanie.*"

"I am so sorry," I whisper.

"Your birthday was… two weeks ago?" He looks at the paper again. "Were you eighteen when we slept together?" His eyes are blazing though his voice is low.

"We, um, met after midnight. On my birthday. So I was technically eighteen." I wish I sounded defiant, but my voice is low and quivery instead.

"Jesus fucking Christ." His chair squeals against the floor as he pushes it back and stands. He comes around the desk and sits on it, directly in front of me. We're only about two feet apart, and something about the closeness makes my heart thud.

He stares into my eyes, and I stare back. Neither of us moves. The radiator in the corner hisses, and somewhere in the building the elevator creaks.

He glances at the door, then looks back at me before speaking in a low rumble. "What the hell were you thinking? Why were you in that bar? You're definitely not old enough."

I shrug. "Fake ID," I whisper. That's not completely true. I have a fake ID, but Jones, the owner, lets me study there sometimes if I promise not to talk to anyone. I don't want to get him in trouble, though. No need to bring anyone down with me.

A muscle in his jaw tightens. We stare at one another for another small eternity, and then I summon my sanity and stand up, slinging my backpack over my shoulder.

"I'll see you next week," I say as I head to the door. I don't look back. And he doesn't say anything. But I'm positive he's staring at me as I walk out.

• • •

Bells Park is a crappy suburb in Illinois, about one hundred miles from Chicago. *Suburb* makes it sound nice. White picket fences and pretty ponytailed moms in minivans driving homemade cupcakes to the school bake sale. But it's ugly here. A railroad runs through the center of town, and long slow freight trains covered in graffiti rumble and screech through day and night.

A decade ago, the downtown was bustling, but things have changed, and now everything's run down or shut down. Or both. The only places open now aren't worth even glancing in. A greasy diner. The dusty antique shop, which is really a secondhand store, where I work part time after school. A real estate office with sun-bleached photos of homes that sold years ago, because nothing sells here anymore.

There's a gas station that features sandwiches wrapped in wrinkled Saran wrap and live bait for people heading down to the river to fish, but even the river is gross now, half-dried and mucky. It always smells like rotten fish and algae.

I walk through the downtown on my way home from class. It's dark out and getting cold, the March air biting. Lamps along the street are dim, and not all of them are working anyway, so I grasp my pocket knife in my jacket pocket once hard for strength. I'm small, but I'm pretty sure I could fight if I had to. I don't have a car, so I have to walk the mile home. And my mom's probably been drinking, so she can't pick me up.

I shiver and pull my hooded sweatshirt tighter around me. Headlights approach from behind, brightening the street, and a car crawls to a stop next to me. It's a cruiser. The front driver window rolls down and I'm looking at Detective Beck.

I turn back to the sidewalk in front of me and keep walking. What the hell does he want?

"It's late. Isn't there someone who can pick you up?" he asks, the car keeping pace with my brisk walk.

"Nope."

"Not the safest neighborhood."

"Don't have much choice." I pick up the pace.

"Let me give you a ride." He doesn't sound convinced that he really wants to.

"No. I'm good." It's fucking freezing, and I'd love a ride. But I don't want to talk about what happened. Or why.

"Suit yourself. See you next week." He drives away, and I watch his taillights fade in the distance.

When I get home, his car is waiting outside my house. He drives away as soon as I get inside.

• • •

"Melanie! Come here. You've got to see this." My mom's got a big glass of wine. I mean really big. When she drinks wine, she doesn't sip. She gulps, like it's Kool-Aid or something. The good thing is she's not a "bad drunk." Not that there's such a thing as a "good drunk," but at least she's not mean or ugly or getting arrested for public indecency or anything. I'm the only one in trouble with the law around here.

"Hey, Mom," I say, setting my backpack down. She's at her computer, and I briefly put my arm around her for a hug. Dirty plates and utensils, stacked haphazardly, look like they'll fall at any minute, and I grab what I can to bring to the kitchen. Like an archaeologist, I can decipher the strata by the crusted stains: Canned noodles and sauce from two nights ago. Brown remains of Salisbury steak gravy in a microwave-meal tray. A coffee mug with dried wine rings instead of coffee dregs.

"Check it out," she says, pointing at her screen, when I return. "Watch."

She pushes the "play" button on a PowerPoint presentation, and music starts—"The Wind Beneath My Wings"—while images, some pixilated, of kittens and puppies interspersed with words flash across the screen. "Love." "Compassion." "Cute."

This is what she does. She collects her disability checks—she had a minor accident at work a few years ago—and makes PowerPoint videos all day long. In between watching reality TV shows and drinking.

"That's nice," I say, but really it makes me want to cry. All of it, but especially, for some weird reason, the fact that "love" and "compassion" are nouns, but "cute" is an adjective.

"Do you really like it? This one's going on my YouTube channel," she says. "I got twenty comments on my last one. I think this one's really going to get a ton of views."

"For sure."

She frowns and bites her lip. "You know, I think I should replace this kitten here," she points at the screen, "with something just a tad cuter, Mel. And maybe have it flash for a second longer?" She clicks, adjusts. "I know the kittens are appealing to people, so I just need to figure out how to increase my viewership."

"I have homework." I head to the kitchen and run water over my mom's dirty dishes. I'll wash them tomorrow morning, maybe, or this weekend. Whenever. I know my mom won't.

I'm suddenly starving, but there's not much in the fridge, so I grab the ends—all that's left—from a bag of bread on the counter and a bruised apple and head to my bedroom.

"Hey! How was your drug class thing tonight?" my mom calls after me.

"Fine. Boring. One down, five to go."

"Good," she says, and I hear her clicking away on her keyboard, consumed once more by her videos.

16

I guess I should be happy she's not on my case about it, but when I explained to her what happened, she accepted it, no questions asked. That's good, right? I'm lucky.

In my room I put the bread and apple on my desk and crawl under the covers, still fully dressed. I finished my homework at school before the drug class, and all I want to do right now is fall into a deep sleep.

• • •

In my locker the next morning is a note. "Sorry," it reads with a sad face at the bottom. That's it. It's taped to the inside of the door to make sure I'll see it. I know it's from Stacey, because she's the only one with the combination to my locker. Other than the principal, of course.

Stacey's locker is on the third floor of the high school, and mine is on the first floor, and we shared combinations so we could store stuff in each other's lockers. Because we trusted each other and that's what best friends do. Until one of them lets the other take the blame for a cigarette pack full of joints.

For a second I consider folding the note up into a small square and sticking it in my back pocket, but instead I crumple up the paper and toss it into a trash can on my way to class. Fuck Stacey. I don't need her. She screwed me over, and I'm done. In my head I picture myself clapping my hands together, ridding themselves of dust and crumbs of the past.

"Melanie!" Principal Evans comes up behind me and puts her arm around my shoulder in a motherly way as she walks me down the hallway. "How was class last night? You went, right?"

I roll my eyes. "Of course I went, Mrs. Evans."

She stops me and puts her hands on my shoulders, looking into my eyes. "I believe in you, Melanie." Her expression is so earnest, like she's waiting for a significant or meaningful response.

"OK." What am I supposed to say?

"Great. Oh, I almost forgot. I stopped at Subway—the one just outside town—and bought a sandwich for lunch, but they

17

accidentally gave me beef instead of chicken, and they let me keep the extra one. I'd be grateful if you'd take it off my hands."

"Oh. Um, sure." I can see right through her, and I don't need anyone to feel sorry for me, but I'm starving. I think of the sad apple and the bread crusts on my desk at home, and I take the bag, swallowing hard, trying not to tear up.

"Well, get to class then," she says with a smile, and I head to Trigonometry. I love math, all the certainty and proofs and correct answers. I like that even though there's more than one way to reach the same conclusion, the end is always concrete and non-debatable. I've actually been working ahead in Trig, mostly because my lunch periods, which used to be occupied with gossiping with Stacey and her boyfriend, have been lonely since we started fighting. Instead, I do schoolwork.

In class, I let my thoughts drift, thinking about the stupid drug class and Detective Beck and what a messed-up situation *that* is. But even though I know I should be horrified about it all, warmth gathers in my belly when I think about that night at his apartment. And how, in class when he stood before us, gun in his holster and scruff on his cheeks, he looked all adult and strict but I *knew*.

I knew the way he kissed. The way his hands felt, tracing rough patterns over delicate skin. The sounds he made when he came. And *he* knew the exact hidden spots to send me into bliss so layered and complex I could barely even breathe.

● ● ●

"Melanie!" A smile brightens Mrs. Hart's wrinkled face when I enter the antique shop, the bell on the door jingling. I work in the shop three days a week after school, from whenever I get there until seven p.m. when the shop closes. It's an easy gig. Almost nobody comes in. Ever. So I don't mind that the pay is way less than minimum wage. I get to finish whatever homework I didn't finish at school, be out of my house, and have peace. And I get paid, even though it's a minuscule amount, for the pleasure.

18

"Hi, Mrs. Hart," I say. "What do you have planned for this evening?" I can't stop the smile that spreads across my face. Mrs. Hart's kindness is infectious, and despite the dust and mildew here, this place is warm and welcoming to me.

"Oh, not much. Going to start the supper for Mr. Hart." She always refers to her husband as Mr. Hart, never by his name or "my husband." It's weird but actually really cute too.

"Are you going to cook that pot roast dish you talked about last time, the one with the pineapple?"

She winks. "I am. But don't tell him what's in it! He thinks he hates pineapple, but every time I cook it mixed in, he never notices. Just says how good it is."

"You could always use that cooking for kids book that's on the shelf over there." I gesture at the bookcase with a grin. "The one about how to sneak fruit and vegetables into food so kids don't notice?"

Her laugh is such a great sound. "I should! He's such a stubborn old man. But at our age, Mr. Hart and I need all the nutrients we can get."

She smoothes her loose flowered blouse over what looks like elastic-waist jeans and shapes her white hair with both hands before heading to the door. "Do you know," she says, stopping and turning to me once more, "that he practically had a fit because I made our scrambled eggs with just the whites this morning? You would have thought I'd served him pigeon's feet or something!" She shakes her head fondly.

"Eggs need the yellows! And they need to be fried in butter, not that spray junk." Mr. Hart appears at the bottom of the staircase that leads to their apartment above the store. He puts his arm around his wife and grins at me. "Is she filling your head with stories about how difficult I am?" He pushes his glasses up on his nose.

"Oh you!" Mrs. Hart playfully dismisses him with her hand. "You can help me with dinner tonight if you're going to be so particular." She starts slowly up the stairs.

19

"Nice seeing you, Melanie." Mr. Hart's eyes are warm as he looks at me.

"You too. Have a good dinner. I've got it covered down here."

"We know you do, Melanie," he responds before turning and following his wife. He closes the door at the bottom of the stairs, and I hear their footsteps till they reach their apartment.

When they're gone, I sit in the chair behind the counter, smiling from my encounter with them. They're so kind, the kind of people who seem to understand you immediately, and who seem to love me despite everything. They don't have any kids, so no grandkids either, and sometimes that makes me a little sad. Anyone would be lucky to be part of their family.

The shop supposedly sells antiques, but with the exception of a few items, there's not much of value for sale. Over the years it's turned more into a secondhand store, and though Mrs. Hart tries to display items so they look fancy, it's still mostly old Nancy Drew books, lace doilies, and oil paintings, the thick paint cracking and dulled with age. Sometimes I'm surprised that the store is still open, or that the Harts manage to pay me the measly amount I get every week.

My homework's all done, and I check outside for Molly, the orange stray cat who stops by sometimes. I've stashed a couple of cans of food for her just in case she shows up. She's nowhere in sight, though, so I check out the bookcase, where each book's price is handwritten in pencil on the title page. I settle on a beat-up copy of *House of Stairs* by William Sleator, which I've read before, but it's so psychologically fucked up that I don't mind rereading it. Instead of sitting on the hard stool behind the counter, I settle into a worn-out armchair next to the cash register and get comfy.

I'm half reading, half dozing, when the rusted bell on the front door gives a flat jangle and I look up.

It's Jake. Or Detective Jake Beck. I slam my book shut and stand up, then head behind the counter to the stool where I perch, looking at him with a forced calm face.

He nods. "Melanie."

"Detective Beck." I smirk, trying to get control over my nerves.

He stands in front of the case with the old pocket knives, each with a string attached to a tiny white tag with the price on it. He's got jeans on again, just tight enough so I can see what he's got, with a black T-shirt tucked in and a holster holding his gun. With our roles so defined now, it's hard to believe that I was in his bed just a couple of weeks ago, that he saw my body. Touched it. Made me come three different times.

We're both silent, until he abruptly moves to the counter and braces his arms on it, leaning toward me.

"We need to talk." His eyes are angry, but hungry too, I think. Or maybe that's just what I want to see.

I shrug, playing it cool. "OK. What's up?"

"You know what's up. Don't play dumb."

"I'm not playing anything," I mutter.

"Yeah? You were playing *something* at Lucy's when you lied about your age. *Aria.*"

"I didn't lie," I argue, though it's probably just a matter of semantics. "You didn't ask. I didn't tell."

"You weren't even supposed to be in that bar in the first place!"

"Fake ID. I already told you."

He holds out his hand. "Give it to me."

"No way. I paid a lot of money for it." The truth is, I didn't pay anything for it. Stacey and I both got IDs from this kid at school who, with some heavy flirting, would have done just about anything for us for free.

"I'm not fucking around, Melanie. Give it to me now."

"Whatever." I pull my wallet out of my backpack and hand him the ID. He sticks it in his pocket without even looking at it. I could have given him my Frequent Flyer card from Boss's Frozen Yogurt, which shut down a year ago, and he wouldn't have noticed. "I don't think it's the ID you're mad about." We might as well get this conversation out of the way.

"You're right. What I'm mad about, Melanie, is that you were barely eighteen when we slept together." His voice is lowered, and he glances out of the corner of his eye at the closed front door to the shop as he speaks.

I shrug. "It's not a big deal. I wanted it. You wanted it. It's over. And I'm, like, legal and everything."

But my nonchalance is belied by the way my pulse picks up when he looks at me, even in anger. At the way it almost physically hurts to say *it's not a big deal*. Because it *was* a big deal. It was desperate and scary and dangerous. And sexy and outrageous and amazing.

There was something about being with Jake that made me feel safe and happy in ways I didn't even know existed. And I'd never, ever been with someone as good in bed. The other three guys I've slept with, all of them in high school, fumbled around while pretending to know what they were doing. Being with Jake made me realize none of them had even a clue.

But it doesn't matter because he's a cop and my teacher, and to him I'm just trouble.

He shakes his head and stands back, crossing his arms over his muscular chest. "Look. We need to clear the air. That's why I'm here."

With my thumbnail I scrape at the sticky remains of a sticker on the counter and studiously avoid making eye contact. Because I want to look at him. I want him to look at me. But he's here to tell me what a big mistake we made—what a big mistake *he* made. And I'm not anyone's mistake.

"It's fine," I finally say. "Just… you know… forget it. OK?"

He clears his throat, and out of the corner of my eye I see him moving a little closer. "Right. I'm sorry. Are we good?"

"Yup."

"We both, uh, could be affected a lot if people found out…"

"I'm not going to tell anyone. *Detective.*" Now I do look up, glaring at him. Somehow the fact that he's worried about people finding out makes me angry.

He looks away, then rubs at the stubble on his chin with one hand. "Dammit, Melanie. Just... I'll see you in class next week."

I nod.

He stares at me for a few moments like he wants to say something else, but then he shakes his head and starts toward the door.

"There's nobody I'd tell anyway, so don't worry." I don't know why I say it. It makes me feel pathetic, but I blurt out the words before I know what I'm doing.

Jake stops and turns.

I'm blushing, but I can't stop talking. "Like, the whole reason I'm in that stupid class is because my best friend betrayed me, and she and her boyfriend were pretty much the only people at school I talk to. And my mom..." My voice trails off. I don't want to get into that.

"What do you mean your friend betrayed you?" He takes a few steps back toward me.

"It was hers. The stuff they found in my locker."

"Did you tell that to anyone?" He looks pissed.

"No. I thought she'd say something on her own. I guess I was giving her the benefit of the doubt." I feel like a fucking idiot now, though.

"And she let you take the fall?" His eyes are blazing.

I nod.

"Some fucking friend," he mutters. "Look, I can talk to the principal and..."

"No. Just leave it, OK? It's over. I'll just finish the stupid class and forget it."

He shakes his head and sighs. "I'll see you next week." He stares at me past the point of comfort, but I don't look away.

It feels like a challenge, and I never back down. It's kind of like playing chicken, two cars speeding toward each other until one of them turns the wheel first. But it's not going to be me.

Jake licks his lips and bows his head. Then he turns and leaves the store.

CHAPTER THREE – JAKE

"Yo, Beck!" James, one of the ten Bells Park police officers, welcomes me as I walk into the station. The usual smell of stale coffee greets me, and I fight back the momentary depression that overtakes me every time I enter this old, grimy building.

The carpeted floor is worn and stained, and all the desks are cheap, the fake wood exterior chipped and peeling. The walls should have been repainted a decade ago. I didn't go into this field for the glamour, but this place needs to be gutted.

I grunt in James' direction, then head to the break room where I pour some lukewarm and watery coffee into a mug that looks clean enough.

Back at my desk I sit down and wait for my computer to boot up.

"How's that fucking drug class going?" James wheels his chair up to my desk and grins.

"It's fucking great." I sip the shitty coffee.

"Not regretting your decision to come out here?" He sits back in his chair and adjusts his belt. "Fucking beer," he says, patting his belly.

"Yeah, it's got nothing to do with the two greasy breakfast sandwiches you eat every morning."

"Ha!" James is a great guy, and even though I haven't known him very long, I like his sense of humor and laid back attitude. He's about my age, twenty-five, and from the beginning he's been easy to get along with.

"And no, I'm not regretting coming here." I'm not sure that's true, but it's too much to think about. I told my uncle I'd help him out while he's building up the Bells Park police force, so I'm sort of on loan from the Chicago PD. I need to stay till the job is done. And honestly, I'm not ready to be back in Chicago yet.

"Who's going to tell you to stop eating shit and lose weight if I leave?" I joke.

"Fuck you," says James cheerfully. "Oh hey. The high school called. The principal, uh…" He rolls back to his desk to pick up a scrap of paper on which he's written some information. "Joan Evans? She's wondering if you can give her a call. About the drug class."

"Yeah?" Immediately I think of Melanie, and I get the weirdest sensation of feeling turned on and sad at the same time. I've never felt that before.

Part of me remembers her as Aria. No. Scratch that. Every single cell in my body remembers her as Aria: the way she smelled, the sounds she made, the silkiness of her skin, the way her body moved under mine. I'd be a fucking liar if I said I didn't think about that. Often.

But her house. Run down, like most of this shitty town. Her mother a drunk, or that's the word on the street. No dad at all. Her job at the thrift store on Main Street, where she can't be making even minimum wage. The fact that she was even in Lucky's that night, and how different she looked then—grownup and sexy—from how she looked curled up in the beat-up chair in the antique shop.

Hardly a trace of makeup on her face made her appear years younger. Made her look her *actual* age, that is. Jeans and sneakers and a sweatshirt with a skull on it. Hair pulled back in a ponytail.

It's hard to reconcile the two versions of her, and my heart could break—or my cock could explode—thinking about it too much.

"I'll go down to the school and talk to her," I hear myself saying. *What the fuck, Jake? You don't need to go there.*

26

James shrugs. "You could just call."

"Not going to sit around on my ass and get fat like you," I joke. But that's not why I'm going. Fuck if it's not because I'm hoping to catch a glimpse of Melanie while I'm there. I'm dying to know which version I'll see at school—the seductress from the bar or the teenager from class? I don't want to admit it, but she's gotten under my skin. And I want just one more glimpse of her, one more chance to peek into her life.

"Later." I head out the door.

• • •

Columbus High School, like everything else in the town, needs work. First, there's the name. I thought it was a well-known fact that Christopher Columbus was an asshole, not a hero, so I'm surprised the name hasn't been changed.

A cracked running track surrounds an overgrown football field, and the bleachers look like they're ready to collapse. The only thing that keeps them still standing, I guess, is the fact that probably nobody attends the games anymore.

"Poor kids," I mutter as I head to the front door and hit the buzzer.

The inside, though old, is surprisingly clean, and an attractive woman in her forties clicks down the hallway in a business suit, hand outstretched and a smile on her face.

"Hi. I'm Joan Evans, principal. Thanks for coming."

"Detective Beck." I shake her hand.

"Let's talk in my office. Would you like some coffee?"

"Please." Anything's got to be better than the swill at the station.

She leads me into the administrative section of the building, stopping at the secretary's desk to request some coffee. Then we head into her office.

"Please sit, Detective Beck," she says.

"Jake. Please."

27

She smiles. "Jake. I wanted to touch base with you regarding our student, Melanie Cannon, who's in the drug program you're teaching?"

I shift slightly and nod.

"She... well... I suppose I want to let you know that if there are any issues or problems, I'm willing to help solve them. I want her to complete the class with you so her record's clean. But she doesn't have much support at home, so I'm offering my assistance."

I clear my throat. "Right. She seems like a good kid." My mind, against my will, flashes back to her on my bed, pale skin on my sheets, dark red lips slightly opened, back arched... *Not now, Jake. Not the fuck now.*

"She is. The fact that she's in the drug class at all might seem to indicate otherwise. But to be honest, I don't think the drugs that were found in her locker were hers. I think she's covering for someone." The principal shakes her head. "Anyway, she's one of our best students, straight A's. And she's been accepted to University of Chicago. A local group gave her a full scholarship. I don't want that to be ruined. She's only got a couple of months left till graduation." Her voice holds a plea and a spark of determination.

"University of Chicago." I'm impressed.

She nods. "Melanie's extremely intelligent."

"Well, we've only had one class so far, but she was fine. Did everything she was supposed to." Of course I don't mention the fact that I knew she'd been smoking in the bathroom. Or that we fucked.

Principal Evans nods. "I'm not asking for preferential treatment for her. Of course I'd never do that. But I'd like it if you'd call me if anything happens. If she misses a class. Or acts out. Anything. Will you call?"

"If anything comes up, I'll let you know." It's obvious the principal cares a lot about Melanie, and I feel the same way, the need to protect her, like despite her tough exterior she's actually fragile, something valuable that could break at any second.

The secretary sticks her head in. "Coffee?" She hands one mug to me and the other to the principal. Then she reaches into her pocket and dumps a handful of individual creamer containers and sugar packets onto the desk before leaving.

I sip the black coffee, relishing the fact that it's actually hot, not lukewarm like back at the station.

Principal Evans studies my face for a few moments as if deliberating whether or not to say something more. Her eyes are kind and intelligent, and I hope she's not intuitive enough to understand that something happened.

"I don't know if you know this." She sets her mug on the desk. "I think it will help you understand Melanie's situation a little more. The scholarship she received? It's from an organization that helps students with an incarcerated parent get through college."

"But her mother..."

Principal Evans shakes her head. "Her father. He hasn't been part of her life for years, as I understand it. Not consistently, at least. One of those part-time parents who comes around just enough to get a kid's hopes up. Then takes off again."

"Jesus," I mutter. "What's he in for?" This wasn't in Melanie's file, but I'm already itching to get back to the station and do some research.

"This time? Burglary. Armed burglary? Is that a thing?"

I chuckle. "Yeah. That's a thing. So he's been in prison before?"

"A few times." She closes her eyes and shakes her head slightly. "So it's a struggle for Melanie. Everything is. She needs to get out of here. We—the responsible adults in her life—need to help her."

Fuck. Me. Responsible adult? Talk about guilt. I manage to nod, keeping my face earnest and neutral.

She stands. "I hear you're on loan from Chicago. Care for a tour of the school while you're still here in Bells Park?"

29

I should say no. Because the only reason I want to say *yes* is the off-chance that I'll catch a glimpse of Melanie. I nod. "Sure. I'd like that."

"Great!" Principal Evans smoothes the pale green skirt of her suit and strides out of the office, gesturing for me to follow. She's so efficient and confident I can't help feeling like I'm back in high school, and I bite back a laugh at the thought.

We pass rows of rusty lockers in the quiet hallways; the kids are in class. Giant framed photos of graduating classes decorate the walls above the lockers. The older ones are in nicer frames, and the more recent are cheaply mounted, like the frames are from the dollar store.

As if reading my thoughts—or following my gaze—the principal says, "There's less money these days for extra. The school needs so much physical work, but we're struggling to get money from the state. Enrollment is way down because the population in our town is down, and there's talk of closing this school and busing the kids over to another suburb."

"This town." I shake my head.

"It's changed a lot ever since all the industry pulled out." She sighs.

The bell rings suddenly, and within two seconds the class doors open and students rush into the halls, laughing and talking. "Hey, Principal Evans!" they say, waving and smiling at her as they walk past.

"They seem to like you," I say. "Everyone hated the principal when I was in high school."

She laughs. "Yeah. We had to let our school counselor go last year—funding issues—so I've filled that role too. Get to know the kids pretty well that way. Luckily I actually have a background in social work."

I'm about to answer when the words get stuck in my throat. Melanie's walking toward us, head down, staring at her beat-up red Converse sneakers, brow furrowed in concentration. Her long dark

30

hair hangs down on either side of her face, shiny and soft, as I well fucking know. A worn-out Station Gray concert T-shirt hugs her curves, and her light blue jeans are torn up.

"Congrats on getting the highest score on the Trig test, Melanie." Principal Evans smiles and it's clear how much she cares about Melanie.

Melanie looks up, and I'm left breathless by those hazel eyes again, guarded but gorgeous. She grins at the principal in the split second before she sees me. And then she freezes, her cheeks turning pink before she glances down at her shoes again.

"You know Detective Beck, right?" asks the principal.

"Yeah. He's, um, teaching the drug class thing at the library," she mutters in her quiet, throaty voice.

"We were just talking about you." Principal Evans puts a hand on Melanie's shoulder.

Melanie looks up at her, and all I see is her face, pale and pretty, framed by her dark straight hair. "Yeah?" Her voice is wary, with a trace of belligerence, but she's polite.

"We both care about you, and we're here to help you. If you need anything, please ask. OK? We just want to get you out of here and into college. Got it?"

Melanie's lips form a small smile. "Got it. Thanks." Her gaze skips from Principal Evans over to me, and she gives me a smile too. A tiny one.

And I realize how screwed I am. How my heart twists in both compassion and lust. How fucked up it is that before me stands a troubled girl, and all I've thought about over the past two weeks is how good it felt to be buried deep inside her. But I can never touch her again.

The loudspeaker crackles. "Principal Evans? You're needed in the office, please. Principal Evans."

She frowns. "I'm sorry. I'll have to cut the tour short. They never call me unless it's an emergency! Can you find your own way out, Detective?"

"I can." I nod. "Thanks."

"I'll be in touch," she says as she hurries away, her heels clicking.

I turn to Melanie, who's chewing on a fingernail and gazing up at me. She looks nervous.

"I can, uh, walk you to class," I say.

"Oh. Yeah. I guess." She shrugs.

"You into Station Gray?" I nod at her shirt as we walk down the hallway.

"They're pretty cool. Yeah."

"I saw them in concert. My eighteenth birthday. It was actually their last major concert."

"Really?" She looks up at me, real interest flashing in her eyes. "Wow. I've never seen them perform. I got this shirt online. And now they don't tour anymore, so."

"They play together, still. But it's all hush-hush. Secret concerts in bars."

"Yeah." She sighs. "God, I'd love to hear them live. So which is your favorite song?" She says it like a challenge, like she's testing my knowledge. But her eyes are lively, eager.

"'Needlepoint.'"

"Uh, don't you teach a say-no-to-drugs class? You know that song's about heroin, right?" She gives me a sly smile.

I laugh out loud. "Yeah. Funny story. So, my grandma heard the song once, and she liked the line *Sharp and pretty, thing of beauty* and the title and thought it was about, you know, needlepoint? The kinds that old women do? So she played it for her friends at their sewing club. It's kind of like their theme song now."

"No way." She laughs, covering her lips with her hand as she does. "I love that so much!"

"It's pretty great." I chuckle.

We stop outside a classroom. The door's open, and I see the students, most already sitting in desks.

"My eighteenth birthday wasn't as cool as yours." She frowns and hesitates, before adding in a lower voice, "I mean, except for the part about meeting you."

I shake my head. "Melanie," I warn, ignoring the flicker of heat that surges through me at her words, glancing around the hallway.

"Sorry." She puts her hand up in apology, and gives me a look I can't interpret. "I just… most of it sucked. Like always. My mom, every year for like the past three years, says she'll take me out for Thai food for my birthday. Cause it's my favorite? We'd have to drive two towns away, because this shitty suburb doesn't have any decent food. But by the time I get home from school, she's had too much to drink and says we'll go on the weekend instead. Except we never do. She still owes me for this year, and last year, and the one before that too. So birthdays kind of suck. And no Station Gray concerts for me." She bites her lip and looks away, her face flushing.

Jesus fucking Christ. If she's trying to make me feel sorry for her? It's working.

I have no idea how to respond, but I'm opening my mouth to say something—comforting, I hope—when the bell rings.

"Gotta go," she says and disappears into the classroom without a look back.

CHAPTER FOUR – MELANIE

When my ex-best friend Stacey turned eighteen in January, her mom gave her a Visa card with a $2000 limit, and we took off in Stacey's Range Rover and headed to Chicago. She rented a room in the Hilton on Michigan Avenue, and we snuck a bottle of her father's Absolut in her suitcase. We drank it on the rocks, grimacing at the taste until it started going down smooth.

Her boyfriend Robby showed up, and she gave me the usual signal—a clumsy wink—so I took off for awhile to give them some privacy.

I know Chicago's not called the Windy City because of the weather, but icy swirls of air bit my cheeks as I walked outside. It was late, past midnight, and not much was open outside the hotel. I was cold as fuck, but I could only think one thing: *this will be my city next year. And until I finish college. And maybe forever. I don't ever have to go back to Bells Park if I don't want to.* I was drunk and ecstatic, and it wasn't just from the vodka.

I wasn't lying when I told Jake at school that the best thing about my eighteenth birthday was meeting him. Other than that, it sucked. Just like I said. My mom promised me dinner, but when I got home she said what I knew she would. "Hey, honey! Can we go out for your birthday this weekend instead of tonight? I'm not feeling well."

"Sure. Yeah." I tried to ignore the two empty bottles—the extra large bottles—of cheap wine next to her computer desk.

"There's some money on the fridge if you want to order something," she said, touching my hair for a second, her voice full of apology, before heading to her bedroom and closing the door.

Underneath an "I Love Singapore" magnet—nobody I know has been to Singapore—was a crumpled ten-dollar bill. The only place that delivers here is Sausage Sausage, a pizza place. But a) I don't like Sausage Sausage and b) ten dollars wouldn't be enough for food and delivery.

It's been two weeks, and we still haven't gone out to celebrate my birthday, but the conversation at school today with Jake made it fresh in my mind once more.

My mom's already in bed, so I'm all alone. I pull my phone out of my pocket and bring up the Netflix app. I don't want to use my mom's computer to watch—seeing her PowerPoint presentations depresses me. And she gets all anxious about people touching her stuff. "My computer's running slower today," she'll say. "Did you do something to it?" Even if I tell her I only used it to look something up, she'll insist I must have broken it.

The doorbell rings, groaning like it's dying. Nobody's replaced the batteries even though it sounds slow and low and has forever. When it stops working completely, I don't think it will matter much. Our house is tiny, so if someone knocked, we'd hear it. And it's not like we have visitors often. I'm curious as I get off the couch.

I open the door, and there's Jake. Detective Beck. He smiles, and my heart feels weak. What the hell is he doing here? And how shitty do I look right now? And thank god I cleaned up the old wine bottles and dirty dishes from around my mom's computer.

"Did you check who it was before opening the door?" He puts one hand flat against the door frame and leans, bracing himself on his arm. He's got a bag in his other hand. His hair looks darker than ever in the lightless night, and his lips twitch, whether in anger or trying to suppress a smile I'm not sure.

"No." I can't tell if he's seriously checking up on me, or if he's joking around.

"Melanie. You need to be careful. Check next time, OK?"

I salute him. "Yes, sir."

"Cut the crap. I'm being serious."

"What's it to you anyway?"

"I'm a fucking detective, Melanie." His voice is low but stern, like he wants to let me know he's pissed but doesn't want anyone to overhear. My mom's probably passed out, dead to the world, but he doesn't know that. "It's my job to make sure people are safe," he continues. "There's been more than one break-in around here this month."

"I'm fine, OK? What do you need, anyway?" I don't know why I feel so bristly around him, like I have to be mean even though I don't want to.

"I don't need anything. I brought you something." He holds out a white plastic bag.

"What is it?"

"It's for you. Thai food."

I frown.

"You said at school that you wanted to go to some Thai place for your birthday, but you never made it?"

I can't move for a second. Did he really drive half an hour each way to get me take-out? I told him my sad birthday story to make him feel a little sorry for me, I guess, but it wasn't a hint.

"Seriously?" I ask. "You got Thai Lagoon for me?"

"Uh, no. It's from Yum Thai. In Bolster?"

"Oh. Thai Lagoon's my favorite." But I reach out and take the bag from him, surprised at how heavy it is. There must be a ton of food in here, and now I can smell it too. My stomach gurgles, and I hope he can't hear it.

He rolls his eyes. "Thank you's the appropriate response."

I smile. "Thank you."

"See you." He's heading down the stairs, and I watch him walk to his car. He's so gorgeous, I can't help thinking it. But at the same time, I want to cry.

My eyes are prickly, and my nose itches, and I hate it that he's done something nice for me and all I want to do is curl up in a ball and sob. *Stupid asshole.*

In the kitchen I put everything out on the table: pad thai and panang curry and spring rolls with dipping sauce. I lean my phone against an empty bottle of wine so I can watch Netflix while I eat.

• • •

On Monday night I walk the mile to the library through cold drizzle. Earlier today it was deceptively warm out, and I opted to wear my other Station Gray T-shirt—the band totally reminds me of Jake now—without a jacket. Now I regret my decision not to go back for a jacket because it feels like tiny slivers of ice biting my skin, and by the time I get to the library I'm shivering and pissed off.

Despite the fact that I'm desperate to get inside and warm up, I stand against the doorway under the awning, where a dirty yellow light emanates from a cracked fixture, highlighting the bumpy and cracked sidewalk. After fishing around in my backpack for my cigarettes, I light one, my hands almost too cold and stiff to work right.

I inhale and blow out the smoke, watching the ghostly tendrils evaporate into the cold night sky.

"Not supposed to smoke within twenty feet of the building."

I whip my head around.

Jake's standing there, his denim-clad legs spread slightly. Drops of rain glisten on his leather jacket. Like usual, he needs a shave—but I like the way that looks on him—and his brown hair is tousled. His lips form a half-grin as he gazes at me.

"What? You going to give me a ticket or something?" I take another drag and feign nonchalance, when really my heart is pounding so hard.

"I could. But I'm trying to help you get out of trouble, not into it."

I shrug. "I don't need your help."

"You need to finish this course so you don't get a record." He shifts his stance slightly and takes a step closer.

"Are you, like, threatening me? Or holding that over my head?"

"Jesus. No, Melanie." He glances around as if to make sure nobody's listening. "I want you to have a clean record, OK? I think you're a good kid, and I think you have a great future ahead of you if you focus and stay out of trouble."

A good kid. I know he didn't mean that as an insult, but my soul feels like it's being crushed. I don't want him to see me that way. Like a kid.

"I'll see you inside." He passes me and heads to the door.

"Hey, thanks," I call out.

He stops, turns. "For what?"

"The Thai food? It was really good." I give him a small smile, hoping I look genuinely thankful and maybe even a little sexy too.

He stares for a second, maybe even a second too long. "You're welcome." His voice is a deep rumble. Then, without another word, he turns and heads inside. I'm alone in the drizzle.

I take a final drag, then flick the butt away, watching it bounce and spark on the pavement. And then my conscience gets the better of me, so I pick it up, grind it out on the ground, and throw it in the trash.

Inside the library it's nominally warmer than outside, but I'm still shivering. In the stairwell I stop at the wrinkled cardboard box on which someone's written "Lost and Found" in black Sharpie. I root through scarves and a few baseball hats and some ugly-ass jackets until I find a decent and plain black hoodie. It's a few sizes too big, but it's warm and comfortable. I pull up the hood and head down into the basement for class.

• • •

About halfway through class I realize I hate the pretty rich girl, the blond who was wearing a suit the first day. Today she's sporting a glossy white blouse tucked into these wool herringbone patterned pants, and she's got a string of pearls around her neck. I seriously thought only old women wore pearls, but there she is, with her frosty hair and glossy lips, like she's a middle-aged cougar. And she's flirting with Jake.

"Does anyone know which drug's usage has increased the most in the United States over the past few years?" he asks. He's taken off his leather jacket so his biceps are showing, and he's doing that thing where he half sits and half leans back on the front of his desk while lecturing.

The blonde raises her hand. Nobody else moves. The stoner kid picks at his nails, and the other misfits, including me, are doodling.

Jake nods at Pearl. I'm sure that's not her real name, but that's what I call her in my head. When I'm being nice, that is. I have other names that aren't quite as friendly for her.

"Um, prescription drugs?" Even her voice is pretty, light and airy.

She wouldn't stand a chance against me in a fight. But in a competition for Jake's attention? I sink lower into my seat.

"No. Though prescription drug use is increasing, it's heroin that's seeing the largest increases nationwide. Let's talk about the dangerous and oftentimes deadly side effects of heroin usage." Jake picks up his information packet—the same one we all have in front of us. He leafs through it trying to find the right page.

"Detective Beck? It's page seventeen." Pearl pushes her chair back a little from her desk and neatly crosses one leg over the other. I can't see her face, but I'm positive she's smiling that innocent-but-flirty smile at him. *Slut.*

"Thank you, Miss Sheldon. Page seventeen, everyone."

I zone out for the rest of class, too annoyed with Pearl for flirting and Jake for letting her. Not that he could stop her. She's not exactly doing anything overtly inappropriate. I just hate feeling jealous—it's such a useless emotion. If I lost it every time I was envious of someone for something I'd probably be dead or crazy by now.

When class is finally over, I pack up my stuff slowly, kind of hoping—without actually letting myself hope—that I'll be the last one out. But Pearl's doing the same thing. I recognize the tactic. Checking her phone even though there's no reception down here. Pretending to look in her backpack pocket for something imaginary she needs. Saying bye to the other students that I know she normally wouldn't deign to talk to.

Fuck it. I'm not going to lower myself, and I'm not going to get into a battle of wills with her. A contest to see who can take longer to put their things into their backpack and leave the room.

I sling my backpack over my shoulder and walk out without a look back at Jake. In my head he stares longingly after me. But I have a really good imagination.

"So Detective Beck? I was wondering if I could talk to you about something," is the last thing I hear, in Pearl's breathless voice, as I head to the stairwell.

• • •

I toss the sweatshirt back into the lost and found box on my way up. Chances are whoever lost it originally has forgotten about it, or has no idea it's here. But just in case, I feel bad keeping it, even if I planned to return it tomorrow.

Once I head outside and the library door clicks locked behind me, I regret my choice. It's even colder than before. Despite the fact that it's stopped raining, a bitter wind has begun, blowing through the still-empty trees and cutting into my skin.

"Fuck." I cross my arms close across my chest and huddle into myself as I start the long walk home. I wish I had a car like Stacey. I wish I had a mom who could actually pick me up at night. I wish I still had my bike, but someone stole it from our garage last summer. Not that it was difficult to do; the lock on the garage door's been busted for as long as I can remember.

40

Headlights from behind light the road, and when I hear a car slowing, I know it's him. But I don't stop; I keep walking, head down, into the cold. I don't want him to know I want him. I don't need his help, or his pity. I can take care of myself.

"Get in, Melanie. I'm driving you home. It's fucking freezing out here."

It is.

He leans over and opens the door from the inside. Gratefully, despite myself, I slip into the seat and slam the door behind me. My teeth are literally chattering—I think Jake can hear it, because he looks over at me, then turns the heat up to high and adjusts the vents so they're pointing at me.

"Why are you out here without a jacket or anything to keep you warm? What happened to the sweatshirt you had on in class?" He starts driving, and when I glance at him his eyes are on the road.

But the fact that he noticed what I was wearing in class makes my stomach flutter.

"Wasn't mine." I hold my hands up to the car vents to warm them up faster.

"Not gonna ask." He glances over at me. "You warming up OK?"

"Yeah. Thanks."

"It's not smart, you know, to be out when it's almost below freezing in just a flimsy T-shirt." I catch him eyeing my shirt. "Even though it's a cool shirt."

When I glance down, all I see are my nipples, hard from the cold, pressing up against my shirt. Did he notice? Is that what he was looking at?

I don't respond.

"You're going to get sick," he continues.

"Being cold doesn't make you sick. Germs make you sick. You know, bacteria or viruses."

"Technically, maybe. *Smartass.* But being cold can lower your immunity and make you more susceptible to catching something."

"I thought you were a cop, not a doctor." I shiver suddenly, the core of my body still chilled despite the warm car.

"Jesus, Melanie. Here." He pulls over and leans forward, slipping his arms out of the leather jacket. "Put this on."

"No. I'm good."

"You're not good, Melanie. You're shivering and need to warm up. Will you please take this?"

"Fine." I sit forward in my seat, and he drapes it over my shoulders. It's really warm on the inside, and all I can think about is how it was against his skin, how the heat in it was generated by his body. I wish I could pull it tighter around me. I wish I could curl up on the seat and close my eyes, take a nap while we drive for hours and hours.

But within minutes we're at my house, where there's not even a front porch light on for me. I can see the bluish glow of my mom's computer through the window, though.

"Someone home? Your mom?" Jake's deep voice breaks through the silence.

"Yeah. Thanks for the ride." I wriggle my shoulders so his jacket falls off them, and immediately shiver, even inside the warm car.

He clears his throat before speaking. "Are you doing all right in the class? Any questions or problems with anything?" It's kind of a weird question, apropos of nothing.

Is it an excuse to talk to me longer? My heart flutters at the possibility, and I glance at him out of the corner of my eye. He's looking straight ahead, and in the lights from the dashboard I can see his shadowed face, his jaw strong, his lips full.

"The class is all right." I turn away from him. I don't want him to catch me staring. "I mean, it's kind of boring, but I expected that."

"You mean an extra two hours a week of reading and taking notes isn't exciting?"

42

I roll my eyes even though he probably can't see in the dark. "I can think of exactly a thousand things that would be more exciting than the class. No offense."

He laughs, the sound low and growly and contagious, and I feel butterflies again. Then his tone gets serious and his smile disappears. "I don't like that it's so dark on your front porch. Tell your mom to put the light on for you next time."

"Doesn't work." I shrug. "It's fine." I reach for the door handle.

"Look at me, Melanie."

I turn my head so I'm staring into his eyes, glinting in the dark. I want to touch his cheek, feel his stubble-roughened skin. I want his lips on mine, even if only for a second. But I know he's not interested anymore, now that he knows I'm only eighteen.

"It's not *fine*." He sounds angry. "It's not fine that…" His voice trails off and he runs his hand through his messy hair.

"That what?"

"Forget it." Jake shakes his head. "Just… be careful. I'll wait for you to get in."

"Bye." I open the car door and slip outside into the cold night. All the way up the front stairs I resist the urge to turn around and wave, to see if he's watching me. The front door's unlocked and I make it in without a look back.

• • •

I don't see Jake all week. Everywhere I go, I look for his black undercover car, but I don't even catch a glimpse of it or of him. Sometimes he drives a cruiser, and my heart skips a beat when I see one, but it's never Jake.

In the antique shop, I keep waiting for the bell to jangle, and every time it does my pulse kicks up till I look up and it's somebody else. It's always people who come in out of curiosity and stay a few minutes longer than they want to out of guilt. I can see the way they pick things up and pretend to examine them, like they'd really want to buy a Smurfs mug from two decades ago or a page-yellowed romance novel from the eighties.

On Monday at lunch I head to Mr. Tallman's room to eat. He's the math teacher, and I'm in his AP Statistics class. In the beginning of the year he said we could have lunch in his room if we needed tutoring or wanted to work on assignments from class. I never showed up for that, but once Stacey and I stopped talking, I wanted some place to be away from the cafeteria, away from her. And it's not like I have any other friends. So I started coming here.

Mr. Tallman's old and bald, with a white beard, and when I told him I don't actually need help, just a place to eat, he left me alone. Usually he goes off, to the teacher's lounge, I guess, and I get to be in peace.

I pull a ham sandwich out of my backpack and unwrap the waxed paper. I made it myself this morning—we actually had groceries today—and take a bite, then set it down and get out my assignment notebook to see what I should work on first. I want to get everything done since I have the stupid drug class tonight. Though honestly, I'm actually excited about it. About seeing Jake. About him driving me home again.

The classroom door opens, and I look up, expecting Mr. Tallman. Instead it's Stacey. *Fuck.*

"I had a really hard time finding you." She stands still in the doorway, somehow managing to look sexy but not slutty in her black leggings and pink Nike crop top. Over it, of course, is an unzipped hoodie, since bare midriffs aren't allowed at school. And she's wearing her pink Converse sneakers.

I shift my feet, aware I'm wearing my red Chucks and remembering how we bought them together at the mall just outside Chicago, an hour's drive away but the closest decent place to go shopping.

"Maybe I didn't want to be found." I squish my index finger down on my sandwich, making a circular indentation in the bread.

"I just wanna talk, Melanie." She walks over to where I'm sitting, her mass of blonde curls bouncing around her shoulders, her lips glossy pink, and flops her Michael Kors purse on the floor before sliding into the desk next to mine. I'm not into purses, and I only know the brand because she dragged me with her to buy it, and even though I've always known her family has money, dropping several hundred dollars on a bag astounded me. It still does.

"There's nothing to talk about." I quickly fold the wax paper around my sandwich and shove it into my backpack along with my assignment notebook.

"Please? Just for a minute?" She lightly grasps my arm with her hand, sporting perfectly manicured nails coated in an effervescent pink.

"What?" I ask, hoisting my backpack into my shoulders but waiting. I'm curious to see what she wants to say to me.

"I'm sorry. I've texted you and I left that note in your locker and I just want you to know I feel really terrible about what happened." Her eyes are pleading with mine.

"But not terrible enough to admit the shit was yours?"

She sighs and shuts her eyes, tilting her head up to the ceiling before looking back at me. "Then we'd both get in trouble, right? You don't want that for me, do you?" Her voice is a plea. She continues, "I said I was sorry, Melanie. And I am. But you've got to understand! If University of Illinois found out about it, they might change their minds about admitting me. And it's been my dream for, like, *ever*. Both my parents went there. They'd kill me. You know that. You know them." She pauses, then says, "They're not like your mom."

"A drunk?" My voice rises and I cross my arms over my chest. "Is that what you mean?"

"No! I didn't mean that. I didn't say that! Your mom is just, I don't know, more casual. About stuff." She looks panicked. "Mel, you know I love your mom. She's, like, so fun."

"And what if University of Chicago finds out about me getting in trouble?" I ask. "What if they revoke *my* acceptance?" I stand up and glare at her.

"I don't *know*, Melanie." She steps back and plays with a curl. "Of course I don't want that to happen! But I can't say anything about me, you know? I can't risk my future! It's like… I'm, like, *expected* to go to college. I can't ruin that."

"So just ruin my chances instead? Because I'm not *expected* to do anything with my life except stay here in this shitty town?" I feel so angry and sad, wondering how this person I've been friends with since third grade could be so selfish and unaware and awful.

"Nothing's ruined! You just have to take that class, right? And then it's over? And, like, I owe you one, OK?" she says.

"I don't want anything from you." I head to the door.

"I'm sorry, Melanie! I swear I'll make it up to you. I'm never going to bring, you know, *stuff* to school again, because I definitely learned my lesson. And I'll… I don't know. I'll have your back, OK?"

There are a million things I want to say. *Fuck you.* Or *kiss my ass.* Or *rot in hell forever you fucking slut.* We used to curse at each other all the time when we were best friends, joking around and seeing who could come up with the worst insult. Only we're not friends anymore. Only now I actually mean them all. I walk away without a word.

• • •

I'm on my way out of school when Principal Evans stops me. "Melanie, I need to have a word with you." Although she's smiling, it's a grim sort of expression, like she's hiding something horrible.

Crap, crap, crap. What the hell is going on? Is this about Jake? Did she find out we slept together? My heart jumps thinking about how much trouble he'd be in, and I'm cold with guilt.

Principal Evans gestures for me to sit, and I balance on the edge of one of the cheap leather chairs in front of her desk. I expect her to continue behind her desk and sit in her own chair, but instead she turns the chair next to mine so it's facing me and sits in it.

"Let's talk," she says, which I take as a cue for me to turn and face her. "Something's come up," she continues. Her eyes are really sad, and that freaks me out.

"K," I say, my voice coming out quieter than I'd intended.

She takes a deep breath. "Melanie, there's no good way to tell you this. So I'm just going to say it. The scholarship you got from Children of Incarcerated Parents? They're revoking it. Something in the fine print about how recipients need to stay out of trouble..."

"But I thought that's what the stupid drug class was about! To keep it off my record!" Panicked, I stand up and pace.

"It is. And that's important. I don't even know for sure how the group found out about you getting in trouble, but it's within their rights according to the scholarship agreement you signed for them to revoke it. I'm so sorry this happened, Melanie."

I can't speak. My throat feels swollen, like anything I'd want to say would be trapped inside me. I can barely even breathe. "But..." I don't know what to say.

"Melanie, I know the drugs weren't even yours. I still don't know why you insisted on keeping quiet about whose they were. It's not too late to try and fix this, if you tell me what really happened." She stands up to look into my face. "Mel?" She sounds hopeful.

"I can't... it doesn't..." What is there to say? My chance—my one and only chance in this whole miserable fucking world—for me to get out of this town and to Chicago for college is gone. "Would it even matter if I said they weren't mine? I mean, they'll just think I'm lying, right?"

"I can help you look for other scholarship opportunities. And there's financial aid. We can also talk about deferring your admittance for a year..."

I shake my head. We both know it's too late for scholarships. And even with financial aid, there's no way I could afford the University of Chicago. I could wait a year, but the thought of that right now, when I was counting on getting away from Bells Park as soon as possible, feels like something in the distant future, so far away I can't see it anymore.

"There *are* other options, Melanie," Principal Evans is saying, but I can't stay here. I can't listen to any more.

"I need to go," I manage to get out, and the last thing I see before I take off is her face, so concerned and sad that it makes my anguish that much worse.

I run out of the office, past the secretary who mutters a bewildered *bye* as I pass her. The hallways are nearly empty, since students evacuate the building as quickly as possible after the last bell, and once I'm outside, I take a deep breath, hoping the fresh air will calm me down. But it doesn't.

My body is freezing and burning up at the same time, like I have the energy to run all the way to Chicago and back without stopping. But I need to calm down. I'm supposed to work at the antique shop for a couple of hours before going to the drug class, though I've already decided I'm not going to that. What's the point?

"Hello, dear!" Mrs. Hart gives me a big smile as I enter, and though I smile back, she frowns. "You don't look well, Melanie. Is everything all right?" Her soft face is comforting, her eyes kind, and I almost tell her. I almost break down in tears and open my mouth.

Instead, though, I nod. "I'm fine, Mrs. Hart. Just tired. Everything's OK."

"All right. Well. If you need to talk, you know where to find me!" She points at the ceiling and smiles.

I force my lips to turn up in response, but I'm grateful when she leaves me alone. Sitting still is impossible. Too much anger and energy is built up inside me, and I need to stay busy. I start with the bookshelves, organizing all the books alphabetically within categories. We've never done that before. A cookbook could be next to a mystery novel, which could be next to a children's book. When I'm done, though, they're arranged perfectly.

Next I tackle the framed artwork, leaning three deep against the back wall. All the landscapes go together. Portraits with each other. Homemade art gets its own stack, and these always make me feel sad. Once a person painted a picture, then later someone stopped caring, or didn't like it, or died, and the art ended up at a secondhand store like this one. Same thing with framed photographs, especially school photos. If it was worth framing once, wouldn't you always want to keep it? What happened that made someone say, "I don't need this photo of my kid when he was five"?

There's more to do—it would take days of nonstop work to organize the whole store—but it's time to close up and not-go to the stupid drug class. I turn off the light and lock the front door, double-checking, like always, that it's secured. Not like anyone would try to rob a place like this, but still.

Molly, the orange cat, appears from behind the building, skinny and loud, mewling at me as she brushes against my shins and calves.

"Molly," I whine, but I can't turn her down, even though I'm sort of in a hurry. "Fine. Come on." I reopen the shop and she glides in, then follows me while I get food and water. Once I set them down, she stops crying and eats vigorously without stopping till it's gone.

"I can't cuddle today," I whisper, petting her back. Her fur is soft, but I can feel the sharp bones right under it. And then, despite myself, I scoop her up and hug her, grateful beyond belief for her warmth, grateful to have *someone* to give me comfort, even if it's only a stray cat.

I clean up the bowls, then let us both back out into the cold evening. The chill air pricks my arms, even through my sweatshirt. Then again, it's practically paper thin since it's so worn out. The antique store doesn't carry clothes, and when people drop them off here we donate them to the shelter in Bolster, so there's nothing to grab.

The library's not far, so I jog there, backpack bumping against my back. Inside, I head straight to the stairwell and grab the black hoodie again. Except now I'm not just borrowing it. I'm going to keep it. I drop my backpack to the floor to pull on the sweatshirt, then grab my stuff and head outside once more, this time down the street to the Save Lot grocery store on the corner. I don't have much money, but tonight it doesn't matter.

Only one cashier is working in the two check-out aisles, though *working* isn't exactly accurate. She's staring out the murky window, and gives me a half-hearted wave as I come in. The store's almost empty, which makes what I'm planning to do much more difficult. But I'm determined. And pissed. And maybe a little desperate too.

I pass by the table of expiring bakery goods, the ones that will be stale even though they're still technically legal to sell, and pretend to browse while I check out the tiny liquor corner at the back of the store. I've got my eye on the smallest, cheapest bottle of whiskey; it'll be easy to hide under my shirt, and even though I'm sure it will taste like shit, I know it will do what I want it to.

Scanning the aisles as surreptitiously as possible, I make my way to the corner, pretending to be checking my phone on the way. I reach out my hand, my fingers grasping the cool glass of the bottle, and snag it quickly, thrusting it up under the sweatshirt and into the waistband of my jeans.

I need to get out of here. I can't get caught. Though what does it matter, really? It's not like I have anything to look forward to anymore. It's not like I'm getting out of this shitty town any time soon.

At the checkout I grab a Twix bar and set it on the belt. I feel like it's less suspicious if I actually buy something. Plus, I haven't eaten all day, the ham sandwich from lunch no longer appealing after my talk with Stacey. It ended up in the trash, and my stomach feels raw.

"That it for you?" asks the clerk. Her eyes are tired, and her hair is in really bad need of a dye job. I think she's about my mom's age, but it's hard to tell. Though I've seen her around, I don't know her name. But I do know she's been here forever. Maybe this will be me someday, staring out the window of the Save Lot at nothing, waiting for people to come into the dusty and pathetic excuse for a store, day after day after day.

"Yeah. Just the Twix."

She rings me up and I pay. "Need a bag?" she asks.

"No." *It's just a fucking candy bar*, I want to add, but I don't say anything except *thanks* as I head back out into the night.

• • •

If you walk east down the railroad tracks, there's a spot where they run along a bridge, and you can climb down underneath it into a wide tunnel. The river's there, and it's gross, but it's receded so much that there's plenty of space to hang out on the cement slabs on either side of the water. Graffiti decorates the walls, and the ground is littered with beer cans and broken bottles. It's the sort of place homeless people would live, but even vagrants stay away from Bells Park. Sometimes kids come here to drink or smoke, but I'm alone tonight.

After brushing a spot clear of glass and debris, I sit down, leaning against the wall, and crack open the bottle of whiskey. I don't drink a lot. Sometimes Stacey and I used to, but it was usually good stuff, wine we snuck from her parents' special temperature-controlled cabinet. This smells strong, but I take a sip, shivering at the harsh bite.

God. It's fucking awful. But I take another sip.

I don't have a plan. Not for my future, and not for tonight. All I know is I don't want to be home. And the drug class? No fucking way. I'm never going back to that. I don't even want to go to school anymore, because what's the point?

I recap the bottle, then pull out my pack of cigarettes and light one, my hands numb from the cold. Huddling into my new-to-me sweatshirt, I inhale and blow out the smoke, watching it float away. Like angels. Or fucking ghosts.

The tears surprise me, unstoppable even before I know they're coming. My body heaves, taken over by uncontrollable sobs.

"What the fuck am I going to do?" My words are a blubbery mess, and there's nobody to hear them. But nobody would have an answer anyway.

"Melanie?" A voice stills me. It's Jake, and I don't want him to see me here like this.

I hold my breath, hoping he'll go away. But the bushes near me rustle until he's pushing through them and walking toward me.

"What the hell are you doing here? Why aren't you in class?" His voice doesn't sound as angry as I'd have thought it would.

"Why aren't *you* in class?" I counter.

"I called in a favor from a friend when you didn't show up."

"It's a stupid class anyway. What's it to you if I skip?"

"If you skip you get a record. Is that what you want?" He comes closer, then sits down next to me on the cement. He smells clean, like he recently showered, and even though we're not touching, my leg next to his feels warmer than the rest of my body.

"It doesn't matter what I want." I take a final drag from my cigarette and flick it into the stagnant river, where it hisses before going out.

"I talked to your principal. I heard what happened."

"Yeah. Well. That's fucking life. How did you know where to find me anyway?"

He laughs. "Cause I used to be your age, and this is exactly where I'd have hung out back then."

"So of all the places I could have gone, you just *knew* I'd be here?" *Bullshit.*

There's humor in his voice when he says, "Well, that and I saw you darting off into the woods. I followed you."

"Stalker. I'm not a kid, you know."

"I know."

"Then why do you treat me like one?"

"What do you mean?" He turns to me, I can see it out of the corner of my eye, but I just keep staring out at the murky black water.

52

"I mean the way you talk about me with the principal. Like you're both so worried about poor little me. When you say things like *when I was your age* like you're so much older than I am. I'm an adult now too, you know."

He sighs. "Melanie, I am older than you. And Principal Evans and I are worried about you. We both know how smart you are. And we both know the pot in your locker was someone else's. We care about you."

"See, that's exactly what I'm talking about!" I turn to him, my heart pounding in anger and something else I can't quite pinpoint. "The whole *we* thing. Like you're working together to help the poor high school kid."

"Fine. *I* care about you, Melanie, OK? Separate from Principal Evans and separate from the class and just the fuck on my own. Got it?" He sounds as mad as I do.

I turn away and pick up the bottle, unscrewing the cap.

"What the fuck, Melanie?" He grabs it from me. "Where did you get this?"

"My mom."

"Bullshit."

"Fine. Save Lot."

"Jesus, Melanie, did you steal it? Or do you have another fake ID?"

"I stole it." I'm past the point of caring what I tell him. What's he going to do? Arrest me?

He stands and strides to the edge of the river, where he upends the bottle and pours the contents out.

"Hey! That's mine!"

He turns back to me. "Let's go."

I shake my head. "You can take the whiskey, but you can't make me go home. I just... can't right now. OK? Just leave me here."

"I'm not going to leave you here. It's dangerous. And cold. And ten bucks says you haven't eaten dinner, and probably not lunch either."

The second he mentions food, my stomach growls, and I clench my stomach muscles to try to stop it. I don't want to prove him right.

"Come on." He steps toward me, reaching out his hand. "I'll get you something to eat."

"I'm not going anywhere. I've been crying, and I look like shit. Any anyway, there's nowhere to go around here."

For a second he's silent, like he's contemplating something. Then he sighs. "Let's go to my place. I've got food, and you can clean up. And then I'll take you home."

"Fine." My heart flip-flops, but I pretend I don't care. When I reach out my hand he grasps it, and his skin is warm, his hand strong as it enfolds mine. With a gentle tug he pulls me to standing, and I grab my backpack.

"Let's go." He drops my hand and starts to climb the embankment.

The loss I feel the second our hands disconnect is terrifying, so I ignore it. I follow him through the mud and brambles and out into the open air along the tracks.

CHAPTER FIVE – JAKE

This is a mistake. I know it with every fiber of my being. But it feels inevitable, like something you can't stop, even if you see it coming. A natural disaster. Hurricane. Tsunami. All you can do is sit back, batten the hatches, and watch it happen.

Of course, I'm full of shit. I could end this at any moment. Could be firm and take her home. But I see in her eyes she can't go there right now, and I don't blame her. She'd be as good as alone with her mom, and leaving her by herself right now would be a mistake. That desperate but sad, defeated but angry look makes it clear.

As I unlock the door to my apartment and let us in, the vivid memory of the only other time she's been here invades my mind. How we could barely make it inside, we were kissing so hard. How desire flooded my brain, my body, and all I knew in those moments was her: wanting her, tasting her, having her. How intimately we got to know each other, every inch of skin touched, licked, caressed.

Fuck. That's not what right now is about, and in retrospect I know it was wrong. But keeping desire at bay feels Herculean.

She sits awkwardly on the couch, sort of balancing on the edge, and looks up at me. Her face is puffy and tearstained, and her clothes, I now notice, are muddy.

"You hungry?" I hang my jacket up and take off my belt holster, setting it on the side table near the front door.

Melanie shrugs, her delicate shoulders barely moving. It's almost like my heart actually breaks a little, like a small fissure cracks open to see her so defeated.

"Hang on." In my bedroom—where I try to forget all the things we did on this very bed—I grab a pair of sweats and put them in the bathroom with a fresh towel.

Back in the living room she's exactly where I left her. "Hey," I say gently. "There's clean clothes and a towel for you in the bathroom. Take a shower, OK? I'll make something to eat. The bathroom's there…" I gesture behind me, but of course she knows where the bathroom is. She's been here before.

"You saying I stink?" The ghost of a smile forms on her lips.

"You're covered in river mud. I don't want to get close enough to see what you smell like," I joke. "Seriously, though, you'll feel better."

"Nothing can make me feel better," she mutters under her breath, but stands and walks toward me. As she passes she puts out her hand, running it along my side briefly as she continues on to the bathroom without a look at me. The door closes and I hear the click of the lock.

Jesus. I take a deep breath, my mind whirling at how quickly she went from bedraggled waif to sexy-as-fuck vixen. She's a contradiction, which confuses me while turning me on more than it should. And it pisses me off that such a small touch can send my mind spiraling in the absolute fucking wrong direction.

I stand still for a few seconds grounding myself until I hear the water turn on, then I head to the kitchen.

The Save Lot, the only grocery store in town, isn't known for variety. There's a minuscule section of supposedly fresh fruit and vegetables, but half of it is already furry or brown, so your best bet is frozen or canned stuff. I settle on something easy and quick: pasta with jarred spaghetti sauce and a bagged salad, only slightly limp, which I pour into a serving bowl and sprinkle with parmesan cheese. I set the table for two and put out a bottle of salad dressing.

Without really thinking, I grab two beers from the fridge, then remember and stop myself. Melanie's only eighteen years old. Not old enough to drink, though apparently she never got that message.

Cursing under my breath, I put the beers back and fill two glasses with some bottled water—the tap water in Bells Park is definitely not safe for human consumption.

While Melanie showers, I stay busy prepping everything for dinner. I need to keep my mind off her. In there. Water running down her body as her hands touch, wash, soothe. I growl, angry at myself, and drain the spaghetti, the hot steam rushing up into my face like a punishment. I toss it with some butter and olive oil, then serve it into two bowls, pouring sauce on top and setting them on the table.

Where the hell is Melanie? I'm about to go check on her, knock on the door and make sure she's OK, when I hear the bathroom door open. Before I see her I smell the spicy scent of my shower gel as it wafts out on a cloud of steam. And then she walks into the kitchen.

Her face is clean, her cheeks pink from the heat of the water. That long black hair is wet and sleek, tucked behind her ears so I can see every detail of her face. The first time I saw her I was taken by her eyes—huge and hazel, the kind of eyes that take everything in, not missing a single thing. Now, too, I can't look away, have to fight the desire to stare into her eyes, to try to figure her out, as though if I gazed long enough I could read her thoughts. Which is fucking ridiculous, but I feel hypnotized. Mesmerized.

Her lashes are so long they almost look fake. And those lips: full and red, even without any makeup. She's the kind of gorgeous that intimidates guys and pisses off girls. And she's not even fully aware of it.

My gray sweatshirt and pants are baggy on her, but there's something about seeing her in them, about the way they're so huge on her that makes my heart pound harder.

"Hey," I say. I have to clear my throat, because my voice is suddenly stuck. "Hey," I say louder. "Food's ready." I gesture at one of the chairs, and she gives me a small smile before slipping into the seat.

"Thanks," she says quietly. "For, you know, the shower and clothes. And dinner. It looks really good."

"It's not much. Sauce is from a jar." I shrug.

"At my house? My mom never cooks. And I don't either. So I usually just have, like, a sandwich or granola bar or something for dinner."

It suddenly occurs to me that though she has curves—ones I can't get out of my mind no matter what—she's not exactly voluptuous. In fact, she's kind of skinny, and I suddenly get the feeling it's not purposeful. There's probably not enough food in her house, and she doesn't have money for nutritious stuff, or doesn't make it a priority. What high school senior uses extra cash for fruit and vegetables?

I feel sad again, but I don't want her to think I'm feeling sorry for her. Sometimes she's like a skittish stray; one wrong word will set her off and she'll run.

"Go ahead. Eat." I gesture at her still-untouched plate. "Here." I push the salad dressing over to her.

She laughs. "Salad! We never have salad at my house." But she serves some into her bowl and carefully pours some dressing on top.

She eats like she's starving, and I suppose she is. When she finishes, I ask her if she wants more.

"No," she says. "That was good, though." One of her fingers runs across her plate, picking up sauce, and then she sticks it in her mouth and licks it off.

I look away. "I'm glad you liked it."

There's a knock on my door, and I sit up straight. I don't have many visitors, and I don't want anyone to find Melanie here in my apartment.

"Stay here," I tell her as I head into the living room. "Yeah?" I ask loudly through the door.

"Jakey! What's up, kid?" It's my fucking uncle Mike. Whom I love. And who normally I'd enjoy inviting in for a beer. But he'd kill me if he found me here with an eighteen-year-old from my class.

I crack the door enough so I can stand in the opening and talk to him, but not enough for him to walk in and get comfortable.

His face is ruddy, his eyes kind but worried. "What happened with class tonight? Everything OK?"

My uncle's been like a second father to me for most of my life, and since my dad died a year ago—was killed a year ago—even more so. He's a cop like my dad was, both of them the reason I went into the profession as well. He's taller than me and beefier, but it's all muscle. When he isn't working, he's working out, and though I join him in the makeshift gym at the station a few times a week, he's in there every single day.

"Yeah. I just, uh, wasn't feeling well earlier." I hate lying to him. I don't think I've ever done it before, and I know he values honesty above all else. The truth isn't something he'd want to hear, though.

"Aw, poor little Jakey." He laughs, then gets serious. "You need anything, kid?"

"Naw, I…" My voice breaks off as the sound of the refrigerator interrupts me, the sucking noise as it opens combined with the jangle of jars in the door knocking together.

Mike tilts his head and raises an eyebrow. "Company? I thought you were sick."

I look down, running my hand through my hair. "I am. I got a, you know, friend over. Kinda taking care of me."

He nods and grins. "A little nursing action?"

I smile and hope with everything in my heart that Melanie doesn't decide to come into the living room right now. "Yup."

"Tell me who she is, I'll tell you all the gossip," he offers. "Small town."

"Ha. It's, you know, casual."

He stares at me for a moment. "All right. I'll see you tomorrow, Jakey."

"Yeah. I'll be in early. And I'm sorry about tonight. You know I wouldn't…"

He interrupts me. "I know. I still owe you for being here at all. It's been a big help having you around."

"I think it's helping me more than you. I really needed to get away…"

He interrupts, patting me on the shoulder. "I know you did. And you're going to have to go back. But while you're here, you've been a big help."

There's a longer conversation we need to have, but now's not the time, so I'm grateful when he nods, then turns and heads down the stairs.

I close the door, then lock it, breathing out hard in relief. Way too fucking close.

In the kitchen, Melanie's moved the chairs so she's sitting on one and her feet are up on another, crossed at the ankle. And she's drinking from a bottle of beer. She gestures at a second bottle, also open, on the table.

"I opened one for you too." She looks up at me from under her thick eyelashes, half apologetic and half flirting. She's definitely morphed all the way into sexy from the sad, crying girl I brought here earlier.

The argument dies on my lips before I can even utter a word. Instead I stare at her, hoping I'm projecting anger, not lust.

"It's just one beer," she argues, tipping back her bottle and drinking. "It's not like I've never drank before. Or been drunk."

"We're not getting drunk." I sit down and pick up my beer, taking a long pull.

"OK." She shrugs lightly, her eyes on mine the whole time. "Whatever you say." Now she's definitely flirting, her tone lilting but just heavy enough to let me know what she really means by *whatever*.

"One beer. And then I take you home."

60

Her face freezes.

I sigh. "Look, Melanie. Do you want to talk about what happened? About the scholarship?"

"Yeah. That'd be great. And while we're at it, do you want to ask me about my dad? He's in prison, you know. And my mom? She drinks wine all day and makes these, like, photo videos with cheesy music, and she posts them to YouTube. Can we talk about her too? Or about how now I'll be stuck in this shitty town forever? Cause that's going to be a really fun conversation." She downs her beer and sets the bottle on the table hard.

I put up my hands in defense. "I just wanted to see if you needed to talk. I know you're disappointed right now, but this is just one setback. You'll still get to college. You'll get out of this town. But you can't give up at the first challenge. Life is full of challenges, and if you let a single one stop you, you'll never go anywhere."

Her eyes fill with fury as she stares at me, but then she takes a deep breath. "You're right. OK? You're right. But it still sucks. What am I supposed to do? Shrug and pretend that it's fine? Because it's not."

"No. It isn't."

When she continues, her voice is small, almost a whisper. "I'm scared, Jake. I'm terrified I'll never, I don't know, *make* it. That I'll end up like my mom or the cashier at Save Lot."

"Melanie." I want to take her hands in mine. I want to cup her face and look into her eyes and tell her she's amazing and smart, that I've never met anyone with a soul like hers. That someday she's going to do spectacular things. But I can't. It's wrong. "You're smart. You know that. Tell me about college. What are you going to study?"

"Social work." She doesn't hesitate.

"You sound pretty sure. A lot of college freshman have no idea what they want to go into."

"I just... I... It's stupid." She looks down at her lap.

"Tell me."

"Fine." She takes a deep breath. "When I was a kid and my dad was in and out of prison all the time, as opposed to now where he's mostly just in, I saw some social workers at school. And I remember thinking that they were always talking down to me. That they never thought I was smart or understood much at all. And then later, there's been some people, like Principal Evans, who are really great. I mean, I see through her, you know? When she pretends she accidentally bought an extra sandwich or something and gives one to me?" Melanie laughs softly. "But I can tell she really *likes* me. And cares. And wants me to do well. I want to do that someday for kids who are going through a lot."

I want to reach across the table and touch her cheek or take her hand, hold it in mine, and let her know I think she's incredible. Instead I clear my throat. "I think you'll be amazing in that field, because you know firsthand how important it is for kids to have support outside the home sometimes. My mom recently became a foster parent, and she has a kid living with her now. As a cop, I've seen a lot of situations where children were being abused or neglected, and it breaks my heart every single time." I look at her intently.

"Why did you decide to become a cop?" She tilts her head and licks her lips, not trying to be sexy, but she is all the same.

"My dad was a cop. And my uncle. He's the chief of police here in Bells Park. I'm here helping him out for a while."

"Oh, so *that's* why you're here. I knew there had to be some reason, because nobody would willingly choose to move here." She rolls her eyes and grins.

"Yeah, it's not the nicest place I've been." I laugh. "I'm pretty sure there are more boarded-up buildings on Main Street than open businesses."

"Right? It's just… dead. It feels stagnant and depressing and lonely, like God forgot about it and so did everyone else." She says it ironically, but her eyes are sad and her voice carries more than a hint of sadness. Then she sits up straight and grins, looking straight into my eyes. "Can I have another beer?"

Gazing right at each other sends a spark straight to my groin. "I shouldn't have let you drink the first one."

She darts out an arm and grabs my bottle, swigging, and setting it back down with a *now what?* look in her eyes. This is definitely not a game I should play. But it's hard to resist the challenge I see when I look at her, red lips holding back a grin as she stares hard, unblinking.

I take a deep breath, hoping to keep my wits, and shake my head. "Get your stuff. I'm taking you home."

With a scowl, she gets up and heads to the bathroom. A few seconds later she goes into the living room, still dressed in my sweats, her clothes in hand.

I grab a plastic grocery bag from the cabinet and bring it to her. "You can put your clothes in here. Keep the sweats."

"I couldn't." Her voice is lower than usual. Throaty. She's up to something as she holds my gaze with those hazel eyes, grinning at me.

"It's not a problem."

"I should really return them now." She grasps the bottom hem of the sweatshirt and lifts it up, slowly. Slow enough, in fact, for me to stop her, but I'm frozen.

I can't take my eyes off the silky expanse of stomach she reveals, slim and tight. I suck in a breath when I see she's not wearing a bra. In one final movement she pulls the shirt up and over her head, tossing it at me.

"Think fast," she says.

I barely catch it, and still I'm too stunned to move as she stands before me in only my baggy sweatpants. I've seen her naked before, but it's as exciting now as the first time to see her topless, her perfect round breasts tipped with hard, pink nipples. I close my eyes briefly, imagining my tongue on them. *Remembering* my tongue on them.

"Melanie." There's warning in my voice, but desire too. I can't hide it. I clutch the sweatshirt as I watch, transfixed, while Melanie's hands move to the waistband of the pants.

Her hair is almost dry now, and it falls across her chest, partially obscuring her tits. How I want to push it aside, stroke her neck, take her nipple between my fingers.

I need to stop her. Stop *this*. But I'm unable to move as she slowly—achingly slowly—pushes the sweatpants down. And, fuck me, she's not wearing panties. Her eyes meet mine, unblinking, as she pushes them all the way to floor and steps out of them.

She bends and picks them up, then makes her way to where I stand, hard as fuck, watching her.

"Here." She holds them out to me.

"You need to get dressed," I murmur.

But her breasts are pressed up against my chest, and through my jeans I swear I can feel the warmth from between her legs. So when she whispers, "Just one kiss," I cave and drop the clothes I'm holding.

I want to devour her. I want to taste every single inch of her. She's so beautiful and clean and ready. Her lips are smoother than I remember, her tongue more demanding, and when I clutch her naked ass, drawing her closer to me, I know I'm fucking lost.

Her hand runs through my hair, clutches a handful, pulling just enough to hurt, spurring me farther, faster. I kiss her harder and she bends one knee, sliding her leg up and wrapping it around me.

Jesus.

Breaking off the kiss, she looks up into my face, her eyes big, hungry. "So, can I stay?" There's confidence in her tone. Teasing too, as if she knows there's no chance I'll say no.

But then I see it. Desperation, or maybe fear, or maybe both. And I recognize the look, the same one she had that first night I met her. Like deep down inside there might be more than just lust driving her tonight. I ignored it that first time, but I can't ignore it now.

64

Nothing in my life has ever been as difficult as it is to step back from her and look away. My entire body wants nothing more than to undo my jeans, push them down and grab her, wrap her legs around me, and fuck her right here in the living room, my belt jangling with each thrust.

But my fucking morality or ethics or whatever it is stops me cold. I pick up the sweats and toss them back at her, trying not to look at her face. "Put these on. I'm taking you home."

"Fuck you." Her words, though a whisper, cut right through me. She unfurls her dirty stack of clothes and begins to pull them on.

I can't look at her. She's hurt, but sleeping with her wouldn't help. It would only make things worse. I can see that now, knowing what I know. I'm not the right guy for her. I'm not the right *anything* for her. I don't know what exactly she needs. But it's sure as hell not me.

When she's done getting dressed she's out the door before I can say anything.

"Wait," I call after her, grabbing my keys. "I'll give you a ride. It's not safe…"

But there's no way she's getting in my car. At a brisk pace she starts down the sidewalk.

"Fuck," I mutter to myself. Should I follow her? I start after her on foot, then change tactic and get into my car, driving at a few miles an hour, just behind her. If I let her run off as angry as she is, she might not even go home. She'd go somewhere else and do something stupid, like she almost did with me.

In my car's headlights she stops suddenly, illuminated, and flips me off, then leaves the sidewalk, darting between two abandoned buildings and disappearing into the night.

Cursing, I drive past the dark space where she went but can't see anything. Instead, I head to her house, where I wait till she shows up and slips inside, without even a look in my direction.

CHAPTER SIX – MELANIE

The second I wake up, the humiliation from last night washes over me. I pull the covers up and curl into myself, wishing I could forget how I stripped—literally stripped—for him, and he still said no.

Fucking pathetic. I don't know if he just feels sorry for me or what, but I hate him. And it's his fucking loss anyway. I could get any guy to sleep with me if that's what I wanted to do.

I pull on jeans and an ancient Chicago Cubs T-shirt that Stacey's dad bought me back in freshman year when he took us to a game at Wrigley Field. He bought hotdogs for us and beer for himself, and even though I kind of hate sports, it was fun to be there, so far away from Bells Park. I hated it even back then.

In the kitchen I scan the contents of the fridge looking for something to bring to lunch. The ham smells weird and looks sort of gray, but there's a little bit of jelly left in the jar, so I make a quick sandwich on only slightly stale bread and wrap it up, then stick it into my backpack.

"Hey, honey."

I turn, surprised to see my mom, fully dressed and with makeup on. She only wears makeup when she goes out, which is never, so this is a strange sight. And she's not usually up and clothed at this point in the day.

She's squeezed into an old pair of black dress pants with a tucked-in white button-down blouse, giving her the look of an overweight waitress instead of a recluse who sits at home on her computer all day long. The blouse is wrinkled, and the toes of her black faux-leather boots are scuffed and peeling.

Her makeup isn't exactly right either: lips too red, blush too dark, eyeliner not quite straight. Her hair, still wet from the shower, is pulled back into a thin ponytail.

At least she tried.

"Hey, Mom. You're up early." I sling my backpack over my shoulder and head to the door. "I'll see you." I'm curious why my mom's up, but I need to leave now or I'll be late.

"I'll drive you. The principal called me yesterday and asked if I could come in to meet with her. I wasn't, well, up for it. So we agreed on first thing in the morning."

Shit. Well, it's not like she was never going to find out about the scholarship. And it's not like she'll even be mad at me. She never gets mad. I think she's too numb from all the drinking she does. Sometimes I wonder if she even has feelings at all anymore.

"Do you know what this is all about?" she asks as she follows me out the front door. "Huh," she adds, running a finger down the railing, where paint is peeling, like she hasn't seen it in months. Maybe she hasn't.

I shake my head. I don't want to talk about it. "Nope."

"How's school going?" she asks as we both get into our shitty car, an ancient Pontiac. The duct tape covering the cracks in the vinyl seat is sticky around the edges, and I crunch up against the window so I avoid getting the gummy residue on my jeans. It'll never come out.

"Fine."

"And that class? The drug class?"

"Oh. Great."

"You had it again last night, didn't you? I'm sorry I wasn't awake when you got home."

"It's OK. The class was fine. It's good."

"You know," she says, putting on the blinker and waiting at the red light on Main Street. "I'm really proud of you, honey. For

67

being a good student. And taking care of as much as you do. And with your father…" Her voice trails off. She likes to talk about him as much as I do, which is not at all.

She turns, and her purse slips from the center console onto the seat next to me. It's this oversized fake white leather bag, with the faux outside cracking and peeling, revealing dark gray thread-worn fabric beneath it.

When I was a little kid, I used to love to rifle through her purse, because she had all sorts of cool things. A hairbrush, inevitably with strands of hair woven and stuck inside the bristles. Pens. Wadded-up receipts. Gum, some partially opened and sticking to the silver foil wrapper, but I could usually find at least one piece clean enough to chew. Random business cards and bookmarks she'd picked up at who knows where. Sales ads from the grocery store. Cigarettes and matches and lighters, usually at least three or four. I used to love the colors of the lighters, especially the neon see-through ones, and wished I had a need for one. They were so pretty.

Around fifth grade, though, I'd find liquor in there too. The individual serving sized bottles of wine. White. Red. Pink. She didn't discriminate. I stopped looking through her purse, because I hated to see them. I'd never been through other mothers' bags, but I was fairly certain they didn't have wine stashed away.

Now, I hear the clink of the glass against a pen or a lighter or something, and I look out the passenger side window until we get to school.

"Bye," I say and get out as quickly as I can.

• • •

I'm not going to school. There's no way. Humiliation about last night courses through me as hot as the knowledge that I lost my scholarship. I thought I could put it out of my mind, focus on my classes instead, but as soon as I see the heavy double doors, I know it will be impossible.

I head around the side of the school, passing the wrecked track and football field. Cutting across the student parking lot, I see Stacey's white Range Rover, sparkling in the morning sun.

"Melanie!" She jogs up behind me, the scent of her flowery perfume so familiar that I wish I could go back in time to when we were still friends, before she betrayed me.

Sighing, I stop and turn. "What do you want?" Really, I should keep walking. I should ignore her. And maybe I'm being pathetic and stupid, but I'm lonely. She used to be my best friend.

"Where are you going?" she asks, slightly breathless. "Are you skipping?" She tucks some of her blonde curls behind her ear, her blue eyes open wide as a smile forms on her mouth.

I shrug.

"Get in," she says, pulling out her car keys and clicking her car unlocked. It beeps, and she nods at it. "Come on. Let's hang out. We'll drive to Bolster and check out some shops or see a movie or something. Like old times. Please? I just… I'm sorry. And I miss you." She presents me with a dramatic frown, her pink lips pouty and sad.

Fuck you, I say, but only in my head. "Fine," I say out loud. I climb into her car, settling into the warm leather interior.

Stacey pulls her sun visor down to check her makeup in the mirror, pursing her shiny pink lips and smiling at herself. Then she snaps it back up again and grins at me. "It's going to be like old times, like we used to be," she says.

I nod. I wouldn't say we're friends again. Not yet. Maybe not ever. But I need to get away. I need to be with someone. And my choices are pretty limited at the moment.

"So where do you want to go? Maybe we should get coffee? Hit the Starbucks they just opened off 51? It's only like twenty minutes? You like Starbucks, right?" She's so eager to please.

"Yeah. Sure." She starts the car, and her phone rings. While she answers the call, I gaze out the window at students filtering into the building. For a moment I allow my eyes to close, to wish I was somewhere else, anywhere else but here in Bells Park with no way to get out.

"So it's okay if we pick up Robby first, right? His cousin is visiting from out of town so he's skipping, and we'll all do something together."

A few months ago I'd have loved an idea like this. A double date. A chance to hang out with Stacey and her boyfriend without being the third wheel. But today, when our friendship is shaky at best, I resent her for ruining this chance for us to bond again.

"Yeah. Whatever."

She pulls out of the parking lot and drives away from the school. "His cousin? He's really cute. He goes to, like, Loyola or Notre Dame or one of those colleges? I think you'll like him."

I can already imagine how the day will go. Stacey and Robby will be all over each other, leaving me and the cousin to have awkward conversations and ignore the fact that Stacey and Robby really want us to get along so everything's smooth and easy for them.

With top forty blasting—Stacey and I used to fake argue about what constituted good music all the time, and she never liked the slightly obscure alternative bands I do—she heads to the nice section of town, which is also the smallest section of town. Though it's technically part of Bells Park, it's like being in a different world. You drive down a country road for a few miles until you get to a gated neighborhood, where fountains and lush greenery, even now in cold and early spring, surround a spotlighted sign that reads *The Grove*.

I'm not entirely sure how they have such a nice neighborhood and houses and are still a part of our crumbling town. I know Stacey's dad is some sort of executive, always traveling and going to conferences, but I never cared enough to get the details. And Stacey's mom is like an older version of Stacey herself, blonde and bubbly. But unlike Stacey, she was always wary of me, even when Stacey and I were little. I slept over there, and played at their house for hours over the summers. But I always felt her hesitance, like she wanted to like me but couldn't quite figure out how.

We pass Stacey's gabled, two-story house, and she pulls into her boyfriend Robby's circular driveway and honks the horn. "Come on!" she says, opening her door and jumping out.

I thought we were just going to pick up Robby and his cousin and go to Starbucks, but I've known Stacey long enough to know plans can change without a moment's notice. So I climb out and follow her to the front door, which Robby pulls open. "Hey, babe." He kisses her on the lips, and I look away. When we spent all our time together, it was second nature to see them make out. Now, though, I feel like an outsider.

"What's up, Mel?" He nods at me, smiling but wary; it's been a while since we all hung out.

"Hi." I force a smile in his direction.

"Come in," he says. "You guys need to catch up."

I'm not sure what he means until we get into the kitchen, large and bright with stainless steel appliances, and I see the bottle of vodka next to the carafe of orange juice. For the record, I can't even imagine using a carafe for orange juice at my house. The rare times we have OJ, it's in the cardboard container, and we pour it straight into scratched-up glasses from the dirty wooden cabinets. Here, it's like being in a TV show kitchen, where everything's shiny and nothing's ever used.

Robby's cousin is cute, and in another world, another time, I might have been interested in him. He's thin and confident, with shaggy light brown hair and matching eyes that look like he's probably a little bit of trouble. He's wearing beat-up jeans and a Fighting Irish T-shirt, which I'm fairly sure is the football team at Notre Dame. College is the last thing I want to think about right now. Well, college and Jake.

"I'm Sam," he says, holding out his hand like an adult.

I can't remember the last time someone my age, or close to it, shook hands with me. I take his hand, and he grins, half cocky and half sweet. Maybe he can be a decent distraction.

"Melanie." I take my hand away and will myself not to blush.

"So you're a senior? What's your plan?"

"Well, I was going to go to University…" I start.

"You going to serve us drinks or hog it all to yourselves?" interrupts Stacey, a weird look on her face. It seems like she does it on purpose. It's not because I lost my scholarship—I'm pretty sure she doesn't know about that yet—so it must be because she doesn't want me to tell him I'm going to University of Chicago. She can't stand to be in anyone's shade.

"What? You saying we're not gentlemen?" Sam winks at me, then fills two crystal cut glasses with ice from the dispenser on the fridge. He pours vodka and then orange juice on top, handing one to each of us.

I don't think I should drink; not after what happened last night, not after how I felt when I got home: So lost, so shitty. But the look on Stacey's face and the thought of my mom in front of her monitor send lurches of depression through my gut, and without thinking I sip the drink, welcoming the warmth from the liquor as much as the refreshing taste of the juice. "It's good," I say, glancing at Sam.

"Yeah?" His eyes are smiling but intense too.

I blush and shrug. "Yeah."

"Let's watch TV." Stacey heads into the big rec room off the kitchen, where a giant flat screen is surrounded by oversized sofas, the kind that are perfect to curl up in and read. With the remote she turns it on and finds *The View*.

"Oh *fuck* no," says Robby with a laugh, reaching over to take the remote from her.

"Leave me alone!" she giggles, bending over so he can't get the controller.

"Fine. But turn the volume off? I can't stand fucking Whoopi's voice."

I sit in the corner of one of the couches, and Sam sits next to me, not quite touching but closer than a complete stranger would be.

"Hey, hey! Listen to this." Robby puts his hands up to shush us, then speaks, pretending to be Whoopi. "And you know, last night, I had sex with my dog. Don't judge, people. Don't judge."

"You're so stupid, Robby." Stacey punches him in the arm, and he pretends it hurts.

"Stupid enough to go out with you, I guess," he counters.

"Jerk."

"You love me." He pulls her to him and they kiss, soft smacking and sucking sounds rising above the sound of the tinny laughter from the TV.

Gross. I used to find their antics funny. Now, though, they're just stupid and annoying. I glance at Sam, and he rolls his eyes. "Get a room," he says, and pokes Robby, who makes a rude comment, but sits up. Stacey wipes her lip gloss and giggles.

Stacey and Robby fight over the remote for the next twenty minutes, flipping through the channels but not settling on anything, while Sam and I watch like they're the entertainment, not the TV itself.

"You guys wanna smoke?" asks Robby finally.

"It's, like, nine in the morning!" says Stacey, but her argument doesn't sound genuine.

Robby shrugs. "Sam? You in? Mel?"

"Let's do it." Sam gets up, looking questioningly at me.

"Whatever," I say under my breath, and I follow them outside.

Robby unstacks pool chairs, big white loungers, and sets them up around the covered pool. It's way too early in the season for it to be opened.

The sun's shining hard, the day warmer than any so far, and I move my chair into the light, enjoying the heat on my body. I lean back in my chair and close my eyes. The feet of a side table scrape on the concrete as Robby pulls it toward him, and though I'm not looking, I've seen this scene enough times to know exactly what he looks like, focusing everything he's got on making the joint tight and perfect.

73

A lighter clicks, and Robby inhales quickly a few times, getting the joint lit. The sweet, skunky smell fills my nostrils.

"Oh yeah," croaks Robby, lungs filled with smoke he's holding as long as possible.

I open my eyes to see him breathe out and grin, then hand the joint to Stacey. My drink is halfway done, and ice has watered it down. I sip it slowly.

Honking geese fly overhead, and I stare at them, at the sky, blue and filled with white fluffy clouds.

Sam gets the joint next and inhales deeply, holding the smoke in before letting it escape his mouth in tiny puffs before offering it to me with one eyebrow raised at me in a half friendly and half suggestive way.

I want to smoke, but I know it'll just make me feel worse later, when it's worn off and I'm lazy and even more depressed. "Nah, I'm good."

"You sure? What's wrong?" Stacey giggles and flips her hair back as she sits up and looks at me.

A feeling of anger starts to bubble through my malaise. I direct my gaze at Stacey, cutting off her laughs. "I learned a lot about weed in my drug class, you know?" My voice holds a challenge.

"Your drug class?" Sam sits up, his eyes seeking mine.

I shrug, keeping my eyes on Stacey. "Wanna tell them about how I got special enrollment, Stacey?" I say lightly, but my smile lacks warmth.

There's silence, and her cheeks burn red. She scowls at me, but checks herself. "Melanie, we're having fun now, right? Let's not get into it?" She gives a weak laugh. "I mean, we should focus on, you know, relaxing right now. Right?" Her eyes search mine earnestly.

"So, what's the deal?" Sam repeats.

I shake my head. "Never mind."

When he tries to pass me the joint again, I think about Jake's face and Principal Evans' expressions and, for some reason, Mrs. Hart laughing with me about sneaking pineapple into her husband's food.

My stomach sours, and my hand jerks, spilling the drink on my jeans. It's cold, and I know later it will be sticky.

"Fuck," I hiss. It's not a big deal, but for some reason it makes me want to cry all the same. Fucking ridiculous. I'm mad at myself for being so pathetic.

"Here." Sam hands me the sweatshirt he brought out with him.

"Thanks?" I squint my eyes at him. "You really want me to clean up with your shirt?"

He shrugs. "It's just a shirt. Robby will wash it for me later."

"Fuck if I will!" says Robby, blowing smoke in our direction. "You'll wash it your damn pussy self."

My phone rings, and I pull it out of my back pocket. It's my mom. I don't want to talk to her right now, so I turn the phone off.

Sam's offering me the joint—it's come around again—and I shake my head. "No. I'm good." A month ago, I probably would have grabbed it and sucked down that smoke as a reprieve from all the shit that's going on, but right now I feel clearer without it.

"Come here." Sam's standing next to me with his hand out, and I take it. He pulls me up so I'm on my feet. "Let's get away from these two for a minute."

Holding his hand feels strangely comfortable, like someone cares about me. Behind us, Stacey and Robby are still smoking, their voices low as they speak in words I can't quite make out.

"I'm glad you're here today," he says. He stops walking and looks down at me. "I'm glad I met you."

"Yeah. Me too."

"Look, Stacey mentioned that drug class earlier?"

I roll my eyes. "Locker search. I had a few joints in mine." Let him think what he thinks. I'm tired of lying.

"Dude, it's legal in some states," he says. "It's seriously not a big deal."

"Yeah. No big deal." I'm sort of surprised she didn't tell him about it already. And I wonder if her own boyfriend knows the truth, that the drugs were hers.

"You just have to work harder at, you know, not getting caught." He grins down at me, then touches my shoulder briefly. When he bends his head toward me, I shut my eyes.

I open my lips to meet his, hoping to lose myself in his embrace, or maybe find myself. But after a minute, it's no use; I'm thinking of Jake, and I feel alone, even though I'm in someone's arms. I pull away. "I'm sorry. This isn't—I'm really distracted."

He shrugs. "It's okay. Let's go inside. Get more drinks. Just, you know, hang out."

The kitchen is warm and bright, and he pours more vodka and orange juice into our glasses, but before I have a chance to drink any, he backs me up against the counter, his lips grinding into mine. "Come here," he mutters into my ear, boosting me up so I'm sitting on the cold marble, and I sigh, give it one more shot.

He smells good, like soap and cologne, but his lips are sloppy, and there's a greediness to his kiss, an inexperience that leaves me cold. Unlike Jake. Who humiliated me last night, for sure, but knew exactly how to touch me that night we first met.

"I gotta go to the bathroom," I whisper to Sam, sliding off the counter and pushing him lightly away from me.

"Can I come with?" he teases.

"Uh, no, I'm really going to the bathroom." I head down the hall and lock myself in the white and lavender restroom that looks like it belongs in a spa, with the muted lighting and fresh flowers and basket of finely sculpted soap.

I pee, then wash my hands and splash some water on my face, drying it on a seriously puffy towel.

Through the sliding glass door in the kitchen I can see Sam outside again, chatting with Stacey and Robby. He's animated, talking about something that's making them laugh.

Before he has a chance to notice me, I hurry into the living room, grab my backpack, and slip out of the house.

• • •

It's about a mile or maybe two back to town, and I walk fast. I half expect Sam to come after me, but the road is silent.

Back downtown, I'm not sure where to go. Not school. Not now. My mom's probably home from her meeting with Principal Evans, and I don't want to deal with her right now, so I can't go to my house.

My jeans feel sticky where I spilled on them, and I can smell pot in my hair. I run a hand through it, thinking about where I can go. And that's when I get the bright idea to go to Jake's apartment.

He's probably at work, though I have no idea what his hours are. But when I knock at his door, hard, several times, nobody answers. A jolt of warning courses through me as I put my hand on the doorknob to the outside door.

This is wrong. This is wrong. This is so wrong! But I turn it all the same, and it gives, the door pushing inward. I smile in victory.

I head up the stairs to his apartment, knowing it could be locked. What cop doesn't keep his door locked? But when I try it, it's open too.

He'd kill me if he found me here. He'd be so pissed. I know it's a huge violation, but something about the wrongness makes it that much more exciting. Also, even beyond that, I remember that safe feeling I got in his arms, when I was here with him in his bed. I want that feeling back, and although I know a place can't confer emotion, thinking of him, while being in his apartment, nearly summons him up in front of my eyes.

His apartment is actually really boring—he has hardly anything here other than furniture. I check out the fridge, which holds mostly beer and a few uninteresting food items. His bed's made, but it's sloppy, the covers just barely dragged up to hide the sheets. Looking at it makes me suddenly tired, and I have to fight the urge to climb in and take a nap, just a short one.

In the bathroom, I strip off my clothes, glad to be rid of the sickly sweet scent, and turn the shower on hot, letting it warm up. Before getting in, I scrunch up the stained part of my jeans and run it under cold water in the sink, then hang them on a hook.

The hot water, once I get in the shower, feels fucking exquisite. I could stay in here all day long, just letting the warmth pour down over me for hours. I forget about everything—Sam, the drug class, Stacey, my mom. The scholarship. All of it. I close my eyes and put my head back and feel nothing but hot and relaxed.

"Open the goddamn curtain *now*."

Jake's voice jolts me, and I jump so hard I almost slip. "Jake," I cry out, my voice strangled with fear over the anger in his voice.

"Melanie?" Now I hear shock.

"Yes, it's just me! It's me." I stick my head out of the curtain and see him standing there, gun in hand, eyes open in disbelief.

"Fuck!" he says. "I thought it was an intruder. Jesus, Melanie, I pulled my *gun* on you! I could have… What are you *thinking*?"

"Sorry," I mutter before disappearing back into the shower. "Can I just—I'll come out, but can I just wash off?" I need a barrier from his anger, and the flimsy curtain is the only protection I have.

"Jesus Christ, Melanie! What the *fuck* are you doing here?"

"I… needed a place to go." It sounds lame. It *is* lame. I can't tell him the thing about how I felt safe here, not now, with that expression on his face.

"This isn't your crash pad for when you decide to skip school." His voice is trembling with anger. "And everyone's looking for you. Your mom. The principal."

"I know. I'm so sorry. I'll be out in a second, OK?"

He mutters something unintelligible.

Shit, shit, shit, shit, *shit*. What the hell was I thinking? Just because he let me shower here once doesn't mean I had permission to just come here whenever I wanted.

I wash quickly and step out, dripping, onto the bath mat on the floor.

There's no towel. My jeans are on the hook where a towel would normally hang. A small cabinet reveals nothing except a few men's items, and I lightly run my finger over the can of shaving cream, shivering at the thought of Jake, towel around his waist, running it over his jaw and staring in a steamed-up mirror.

"Jake?" I pull the door open a crack and call for him.

"What?" He still sounds pissed. His steps creak across the floor until he's right outside.

"Do you have a towel?"

He grumbles something I can't make out, and then I hear him walk away, open a closet in the hall, and return.

The crack of the open door widens, and his hand enters the room, holding out a thick blue towel.

I'm not sure if I'm trying to get over yesterday's sting of rejection, or if I'm trying to convince him not to be mad anymore, but without even really thinking I pull the door open all the way. All I know is I'm dying for his touch, right this second. He's framed in the doorway, still holding the towel, and I'm completely naked and dripping in front of him.

"Jesus, Melanie." His eyes spark before he turns his head, shielding his view with one hand.

"Jake, I…"

"Just take the fucking towel."

Instead I reach out and grab a handful of his T-shirt, pulling him toward me until he's close enough so I can shut the door. "Please." I look into his eyes, put one hand on each cheek. "Please, Jake. I need you. *You're* the reason I came here. I need you."

At first, he resists, but it's like pulling something heavy, something that gains more and more momentum until it's moving so fast you can't stop it anymore.

The towel's on the floor, and we're standing face to face in swirling steam.

"I can't do this," he mutters, but the next second he kisses me, his lips hungry.

My body presses against him, his T-shirt growing damp from my still-wet body. I've never been kissed like this, never felt this much need from another person. It's like he wants to devour me, and I want to let him. I want to give myself to him.

Desperate to feel his skin against mine, I pull his T-shirt the rest of the way out of his jeans, then push it up so he grabs it, ripping it off and dropping it onto the floor. His hands hold my face as he gazes into my eyes. It's like he's waiting for confirmation, for my consent, and instead of saying anything, I reach out, touching his hard stomach with my fingers. My hand flattens against his skin and I explore, moving up to touch his chest, then lower once more, my fingertips dipping into the waistband of his jeans, teasing.

With a groan, Jake bends his head, finding my right nipple with his tongue, which he flicks over the sensitive skin till I can barely breathe. He sucks it gently, the skin tickling, puckering, sending electric shocks throughout my body.

My knees grow weak as he moves to the other nipple, teasing it, his lips pulling gently. When I touch the front of his jeans I can feel his hardness, and when I rub him through his clothes he moans.

This time when we kiss his fingers explore, traveling down my stomach to the damp trimmed hair between my legs, which he gently pushes apart for better access. His thumb caresses my clit while a finger travels farther, dipping into my wetness. Shamelessly I moan, my head falling back as I do, the feeling so exquisite. How does he know how to touch me exactly the way I want to be touched?

"You like that," he whispers against my neck. It's not a question. He knows I do, and his confidence turns me on even more.

"Yes," I reply, my voice hoarse. I reach for the buckle of his belt, but he takes my hand away.

With one swift motion he pushes everything on the sink counter into the sink: soap dispenser, toothbrush, toothpaste. Then he lifts me so I'm sitting on the cool marble surface. His eyes on mine, he touches the inside of my thigh, urging me to open my legs wider, so I do.

And then he kneels in front of me. *Oh god.* His fingers touch me first, gently opening me, finding my sensitive clit and ever so slowly teasing it. But when his face moves forward, I tense up.

I've never done this before. Had this done for me, I mean. I've given blow jobs, but no guy has ever reciprocated. Maybe high school guys aren't into that. I don't know. But here's a man, kneeling in front of me, and for some weird reason I feel nervous.

"Relax." He must sense my anxiety, because he continues to touch me, his fingers knowing exactly what to do, until I melt, until I don't care what he does as long as it feels this good.

And then his tongue. It flicks over my clit and I cry out at the sensation, better than anything I've felt before. One of his fingers moves to my wetness, pushing in a little, then all the way, while his tongue continues to pleasure my clit.

"Oh," I murmur, my body tensing again, but not from fear this time. Already I feel an orgasm building, quicker than it's ever happened before.

He continues, and I can't help my body from writhing at the exquisite sensation.

"I'm going to come, Jake," I whisper. It's almost like I'm warning him, like I feel the need to let him know it's going to happen, and soon.

"That's the plan." He stops only long enough to respond to me, and then his tongue finds the spot again, his fingers too, and just as quickly as before he builds me up, closer and closer to bliss.

I fight it at first, wanting the sensation to last forever, or at least for a few more moments before I crash, hard and fast. But I can't hold on. It feels too good, and within seconds I'm there, my whole body clenching in that bliss of just-before, and then exploding, my head back, my damp hair behind me, my hands bracing myself on the bathroom counter.

His lips are salty when he kisses me, my pussy still contracting in the aftermath of pleasure, my body weak. I'm not even sure I can stand. But Jake lifts me down, holding me upright for a few seconds before letting me go.

"Get dressed." He picks up the towel from the floor and hands it to me, leaving the bathroom without a word.

Wait. I want to say it out loud, but I don't have the energy. Instead I pull on my clothes, the jeans still slightly damp.

In the living room, Jake's already put on a dry T-shirt, and he's got his holster on, as well as his leather jacket. His key are jingling in his hand like he's anxious to get going. "You ready to go?" He barely looks at me.

"Yeah. Let me just put on my shoes." I sit on the floor and pull on my red Converse sneakers. I try to pretend he's not being suddenly cold.

"Your principal just called."

Fuck.

"She and your mom are worried that you didn't show up for school."

"What did you say?" I ask.

"I lied, Melanie. And I never lie. I said I picked you up walking on Route 51 and I'm bringing you to school now."

"I'm sorry."

"I'm sorry too. This was a mistake. Again. And it's not going to happen anymore."

"Right." My heart hurts when he says that, but I know he's right, so I finish tying my shoes and stand up. "My hair's wet, though. How will I explain that?"

"Fuck. I don't know. I don't have a hair dryer."

"Wait." I dig in my backpack and pull out a black knit winter cap that I keep in there for colder days. I pull it on over my hair. "Perfect!" I smile at him, hoping to entice him into a slightly better mood, but it doesn't work. He just opens the front door and gestures for me to leave.

"I need to bring you to the school, where we need to meet with your mom and the principal." His words are angry.

And suddenly I realize this position he's in, with me like this, is dangerous for him. He could get in a lot of trouble, or, at the very least, lose the respect of a lot of people. And I don't want that for him. I was only thinking of myself; what I needed. God, I hope it's not too late to change that.

"I'm sorry," I say again, and this time it's not just words. I follow him out to the car, and he opens the passenger door for me.

"Just get in."

As soon as he gets in too and slams the door closed, I say, "Look. I'm not going to tell anyone anything. There's no way. OK? You can trust me." My voice is earnest. "What we do is personal, between us."

"It's still wrong, Melanie." His voice is really cold.

"I *said* I'm sorry! What else do you want me to do? It's not like I forced you into anything!"

"That's exactly it. I should have known better." Even though he's pissed, he's so freaking handsome. Out of the corner of my eye I stare at him in profile, his strong jaw, his brown eyes. That messy hair, just slightly wavy, that he runs his hand through when he's frustrated or angry. The stubble on his face fascinates me, turns me on; it's so rugged. Such a reminder of what a man he is.

He catches me staring, and I look away quickly, staring out the window as we get closer to the school.

CHAPTER SEVEN – JAKE

This is the last fucking thing in the world I want to do. At Columbus High, I park and we get out of the car. How the hell is it that I'm walking into a meeting with the principal and a parent to talk about a student—a student who was just in my bathroom, legs spread, while I licked her until she came? *Jesus fucking Christ.*

I'm not going to think about how she tasted, how I thought I'd come too just from the sounds she made and how wet she got. I'm not going to think about whether I regret not unbuckling my belt, pushing down my jeans, and shoving inside her as hard as I could. No. I'm going to act like the respectable adult I supposedly am and pretend I'm not a fucking pervert who can't keep my hands off Melanie Fucking Cannon.

We're buzzed in before we even have a chance to ring, and Principal Evans smiles at me, then turns to Melanie with a concerned expression on her face.

"Melanie, we've been worried about you."

"Sorry." Melanie looks at her feet as she says it. "I didn't mean to make anyone worried."

"Thank you, Officer Beck, for bringing her here. Let's all go into my office to talk."

I follow them into the principal's office, past the secretary who looks at us curiously. A woman, whom I assume is Melanie's mother, sits in a chair waiting for us. The first thing that strikes me about her is that she looks uncomfortable. Her clothes don't seem to fit her right, and her makeup is too noticeable, like she doesn't know how to wear it or maybe usually doesn't. She's clutching a worn-out white purse on her lap like a lifesaver.

"Mrs. Cannon," says Principal Evans, "this is Detective Jake Beck. He's teaching the drug education class that Melanie's in at the library."

"Nice to meet you," says Melanie's mom, with a nervous smile. "Melanie, I was really frantic." She looks at her daughter. I see a faint tremor in her hands as they clutch her bag. "Are you all right?"

"Let's all have a seat." Mrs. Evans has already arranged two other chairs in front of her desk, and Melanie ends up in the middle between me and her mother.

I clear my throat. "I found her out on Route 51, walking toward town."

"I was at Stacey's," she whispers.

Principal Evans speaks. "It looks like we need a plan to make sure Melanie's staying in school. And a plan for next year. For now, though, let's worry about making sure she finishes senior year."

"I'm *going* to finish. I wouldn't not, OK?" Melanie taps her red Converse tennis shoe on the floor, then looks up at the principal. "I'm gonna do it. I'm sorry I caused you all to worry. I just needed a day to think things over. I apologize for doing it in an inconsiderate way."

"OK, Melanie, but you skipped today, and if I understand correctly, you didn't attend your class Monday night. Is that right, Detective Beck?" She looks at me.

"Uh, yes. Correct."

"Is she out then?" Principal Evans' eyes plead with me.

I take a deep breath. "Technically, I... Look. As long as she continues to show up from here on out, she can stay in the class."

"Melanie, that's a generous offer." Principal Evans lets out a breath and stares at Melanie, folding her hands in front of her on the desk. "I hope you can see that he's going above and beyond and making a *huge* exception to help you out." Her voice is firm, almost angry. Disappointed.

"I know. Thank you." She glances over at me, then looks quickly away again.

"How have you been getting to school in the mornings?" asks the principal, her voice softer.

Melanie sighs. "I walk. It's only a mile? Today I just had a lot on my mind, and when Stacey—uh, never mind."

Principal Evans turns to Melanie's mother. "Can you give her a ride for the remainder of the year? Just to make sure she actually gets here?"

"No. It's fine. I'm going to come to school, OK?" Melanie sits up straighter. "She doesn't need to do that." She puts a hand on her mother's arm, as if to prevent her from talking, and it reminds me of a parent bracing a child at an abrupt traffic stop.

"Oh, I, uh…" Mrs. Cannon looks surprised, like she didn't expect to be asked this question. "I don't. Melanie? I mean?" She twists her purse strap, looking confused. "Do you think that's necessary, though?"

My heart fills with pain for Melanie that her mom didn't immediately say, "Yes. Of course." That, instead, she struggled with a response.

"I can help." I hear my voice saying it, but I curse myself inside. *Fuck.* Why the hell did I say that? The words were out before I even knew they were coming. "I can give her a ride. Help make sure she gets to school."

"I do *not* need a police escort. Just give me a chance. I'm sorry." Melanie sits forward in her chair. "Please. College means a lot to me." She sounds fierce. "I will graduate. I won't miss any more days. I promise."

Principal Evans sighs. "Thank you, Detective Beck. It's refreshing to know how much you care about the students. Melanie, let's see how things go for the next week, all right? But I do want you to check in with me every morning when you arrive. If you're late, I'll send Detective Beck out to look for you." She says the last part in a half humorous and half threatening way.

I stand. "I'm here if you need me."

"Thanks." Melanie's mom gets up too, dropping her purse as she does. Something rolls out and under the principal's desk. Mrs. Cannon bends down, her face red and sweaty, as she swipes her hand out trying to reach it.

"Here." Joan Evans retrieves the object—an airplane-sized bottle of vodka—and hands it back to Melanie's mom.

"Thanks." She thrusts it back into her purse, her cheeks flushed, and she looks at me before glancing away quickly. Her face is tired and older than I guess she is, and I try to feel sympathy for her.

But when I look at Melanie, head hanging and staring at her sneakers, all I feel is angry.

• • •

"Where the hell were you?" My uncle's sipping shitty coffee back at the station.

"Good to see you too." I sit at my desk and smile at him.

"No. Where the hell were you?" He's serious, and I'm fucked.

"Driving around looking for some kid. Then meeting with her mom and the principal at the high school." Do I sound casual like I hope, or can he tell by my tone that I was up to no fucking good with an eighteen-year-old? That I had my face buried in her sweet pussy just a few hours ago?

"What's going on, Jake?" He pulls his chair up to my desk so we can talk, which is exactly what I don't want to do.

"Like I said." I sit back in my chair and meet his eyes. "Some kid didn't show up for school, and the principal has kind of taken her under her wing. She was worried and called me up."

"Which kid?"

"The Cannon girl. Melanie."

My uncle nods. "Her mom's a drunk. Years back we used to be called to their house all the time because her husband was beating up on her. He's in prison now. That poor kid, though. She's been through a lot."

"Exactly. I was just helping out. Brought her back to school. Sat in on a meeting with her mom and the principal."

"You've always had a real kind heart. But look." He scoots even closer to me, looking me directly in the eyes, his face filled with stern warning. "Don't be fucking stupid. You understand?"

Shit. "Yeah. Of course." I shake my head like *what the fuck are you talking about.* But I know exactly what he's talking about.

"Jakey, you've always had a soft spot in your heart for strays. Your mom used to get so fed up with you always bringing cats and dogs home. You remember?"

I laugh at the thought. "They knew me by name at the shelter by the time I was ten years old!"

"And then you volunteered there in high school. And that's great. It's one of the best things about you. That you're tough as fucking nails, but underneath it you've got a really good heart."

"Thanks."

My uncle frowns, his weather-worn face looking suddenly older than usual. "There are some strays you need to leave alone. You get what I'm saying?"

"Jesus, Mike, she's not a fucking stray animal. She's a person."

"Yeah. A kid. Barely fucking legal."

"Dude, you don't need to worry about me, OK?"

"Dude?" He laughs, but then his face gets serious again. "Don't give me reason to worry, Jake. You never have. Don't start now."

I nod. "It's all good."

CHAPTER EIGHT – MELANIE

"Melanie, dear, I've been meaning to tell you what a fantastic job you did organizing and cleaning last week!" Mrs. Hart smiles at me broadly from the front counter as I enter the antique shop.

"Oh, it wasn't a big deal." I shrug, but I'm so glad she's happy.

"Not a big deal? It's perfect, and I've been wanting to do something similar, but it's hard at my age to get stuff done. Thank you."

"Mrs. Hart, you can always ask me to do stuff. I don't mind." I set my backpack down next to the counter and glance around the shop. "Are there any other projects you want me to do?"

"Well, if I think of anything, I'll let you know." She tilts her head and smiles fondly at me. "It's going to be awfully hard to find someone as wonderful as you to work here when you head to Chicago in the fall."

"Looks like I won't be going after all." I don't want to talk about it. I wish I could keep it a secret forever. But eventually people will find out, and I'd rather it be sooner than later.

"What are you talking about?" Her soft white forehead crinkles up in confusion.

"Well, you know I got in some trouble at school…"

"I know it wasn't your fault." Her eyes stare deeply into mine. She believes in me.

"Anyway, the group that gave me the scholarship found out about it somehow and decided to revoke it. So yeah." I sigh and look down.

"Melanie." She steps toward me, taking my hand between her two gentle ones. "I'm so sorry to hear this. Can you appeal? Is there anything you can do?"

I want to crumple onto the floor. I want to cry and let her comfort me. I want some relief from this sense of dread that's been following me around. But I pull away.

"No. It's over. It's all right. I'll figure something out. Maybe wait a year and then go. See if there are scholarships or financial aid or something."

She shakes her head, and her eyes are so sad I can't look at her any longer.

"Look," I add. "Mr. Hart is probably waiting for you! He worries when you're late getting home."

She chuckles. "Even though he knows I'm right downstairs. Now you take care, Melanie. Don't forget to lock up."

"I won't."

She turns to leave, but as she approaches the stairs to her apartment, she turns. "Remember that things have a way of working out sometimes. Don't give up. Don't ever give up. Keep your head high."

I sigh. "It's hard, but I'm trying."

She takes a few steps closer. "I have a friend, my best friend from high school, so I've known her forever. She's really irreverent, and I probably shouldn't repeat what she says. But the advice she likes to give people is to *take the world by the balls*."

My eyes open wide. "Mrs. Hart!" I laugh.

She giggles. "I know, I know. But the sentiment is wonderful. Grab the world and make it yours."

"Thanks. Mrs. Hart, I really appreciate you and Mr. Hart. For giving me a job, and for making me feel comfortable. And confident. I just, you know, want to tell you that." I blush, unused to expressing myself so openly.

"Melanie, dear, we love you. Now you have a good night, all right?"

I smile at her as she leaves, and as soon as she's gone my face falls back into its now-permanent frown and I breathe deeply.

The warmth I felt talking to Mrs. Hart is replaced by the pissed-off feeling I've had all day. I'm pissed at Principal Evans for getting so involved. I'm pissed at my mom for being my mom.

I'm pissed at Jake for... I can't even articulate what it is. For caring, but not enough. For being hot, then super cold. I don't understand him, and I don't want to need him. But I do. My body and soul feel empty without him around, and that scares me, because I've always sworn I'd never rely on anybody. I'd always take care of myself, and I would never need another person.

I turn to the front door when I hear a light scratching on the glass, and my face breaks out into a grin. It's Molly, her mouth opening in a meow I can't hear through the door. When I open it, she steps inside, then rubs against my leg, looking up at me and mewling.

"You're hungry, huh?" I fill bowls with food and water and set them down on the floor. She eats quickly and voraciously, and I smile while she does.

After eating and drinking, she jumps up onto the old armchair I usually sit in, curls up, and goes to sleep. I pet her gently and she rouses slightly and begins to purr. It's nice not to feel her bones so much, to know I'm helping her survive.

My phone beeps with a text. It's Sam, Robby's cousin. *Hey*, he writes, *I'd like to take you out for dinner. Tomorrow work?*

Sure. Pick me up at 7? I respond.

I don't really want to go. I want to be with Jake, at his apartment again. Like it was the first time, when he didn't know anything about me. When he didn't think of me as a kid. When I could have maybe had his love, not just his pity.

None of that's possible, though. So I'll settle for a little fun instead.

• • •

When it's time to close up, Molly doesn't want to leave. I hold the door open and click my tongue, but all she does is look at me once, then close her eyes again.

"Come on," I say. "It's time to go." But I know the Harts wouldn't be happy if I let a cat stay overnight, and my mom is allergic so I can't bring her home. "I'll be back, OK? Not tomorrow, but the next day, all right?" I know it's silly to talk to an animal, but I swear she understands me.

When I scoop her up she meows, and it kills me to set her outside on the cracked pavement in front of the store. "You'll be fine," I say. But she looks up at me with sad eyes and I want to cry.

I don't look back as I walk away. And I try not to be disappointed that Jake doesn't appear in his car, following me home, making sure I'm OK.

• • •

My mom's at her computer, a photo of a kitten wearing a knitted hat up on her screen. There's an open wine bottle near her feet, but in the darkened living room I can't tell if it's full or empty, and I don't know if it's from last night or tonight.

"Let's talk, honey." She turns her chair toward me.

I set my backpack on the floor and sit on the couch.

"How was work?" she asks.

"Fine."

"That police officer was nice. The one at school? I didn't know you'd skipped a session of that drug class thing you're in."

I shrug. "I was upset. I'd just found out about the scholarship."

"I'm really sorry that happened." She pats at the top of her head, where her hair is pulled back into a greasy, bumpy ponytail. It's weird. Sometimes I look at old photos of her, and she was so pretty.

So happy. She was a real person, all those years ago. Now, she doesn't seem real at all. "That was a good scholarship," she adds.

"Yeah. So now… I don't know what I'll be doing next year."

"Oh, honey, there's online colleges, you know. They're probably not that expensive. You could keep working at the shop, or maybe at the Save Lot if it pays better, and take some classes. Or that community college? It's only maybe a half hour away. You could go there."

"Yeah. I could." I can. And I probably will. But the loss of my bigger dream is still too raw, and hearing her say it like this, so casually, hurts.

"So hey. Can I show you my latest video?" She spins her chair again so she's facing the computer and presses *play* in her video editor program. "I didn't add any music to it yet. I'm still trying to decide what to use. Something with *hat* in it, I think. Obviously."

This one is a series of photos and drawings of kittens and cats wearing hats. Some are crocheted or knitted, some are baseball caps. A few have wigs, which doesn't quite fit the theme, but I suppose it's close enough.

"What do you think?" Her eyes are bright and excited—even in the dark living room I can see that. "And any ideas for what song I should use?"

"It's great, Mom. I like it a lot. If I think of any good songs that would work I'll let you know, OK?" I pause. "Is there anything, you know, for dinner?" Unbidden, my mind flickers to the meal at Jake's: the spaghetti, the salad. The laughter.

She doesn't turn around. "Oh, honey, I got so busy with my project that I didn't eat. You can make anything you like, okay?"

"Sure." I take a deep breath and let it out slowly.

"Good night, honey." She's back at work, clicking and dragging.

"Good night." I head to my room without even stopping in the kitchen.

CHAPTER NINE – JAKE

After our shift, James asks me if I want to grab a bite to eat.

"Where?" I ask. "The shitty diner?"

"Nah. Let's hit the Baker's Square on 51."

"It's fucking far, man." There's nothing decent in or near Bells Park.

"It's only a fuckin' twenty-minute drive. What else you gonna do tonight?"

That's a good question. The only thing I'd do is sit around and think about Melanie. My night would consist of drinking one too many beers and seeing how long I could hold off watching shit television before I had to get in the shower and jack off to the memory of how good her pussy tasted.

And then I'd feel guilty because even though she's hot as fuck, she makes me sadder than I've ever been before. Her life. Her situation. Her Converse sneakers and her sad eyes and the fact that she's almost—not quite but almost—given up.

"Yeah," I tell James. "Let's get the fuck out of here."

The Baker's Square is packed. It's Friday night, and I guess there's not a whole lot to do around here. We wait at the front by the glass display showcasing the pies, and James checks them all out.

"I'm taking one of these home," he says.

"Dude, you need to lay off the pie and work out with me instead," I joke.

"What. You think I'm too big to get a girl?" He glances around the restaurant. "Too bad this isn't a bar. I'd show you how easy it is for me to get laid."

"Oh yeah?" I laugh.

"Yeah. I mean, maybe not as easy as you. Fucking hotshot from Chicago."

The host, a pretty blonde, with milky skin and pink cheeks and that all-American girl next door look calls us. "Table for two?" she asks.

"Yeah," says James. "But, uh, we're not together. You know what I mean?"

She looks blankly at him. "So you want to sit at different tables?"

"No. I mean, we're together. But not, you know, together."

She shakes her head and frowns, still not understanding what he's getting at.

I sigh. "He wants your number," I say with a grin at him.

"Dude," James hisses at me.

The girl pretends she doesn't hear us and slaps the menus on the table before stalking off.

"What the fuck you doing?" asks James, but he's smiling. "I could've had that."

"You think so? You really think she'd have given you her number?"

"Yeah." He opens his menu.

"Maybe she'd have given you *a* number. But not hers." I scan the menu before closing it and deciding on a burger.

We order beers and our dinner, James trying to catch the server's eye, but she's having none of it. Just to fuck with him, I consider flirting with her, because I'm pretty sure she'd respond to me. But I'm not a dick.

"So how long you planning to stay anyway?" James takes a huge gulp of his beer, then sets the pint glass down on the cardboard coaster.

"Not sure. There wasn't really an end-date figured out. My uncle just said he needed to borrow me until he could build up the force. We've got two new recruits starting next week, so I'll have to meet with him and see how much longer you guys need me here."

"And your job back in Chicago is still waiting?"

"Yeah. They love me there." I know I sound cocky, but it's true. My uncle is my actual family, but my precinct back in Chicago feels like family too. It's where my dad and uncle started out, and I've known some of the guys my entire life. Still, the thought of going back there, of how different the station felt without my dad around, of seeing my mom, hurts my heart. I want to change the fucking subject.

"We'll miss you. It's been nice having you around."

I sip the beer, cold and crisp, and nod. "Yeah. It's not as bad here as I thought at first." I wink at James. "I mean, the town's shitty. But the people are nice."

"And you don't mind getting stuck with the crap job teaching that stupid drug class?" James loves teasing me about that. "Speaking of which…" His voice trails off and he stares at something behind me.

"What?" But my heart, stupid fucking thing, has already kicked up a notch, as if I know exactly what he's going to say next.

"Isn't that the Cannon girl? From the class?"

Fuck. Me. I turn around and there she is, glammed up like the first night I met her. Fucked her. Her long black hair is straight and shimmery, hanging in two long sheets on either side of her face. Her lips are dark red, her skin pale, her eyes outlined in dark black that gives her a half sexy and half haunted look. She's got on a low-cut black v-neck shirt, tight jeans, and those same fucking tall black boots. *Christ.* It's hot as hell, but I also know it's the look she has when she's desperate. Scared. Looking for a way to forget.

"Her date looks like a douche," says James.

But I've already noticed that. He's a pretty college kid, wearing a goddamn polo shirt with khakis. He looks friendly and nice but I know what he's after. Probably going back to school after spring

96

break, so he doesn't want a relationship. He wants Melanie, for one night, or maybe a few. And it fucking kills me to think about that.

"You OK, man?" James eyes me carefully.

"Yeah." I chug my beer, practically finishing it in one swallow. I try not to watch as the host walks Melanie and that little asshole down another aisle—at least they don't walk right past us—and seats them in a booth near the window. Right the fuck in my line of sight.

When the waitress comes with our food, I've lost my appetite, but I order another beer right away. James is so into his food that he doesn't notice I'm barely eating. I hate that I'm so messed up about seeing her here with someone else. But every cell in my body wants to go over there, pull him up by his shirt so he's standing, and punch his stupid fucking face.

I mean, it's not like I'm the right guy for her. But that fucker isn't either.

"You gonna eat those?" James points at my fries, and when I shake my head, he grabs some and stuffs them in his mouth.

I push my plate closer to him and watch as Melanie gets up, leans down to say something to the dude she's with, and heads down the aisle. She must be going to the bathroom. And, against my better judgment, I get up too.

"Be back," I say.

"Yup." James keeps eating.

I walk past tables filled with cheerful people, families and kids, until I get to the small hallway where the restrooms are. Melanie's already disappeared into the women's room, so I stand against the wall and wait for her to come out.

I have no idea what I'm going to say to her. No idea what I'm doing. And when she finally does emerge from the bathroom, looking startled to see me, I still don't know.

"Hi." She pushes the hair on the right side of her face behind her ear, and her hazel eyes open wide. For a second she smiles, but then her brow wrinkles. "What are you doing here? You didn't follow me, did you?" A slight tinge of anger coats her words.

"No. I didn't follow you. I'm here having dinner with a buddy from the station."

"Okaaaay." She draws out the word. "Cause this feels really stalkerish. Bells Park is small, so running into each other there makes sense. But here?"

"Stalkerish? You're the one who broke into my apartment."

"It was unlocked. I didn't have to break in."

"It was still trespassing." I don't know why I'm arguing about this with her, but I can't leave. I'm frozen, locked in place by her eyes, so deep and sexy and tender and vulnerable all at once.

"Is there a line for the bathroom?" She points to the men's room.

"No. I just, uh..." My voice trails off. Unsure what to say, I run my hand through my hair, then rub the back of my neck.

"You what?"

"Melanie, look. I happened to be eating here when you walked in with your... date. And I wanted to talk to you."

"About what?"

I feel fucking stupid. I don't have anything specific to say. So I go with the thing currently on my mind, even if it makes me sound like a jealous asshole. "Who's the guy?"

She shrugs. "None of your business."

"You're too good for him."

She shakes her head and purses her lips. "He goes to Notre Dame, for your information. He's not some stupid loser. So no, I wouldn't say I'm too good for him. Maybe the other way around."

I grab her shoulder, not hard, but I need to get her attention. "No. You're wrong. You have no idea what you're worth, Melanie. No idea how fucking spectacular you are."

"Spectacular?" She lifts my hand off her shoulder, letting it drop down to my side. "If I'm so fucking spectacular, then why do you run all freaking hot and cold with me? One minute we're, you know, and the next you won't even look at me. There's nothing spectacular about that."

98

"Jesus," I hiss. "It's because of the situation. Because you're barely legal. And you're still in high school, for god's sake. And I'm the teacher of a class you're taking so you don't get a criminal record. There's so much wrong about it. About us. But I still hate seeing you with some asshole who only wants one thing."

"And why are you so sure he only wants one thing?" Her words are angry.

I know I've said something wrong, but I'm not exactly sure what. "Because that's what all guys want." It's the only answer I can come up with.

"Or is it because you know I'm a loser. I'm a druggie. I'm a pathetic girl who lost her scholarship and isn't going anywhere. Ever. So of *course* he'd only be interested in having sex with me. I'm not, I don't know, polished and perfect."

"Polished and perfect is overrated. You're just... rough around the edges. But inside you're pretty fucking amazing, Melanie." My words sound urgent.

"You really think that." Her voice is mocking, defiant, but I hear a thin reed of hope.

"I *know* that." My tone is rough, but my hands on her shoulders are soft. I lower my voice. "And don't you fucking forget it, for one single second, okay?"

She looks at me for a long time, and her eyes well up. I think she's about to speak, when two women come out of the ladies' room, brushing past us and leaving a cloud of their too-strong perfume.

"I have to leave," she says, but her voice is soft. She touches my arm once, and then she's gone.

"God fucking dammit," I whisper. Then I take a deep breath and head back to my table, where James has finished my dinner.

• • •

After dropping James off, I drive aimlessly through Bells Park. It's even more dead after dark than during the day, and sadness settles over me. I hate this fucking town. I end up parked across the street and down a few houses from Melanie's, behind an overflowing dumpster, the kind that are supposed to sit somewhere for the duration of a project and then get removed, but this one looks like a permanent fixture.

The houses on the block are all small, with tiny front yards that are really just patches of mud, and front porches that are so old and rickety a single chair would fall right through. On some, splintered banisters hang like broken limbs. You can't see it at night, but the sidewalk buckles and splits, and I imagine that during the summer weeds fill in the cracks and grow tall and proud in neglect.

I don't know what I'm doing here. I tell myself I just want to make sure Melanie's all right, but I can't help feeling like a fucking dirty stalker, sitting outside her house and waiting for her to get back from a date. With a useless little shit.

I hit the steering wheel with the heel of my hand. *Fucker*, I mutter.

Headlights appear in my rearview window as a car slows down and stops in front of Melanie's house. It sits there for a few minutes, and I'm glad I can't see what the people are doing, because if it's Melanie and that kid making out, I'm not sure I could sit here without dragging him out of the driver's seat.

And I'm not a violent person. So feeling like this is disconcerting. But I can't fucking help the surge of anger—and jealousy—that fills my chest when I think about it.

Finally I see the passenger side door open, and Melanie gets out. She turns and waves to the car, but it's already pulling away, rushing past me with a screech and leaving her standing there all alone. He didn't even wait to make sure she got inside safely.

She starts for the front stairs, but then she freezes. When she moves again, it's back onto the sidewalk where she begins to walk toward town.

Where the fuck is she going? A glance at the dashboard clock lets me know it's eleven p.m., way too late for her to be up to anything safe. Nothing happens in Bells Park this late, except trouble.

She's not wearing a jacket—*why does this girl never fucking dress warm enough?*—and she looks cold as she hurries down the street. I tail her in my car, staying far enough behind so she doesn't know she's being followed. I have to be careful because she's smart, though walking around at late in this crappy neighborhood is pretty fucking stupid. From time to time she darts her eyes around, checking the empty sidewalks, and inserts her hand into her pocket, and I'm pretty sure she's got a fucking knife. I chuckle to myself, even as I shake my head. Jesus.

On Main Street she slows down, like she's lost some steam or is having second thoughts. And then she turns the corner, walks halfway down the block, and stops. In front of the three-flat where I live, the sole renter in the building.

Holy shit. My heart beats like a fucking teenager's at the realization that she's here to see me.

She puts her hand up to knock, then stops herself. She backs up against the door and pulls out a pack of cigarettes, struggling with her lighter in the wind for a few moments before getting one lit. In the wan light from the moon and the few streetlights that aren't burnt out, her milky breasts rise just above the v of her black shirt. She bends one knee, still leaning against the door and placing the sole of her boot against it too. She could be a model. Or a movie star. Instead she's this poor kid in a crappy town.

I get out of my car. "Melanie."

She startles at my voice. "Oh. What are you doing here?" Her eyes are big, her face surprised.

"I live here."

"Yeah, of course. Right." She laughs and takes another drag from the cigarette.

"What are *you* doing here?" I walk toward her so I'm standing in front of her. Close but not touching.

She turns her head and blows out smoke. "I wanted to see you." She rubs the lit end of the cigarette against the brick wall next to the doorway.

101

"Yeah?" I want to kiss her. I want to taste her, smoky breath and all. But I hold back.

"Yeah." Most of her lipstick rubbed off on the cigarette, or maybe just wore off over the course of the night since I saw her at Baker's Square. But her lips are still so perfect.

"What happened to your date?"

She shrugs. "He dropped me off."

"And didn't even wait to make sure you got inside." I realize too late I've given myself away, but I don't really care.

"How do you know that? Were you following me?" She frowns, but her eyes light up, like this makes her happy, or maybe relieved.

"This time, I was. I didn't like that kid. He's an asshole."

"Geez." She rolls her eyes. "You just can't stop, can you?"

"I can't, Melanie. I know I should, but I can't." I reach out and touch her bottom lip, tracing it softly with my finger. "And besides, if you really wanted me to stop, you wouldn't be here right now."

Her lips open slightly, not as if she's about to say something but as if she wants me to kiss her.

"Do you want to come inside?" I ask.

"Yes."

• • •

Her mouth tastes like cigarettes and cinnamon—I wonder if she had pie for dessert. For days I've wanted to run my hands through her long black hair, and now I can. I do, the softness almost unbearably erotic between my fingers. My body struggles between rushing this—it's practically impossible to hold back—and taking my time, because I want every single second to last an eternity. I want to be here forever with Melanie, touching her, kissing her, making her understand how fucking beautiful she really is.

For a long time we just kiss, and holding back makes me lightheaded. The living room is dark, and from the kitchen the

102

refrigerator hums. A car drives past outside, its engine getting louder as it approaches, then quieter and quieter until it's gone once more.

When I can no longer stand it, can no longer stop my hands, I run my fingers up her side, from the top of her jeans to the bottom of her right breast. I touch the sleek fabric of her shirt, imagining how this same move would feel on her bare skin and knowing I'll find out in just a few minutes.

Her nipple is hard—I can feel it even through her shirt and bra—and the way she moans slightly into my lips makes my cock throb.

"Jesus, Melanie," I whisper as my hand travels up under her shirt, the lace of her bra rough against my fingers. "You're so goddamn beautiful."

"Jake." My name is just a whisper on her lips, and she doesn't say anything else. Yet it's one of the most erotic things I've ever heard.

Her fingers flit against my stomach, lightly through my shirt, and I breathe in hard. It's such a simple touch, but the way it makes me feel is anything but simple. I knew she turned me on. I knew that from the first second I saw her.

But what I didn't expect was to feel so much emotion too. I don't know how to deal with that, and now isn't the time to think about it, especially as her hand moves under my shirt, exploring my stomach and my chest.

When her fingers run along the waistband of my jeans, I grab her shirt by the bottom hem and pull it up. Her arms lift so I can get it all the way off, and I do, dropping it on the floor next to us.

Like an inexperienced kid I fumble with her bra clasp for a few seconds before it finally gives away. She slips her arms out and it, too, ends up on the floor.

I stare into her eyes as I reach out, touching one nipple with my thumb, rubbing it and watching her eyes widen, her lips open slightly. I like knowing I can take her breath away. I like knowing I can make her feel so much, feel everything.

"Are you sure this is what you want?" My voice is low, raspy.

She nods. "Yes. I want this. You. I want you, Jake." She moves up against me, writhing slightly, and again we kiss, desperate and hungry.

I pull my shirt off, then put my arms around her, urging her closer, so I can feel her skin against mine.

"You know this is wrong, don't you?" I ask. I'm not sure why I need to say this, need to make sure she knows what she's signing up for.

"It's not wrong. It's what we both want. How can that be wrong?"

How the fuck indeed.

Her hand is small as she grasps mine, pulling me toward the bedroom. There's no mistaking her desire.

"I want to take these off," she whispers as we stand next to the bed, running her hand along my crotch. Her hands move to my belt, and it seems to take her forever to undo the buckle and unzip my jeans. She kisses my neck, then my chest, then my stomach, and before I know it she's kneeling in front of me, pushing my jeans and underwear down.

My cock is rock fucking hard when she releases it. I stare down at her on her knees in front of me, grasping me in her hand. When her head moves forward and her tongue darts out, licking the tip, I groan.

"Jesus, Melanie."

Her tongue swirls around the tip, and then she licks my balls, sucking at them gently before running her tongue all the way back up to the head once more.

"Take me to bed," she says, standing up in front of me.

She doesn't need to ask twice, but first I kiss her wildly, unable to get enough as I undo the button and zipper of her jeans. I peel them off her skin as quickly as I can, and it's only more difficult because they're tight, hugging her body. She wriggles her hips as I tug the jeans down and off, kneeling in front of her as she steps out of them. Her underwear comes down next, the silky fabric damp where it was nestled between her legs.

Still on the floor in front of her, I kiss her stomach, caressing her ass and feeling intoxicated from her smell.

CHAPTER TEN – MELANIE

When Jake kisses my stomach, kneeling right in front of me, I can barely stand. My knees go weak, and I want him to move lower, to find my clit with his tongue again, to taste me, to tease me, to make me come like he did in the bathroom.

But I'm afraid he'll stop again. He'll end it as soon as I orgasm. And even more than wanting him to lick me, I want him inside me. I want him on top of me, covering me, his skin on mine as we breathe and move together. I have to have him.

I grasp his hand so he's standing, then turn and push the covers aside before climbing onto the bed and lying on my back with my head on the pillow.

For a moment he stands still at the side of the bed. I'm not sure what he's waiting for, but I reach out and grasp his cock, hard as fuck, and move my hand up and down his shaft. There's a drop of pre-cum on the tip, and I touch it with my index finger, spreading the glossy liquid out over his head.

When I meet his eyes, they're fixed on mine. Deep. Intense. Focused on me like he's a blind man suddenly gifted with sight.

I roll onto my side and prop myself up so my mouth is even with his cock, and I lick the cum off slowly, knowing that the slower I go, the more he wants it. This. Everything. His groan lets me know I'm right, and I smile in victory.

"You're teasing me, aren't you?" He must have seen my smile, and now he pushes me on the bed, his hands on my shoulders, and gets on top of me. His thighs are on either side of mine, his hands braced on the mattress next to my head.

"It's only teasing if I don't plan on following through. But I could drive you really crazy by sucking you until you're about to come, and then stopping. I'd do that over and over again until you couldn't stand it, and you pushed me on the bed and fucked me as hard as you could."

"Jesus, Melanie. Is that what you want to do?" His voice is filled with desire and disbelief.

"I'll do the sucking part another time. And I'll make you insane. But I do want you to fuck me, as hard as you can. Now."

He growls, his eyes locked on mine. His hands push my legs open wide, and his fingers find my pussy. One, then two, make their way inside, and I close my eyes and moan in pleasure and desire.

Jake grabs a condom from the nightstand and rips open the foil before putting it on. His lips kiss my neck as he guides his cock to my entrance and, slowly, he pushes inside.

"You're so fucking tight," he whispers. "God, you feel so good, Melanie."

"You too." I cling to him as he fills me, my toes curling in ecstasy, my fingers digging into his arms.

All the way inside, he holds still for a few seconds before pulling out and thrusting in again. I writhe against him, under him, wanting the pace quicker.

But he just grins at me. "Be patient."

Except I know he's barely holding back. His jaw is tense, and his eyes are filled with concentration, like he's trying hard not to go too fast too soon.

"I just... please..." I need it to be more intense. I need it to be hard. I need it to take my breath away.

"Hang on." He pulls all the way out. "You're so... I could come right now. Just give me a second."

Something about him being that turned on makes me even crazier. I flip over onto my stomach, pushing my ass up against his cock.

"Melanie," he moans, gripping my hips and teasing the lips of my pussy with his cock.

I drive back, his cock sliding into me, and he holds on to me tight, thrusting inside me farther than I thought possible. One hand holds my left hip while the other moves to my stomach, then lower until he finds my clit, massaging it in gentle circles while he fucks me from behind.

"I'm going to come," I whisper as my body starts to tense.

His thrusts are harder but slower now, as he holds himself inside me for a split second longer before pulling out and pushing in again. His finger continues to caress between my legs, and my body gets tighter and tighter until I come hard, pushing back against him to force him inside me as far as he can go.

I contract around his cock, over and over again. Slowly he pulls out, then pushes in again, and once more and he's coming too.

He collapses on top of me, his heart pounding against my back. His lips kiss the back of my neck, pushing my hair aside gently to caress my skin.

After a few minutes he rolls off onto his side, pulling me to him, my back against his chest. We lie like that, very still, as our hearts slow and our breathing becomes even and quiet. And then we stay like that longer.

It's one of those moments, the kind you wish you could live in forever, because everything single thing about it is perfect. You can forget all the fucked-up events that got you there. And you can ignore all the horrors up ahead. It's one pure perfect moment of bliss. And I wish it would never end.

"No guy has ever made me come before," I admit. "I've only, you know, made myself come."

He's silent for a few seconds before he says, "I fucking hate thinking about you with some other asshole. But I like thinking about you touching yourself."

I laugh, and he strokes my hair.

After a while he pulls away. "I gotta clean up," he says, getting out of bed. He walks to the bathroom, his naked ass so grabbable, his muscled thighs so gorgeous I actually sigh. I hear the bathroom door shut and the toilet flush. The water runs, then shuts off, and he comes out of the bathroom, still naked but minus the condom.

He smiles at me from the hallway. "You want something to drink?"

"A beer?" I smile broadly at him.

"I'll get you a water." He disappears, and I hear the fridge and then a cabinet opening and closing. He returns a few moments later with a green frosty bottle of beer and a glass of water, which he hands to me.

"Asshole." I grin at him.

"You're right. I am an asshole to have done what I just did with you. I don't need to make it worse by giving you alcohol too." But he doesn't resist when I take the bottle from his hand and take a long drink.

"I'm old enough to make my own decisions." I hand the beer back to him. "I'm not like a normal eighteen-year-old. I've pretty much been taking care of myself, you know."

"If you call ditching school and jeopardizing your college education taking care of yourself," he says, then his eyes widen. He expects me to lash out, I can tell.

But his words don't make me angry, not this time. I laugh. "Asshole," I say again, poking his shoulder. "No, seriously. I know I've made some mistakes lately. But I've been through a lot, and even though people have helped me, I'm proud of where I am now. Aside from losing the scholarship, that is." I still feel sick about it, but it's getting easier to talk about.

"And that wasn't your fault. I'm still pissed that you took the blame for your friend. I don't understand, Melanie."

I sigh and drink a big sip of beer, crisp and clear and bubbly in my mouth. I shrug. "I don't know how to explain it. It was stupid. I know that. I just thought, at first, that she would tell the truth. And when she didn't, I still wanted to give her a chance to make it right. And then, when I realized she wasn't going to come forward, I felt too… I don't know. Defeated? Depressed? Worthless? Like I deserved to get screwed over or something." I hand the bottle back to him.

"Because you got screwed over so many times before." His hand strokes my cheek, and I look into his eyes, filled with compassion.

I want to cry, but I swallow hard instead. "Yeah. I never had much luck, you know? Anyway, it's over. I just need to move forward."

His hand on my cheek turns my face to his. "You've been through a lot, Melanie. It's a wonder you're not completely fucked up by now."

"Who says I'm not?" I smile, but the urge to cry is still there.

"You're not. You're gorgeous. And smart. And mature. And funny…"

"You mean sarcastic?" I interrupt.

"That too." He leans forward and brushes his lips over mine.

I take the beer back from him and drink a little more, raising my eyebrows at him.

"That's enough." He takes the green bottle from me.

"What are you? Like, my teacher or something?" I run one hand down his torso.

"Yeah, and you're going to be in big fucking trouble if you miss the next class." He's kissing me again, then putting the drink on the nightstand and pushing me so I'm lying on the bed again, and his kisses are traveling down my body.

His tongue darts into my belly button, and I writhe because it tickles but also because I know what's coming next. I open my legs, and even though I just orgasmed, the way his tongue moves over my sensitive skin lets me know the night has only just begun.

• • •

On Monday, I can't stop smiling. It's stupid to be happy about going to the drug class tonight, but I can't wait to see Jake again. I haven't seen him since Friday night, when we fell asleep until three in the morning, then woke up so he could drive me home.

It's the second half of April, and the day is actually kind of warm—warm enough, at least, that I don't need a jacket and won't be freezing later without one like usual. Instead of an old rock band shirt, I wear a tight lacy black top that's, of course, low cut. I opt for a black skirt, kind of flouncy but short, and pull on my knee-high boots instead of my usual sneakers. I won't be coming home after school, and I want to look good for class tonight.

At school, even though it almost physically hurts, I stop by Principal Evans' office to let her know I'd like some information on local community colleges. A few years ago the school let the school social worker and the college counseling officer go, because funds were short, I guess. So Principal Evans does it all. And I ignore the mixture of sadness and kindness in her eyes when she tells me to stop by later and she'll have a packet of information for me.

"Melanie!" Stacey stops me in the hallway before English class, hugging me briefly then standing back to take a look at me. "You look hot! Why are you so dressed up? Are you seeing Sam after school or something? I thought he and Robby were going to catch a movie."

"Sam? Oh. No. I just, you know, wanted to look nice." I shrug.

"Okay." She squints her eyes at me for a moment before continuing. "So, how was Friday night? Dinner with Sam? I saw him over the weekend, and he didn't say much about it. Said he doesn't like to kiss and tell. So? What's there to tell?"

111

I hope my laugh doesn't sound nervous. "He's nice. We went out for dinner. And there's nothing to tell."

"Seriously? He's hot, Melanie. And you're telling me *nothing* happened? At all?"

"Nothing, Stacey. I swear. We had dinner, then he dropped me off. We talked for a few minutes in the car. And then I went home." Or didn't. But I'll never tell her where I really went. I'll never tell anyone.

"Hmph. Well, his spring break will be over soon, so if you want to get on that, you better hurry." She winks at me, then laughs, her blonde curls bobbing up and down. Then her face gets serious, and she takes my hands in hers. "I'm still sorry. I want you to know that, Mel. And I'm going to keep saying it, like, forever. Or until you forgive me."

"I do forgive you, OK? It's fine." It's not true, but saying it makes her smile, her glossy lips perking up as she squeezes my hands, then turns and practically skips away. She turns back once. "See you later!"

"Later." But I say it quietly, and I'm pretty sure she didn't hear it.

After school, I stop by Mrs. Evans' office to pick up the packet. She's put a ton of pamphlets and information in a manila envelope, and when she hands it to me she looks straight into my eyes. "What are you doing right now?" she asks.

"Um, working? At the antique shop?"

"And after that?" She raises an eyebrow at me.

I roll my eyes but smile at her. "I'm going to the library for the drug class."

"You better. Don't let me find out tomorrow that you didn't show up, OK?"

"I promise."

"Detective Beck is being extremely generous by allowing you to continue in the class even though you missed one session. You know that, right?"

"I know." *Thank god she doesn't know why he's being so generous.*

"All right. I'll see you tomorrow. Oh, I also put some information in that envelope about the process to defer admittance to University of Chicago. Make sure you follow up on that, OK?"

"Yup." I head out of school and to the shop, opening it with my key. The Harts are out of town, on a very rare trip—they never go anywhere—to the Grand Canyon. So the shop is only open in the evenings when I'm there. Honestly they probably should have just closed up for the week, since nobody comes in anyway. But I don't mind being there. It's nice to be alone, and to have time to think or get my homework done or rest.

Today, my mind won't stop focusing on Jake and what happened between us on Friday night. I can't get over how perfectly he knew how to touch me, how to make me respond. It felt like we'd known each other for years instead of mere weeks.

It's hard to sit still; it feels impossible to wait the three hours until the class starts. I'm a bubble of energy and excitement, ready to burst with the tension I feel. How will Jake look at me? What will he say to me? What will happen after class? I think I'll die if he just says, "See you next week, Ms. Cannon," and lets me leave.

When it's finally time to head over to the library, I'm filled with a mixture of fear and excitement.

Jake's not here yet. I take my seat toward the back of the classroom and rip a sheet out of my notebook. I write, "I'm not wearing any panties," on it. Does that sound too juvenile? I consider tearing out another sheet and writing, "I can't wait for you to come in my mouth," but I worry that sounds way too dirty.

The first note's fine, I decide, folding the paper in half, then in half once more. I run my finger along the creases, making them flatter and flatter, as I anxiously wait for Jake to appear.

And when he does, I feel like I'm not prepared. I'm breathless for a moment, my head floaty and dizzy. He's such a *man*, so sexy and controlled and powerful. Just seeing his gun, holstered at his side, makes me realize this isn't a game. He's an adult. And while technically I am too, his job, his position, the fact that he's teaching this very class I'm in reminds me of how much more of a grownup he is than I am. And that, even though it shouldn't, turns me on.

His jeans are faded, and today he's wearing a Chicago Police Department T-shirt. After setting his bag down on the desk, he glances up at the classroom, scanning over everyone. For a second his eyes land on me, but in an instant they've moved on. My heart squeezes, and I try to remind myself that he can't give me the smile I want here, in front of the entire class.

I take a deep breath and bring the folded paper to the front of the class. "I'm supposed to give this to you," I mutter, dropping it on his desk and immediately heading back to my seat.

Some students are already seated, some are still straggling in, and I watch while he unfolds the note, his face completely even as he reads it. He doesn't even look up at me.

Oh god. It was immature. What the hell was I thinking? I want to curl up in a ball and hide, but it's too late. I just made a fool out of myself, and there's nothing I can do about it.

Jake takes a stack of photocopied handouts from his bag. "Take one and pass them on," he says, handing the stack to Pearl, who's taken up her seat right in front of him. *Bitch.*

"Of course." I can only see the back of her head, but I'm sure she's smiling at him, maybe biting her lip to try to be more desirable to him. I hate her, even more than last week.

"Melanie?" he says.

My eyes dart to his face. "Um, yes?"

"Come here, please."

My heart pounds as I make my way to the front of the class. He gestures for me to stand next to him, and I do, wondering what's going on.

"Ms. Cannon, this is from last week. I expect you to read it and answer all the questions at the end. Legibly. And turn it back in to me next week. I won't accept it late. Understand?"

114

"Yes," I whisper, taking the stapled papers from him and heading back to my desk. I slink into my seat, putting the papers down and taking the stack from the stoner kid who's reaching over to hand it to me. I take one, then pass the rest on to the girl to my right.

When I look down at last week's paper, the one Jake just gave me, I read what he's written on the bottom. *I can't wait to see for myself.*

· · ·

After class, Jake says, "Ms. Cannon? Can you stay after? We need to go over some things from last week."

"Yeah. Sure." I shrug nonchalantly as I load up my backpack.

This time when Pearl stops at his desk, smiling and wiggling her hips, I don't even care. Because he asked *me* to stay. And because *I'm* the one who spent most of the night at his house on Friday.

When everyone's gone, he stares at me for a second, his eyes so intense I can't sit still under his gaze. "Don't move," he says. "I'll be right back."

He leaves the room and is gone for about five minutes, during which I look around the room, trying to keep my mind occupied and my heart from jumping out of my chest. The possibilities of what tonight holds in store are endless and endlessly exciting.

"Where did you go?" I ask when he finally returns.

"Made sure everyone left the building. I'm locking up tonight. The director gave me the key." He stands in front of the desk where I'm seated, reaching out a hand and pushing a strand of hair behind my right ear. "You make me insane, Melanie. Did you know that?" It's a rhetorical question.

"I thought about you all weekend."

"Yeah?" He briefly touches my lips, then backs up, leaning against his desk and staring at me. "What did you think about?"

"Friday night." I bite my lip, hoping it's the right answer, the one he wants to hear, the one that will make him want me even more.

"What part?" There's a hint of challenge in his voice.

"All of it."

"Were you lying?" he asks.

"Lying? About what?"

"The note you gave me. Is it true?"

One corner of my mouth turns up in a grin as I grab the bottom of my skirt and pull it up for a second, just long enough for him to see I was telling the truth.

"Fuck," he whispers, his body straightening slightly, his eyes filled with heat.

I slip out of the desk and move right in front of him. "I've been thinking about *this* for a long time." I feel brave and sexy and confident as my hands undo his belt buckle. I push his jeans and underwear down just enough so I can free his cock, already hard.

When I kneel down in front of him he hisses out a breath.

"It's dangerous to do this here," he whispers.

"Do you want me to stop?"

"Fuck," he groans as I lick him from the base all the way to the tip and swirl my tongue there for a few seconds. "No, I don't want you to stop. Please don't stop."

"Are you sure?" I ask with mock concern in my tone, before taking him all the way into my mouth and deep into my throat, then popping him out of my mouth again.

"Jesus, Melanie. Yes, I'm sure. I've never been surer of anything before in my life."

I glance at the small dingy window in the door. The hallway's pitch black, and I know nobody's in the building except us. So I bend my head once more and swallow his cock, gripping the base as I move my mouth up and down, sucking as hard as I can.

"Am I doing it OK?" This time I'm not trying to tease him. I suddenly feel insecure. I've done this before, but I never really *wanted* to. And I didn't really care if the guy liked it or not. But with Jake? I want it to be good. I want to make him feel amazing.

"You're, uh, perfect." His words sound strangled, like it's hard for him to speak.

I take him in my mouth again, as far as I can again, and suck, moving my tongue along his sensitive skin as I do. Then I find a

116

steady rhythm, fucking him with my mouth while I grip the thick base of his cock.

His hand is in my hair, his cock twitching in my mouth, my knees cold on the hard floor of the library classroom, my pussy throbbing every time he moans in pleasure. I'm doing this to him. I'm making him feel this way.

"I'm going to come," he mutters after a few minutes. "Fuck. I'm going to come now."

I've never let a guy come in my mouth, but I want Jake to. His cock hardens even more and he grasps a handful of my hair, pulling but not too hard. And then my mouth fills with his cum. Under my left hand his quad muscles tighten, and he groans, cursing under his breath.

I dare to glance up at his face, my mouth still filled with him, and see his head thrown back, his lips open in pure bliss.

I wipe my mouth with the back of my hand as I stand up, feeling weirdly proud and more than a little turned on. He's already pulling up his jeans, fastening his belt and glancing at the still-dark hallway through the little square window in the door.

"Come here." He pulls me to him, into a rough hug.

I bury my face in his worn, soft T-shirt, smelling the masculine odor of his deodorant and the scent of his skin. Already, I think I've committed to memory the way he smells. I think I'll remember it forever.

He kisses the top of my head. "Melanie. Jesus. You're amazing."

"So you think I'm going to pass this class?"

He pulls away and laughs, looking into my eyes.

I reach up and touch his rough cheek, then run my finger down along his jaw.

"Yeah," he says. "I think you're going to pass this class. Now let's go. I'm driving you home."

As we walk outside, I wish he'd take me back to his place. I wish we could hang out all night long. But I know without him saying it that he needs to be careful, that we can't be seen together too often. Or at all.

When we pull up to my house he says, "Turn on the porch light when you get inside."

"It's burned out. It's been out for ages." I grab the door handle.

"I fixed it a few nights ago."

"You what?" I look curiously at him.

He nods. "Just needed a new bulb."

"My mom didn't mind?"

He blows out a breath. "She didn't notice I was on the porch, Mel." He starts to say something, then checks himself. "I knocked and she didn't answer."

"Thanks?" I get out of the car slowly. I turn to wave at him before going inside, where I flick on the switch. Light illuminates the falling-down porch and I smile, even though he can't see me from all the way inside the house.

I watch him drive away, then head into the living room, where my mom barely looks up from the computer to say hello.

CHAPTER ELEVEN – JAKE

"Jake! When you coming back to Chicago?" My buddy Saul from back home answers my call right away. We grew up together on the north side of Chicago, and we've been friends ever since. He runs a few bars in the city, and I'm calling for a favor.

"Soon, man. I'm just doing some shit for my uncle. You know." I open a beer and walk to the window, looking out at the dirty street.

"You doing OK? How's your mom?"

"Yeah. Fine. We're fine." Truth is, I haven't really spoken to my mom in a while, but I don't want to get into it, so I change the subject fast. "Dude, I got a favor to ask."

"Yeah? Anything, man. What do you need?"

"Any chance you've heard something about Station Gray playing anywhere soon?"

"You fucking got ESP or shit?" Saul laughs loudly.

"Huh?"

"Fucking ESP? You read minds or whatever?"

"No, man, why? They playing at one of your clubs?" *Yes.* I grin and swig some beer.

"Dude, yeah. They're going to be at Velvet, uh, Friday night. Eleven. They're gonna fucking pack the place, but I'll save a table for you. Bringing someone?"

I clear my throat. "Yeah."

119

"A date?"

"Yup."

"Aw, Jakey!" He sounds way too excited. "Dude, you haven't brought a fucking date date around in, like, years. Getting tired of mindless flings or what?"

"Something like that," I mutter.

"She from that fucking little town you're working in?"

"Yeah."

"Nice. Bring her to Chicago, show her the city. Glad you thought of taking her to my place, Jake."

"She's a huge Station Gray fan," I tell him.

"Good taste, man. Except for being with you." He guffaws. "So I'll see you Friday?"

"Yeah. Thanks." I hang up, thinking of what Melanie's face will look like when she realizes we're going to see Station Gray live.

• • •

I debate the intelligence of taking Melanie to Chicago, to a bar where she'll be underage. But honestly, it doesn't take me long to make up my mind. Getting her away from Bells Park, even for one night, and taking her to see her favorite band ever will be amazing. Maybe it will make up for some of the things she hasn't been able to do. For the things she's missed out on.

And I'd be lying if I said I couldn't wait to get her away from here, somewhere we can be together and not worry about who sees us.

I pick her up outside the antique shop. I would have picked her up at home, would have risked her mother seeing us, but Melanie insisted I meet her here. She smiles the second she sees me pull up, an expression so bright it's visible even through the cloudy glass of the front door.

She looks fucking amazing. Tight jeans. Those boots again. Hair shiny and straight. Red, red lips. And that sweater, that white sweater she was wearing the first time I met her.

120

I take off the second she gets in the car, then feel shitty for driving away so fast, mostly out of fear of being seen, but she doesn't seem to notice. She's giddy, almost shaking as she looks at me with those huge hazel eyes.

"Tell me where we're going!" she insists.

I shake my head and bite back a grin. "Nope."

"Please?"

"It's a surprise."

"I fucking hate surprises." But she laughs.

Part of her good mood, I know, is derived from the same place mine is: the fact that we're *going* somewhere. Together. It's like being on a first date, and I feel like a teenage boy, like I'd do anything to impress her.

"You look pretty," I say, resting my right hand on her leg, just above the knee.

"Really?" She scrunches her nose a little, and I know she's not just asking to hear me say it again; in part she's really not sure it's true.

"Really. Actually, *pretty* isn't the right word. You look absolutely fucking unbelievable, Melanie."

"Oh," she sighs, clearly surprised by my words, or possibly the strength of my tone. "But you still won't tell me where we're going?"

I shrug and grin, keeping my eyes on the road as I get onto the expressway. "Chicago."

"Wait. What?" She turns almost completely in her seat so she's facing me. "Are you serious?"

"Yeah." I can't stop smiling; I love seeing her so excited.

"Oh my god, Jake! This is so awesome. What are we going to do there? Can I see your apartment? This is so cool." She's practically bouncing up and down.

I laugh. "We're going to hang out. Have dinner." I don't want to tell her about seeing the band yet.

"What was it like, growing up in Chicago?" she asks.

"Uh, it was great. I mean, I don't have anything else to compare it to, you know? I was an only child, and my parents were great. My dad was a cop. My mom was always baking stuff, so all the kids wanted to be at our house. We were, you know, typical middle class." Guilt washes over me thinking about what a great life I had compared to Melanie's.

"That sounds so nice." Her tone is wistful. "I always wished I had a house that I could bring people to. But even now, I'm embarrassed. About my mom. Like, even if people know she, well, drinks? I don't want them to *see* it." She's quiet for a second before adding, "I've never told that to anyone before. I've never admitted I'm embarrassed of my mom. And dad."

"How well do you know your father?"

She shakes her head. "I don't. He left my mom when she was pregnant with me, and I've met him a handful of times when he came around for... I actually don't even know what he wanted. My mom never said. Sometimes he'd stay for a few days. Once he lived with us for a few months."

"What was that like?" I ask.

"I was in maybe fifth grade? And I remember thinking that I should care that he was there. That I should try to bond with him or something. But I only felt weird around him. Uncomfortable. And I could tell he felt the same about me."

She's quiet, looking out the window, before continuing. "He and my mom drank a lot. And fought. And finally he left. I thought I should be sad that he was gone—he was my dad, after all—but all I felt was relief. Is that bad? To be happier not to have a father than to have one?"

"He wasn't really a father, though, was he?"

"No. He wasn't." She reaches out and takes my hand.

My heart fucking flutters. It's ridiculous, how much a touch from Melanie does to me. How much I feel when I'm around her. I squeeze her hand but try to focus on the road, on driving, and not on how small her hand is, on the smoothness of her skin.

"You hungry?" I ask when we finally exit 290 and are in the city.

"Starved." But she doesn't look at me; she's staring out the window at the urban landscape, and I think if I let her, she'd get out and walk, just to be somewhere new, somewhere that's not Bells Park.

"You like burgers?" I have a perfect place picked out; it's kind of a dive, but it's got the best burgers in the city, and it's close to Velvet, my friend's bar.

"Yeah, I love burgers."

I drive down Western until we're in Wicker Park, a section of the city, and find a place to park, no small feat on a Friday night.

Burgers Seven is kind of a hole in the wall that straddles the line between hipster paradise and complete and total dump. But it's been written up in several big publications as having one of the best burgers in the city. It's packed, but the line moves quickly, and I order two burgers and fries, and one beer and one soda. We find two barstool seats by the window, facing out so we can see the sidewalk.

"Oh my god, I love it here!" Melanie stares out onto the street, where couples walk by laughing and cars light up the pavement. There's a bar across the street, and from here we can see inside the big windows where people are hanging out.

"What do you like about it?"

She looks at me like I'm crazy. "It's not Bells Park, for starters." Her laugh is sarcastic but lovely. "There's just so many people. And things to do. And, I don't know, *life*." She takes a big bite of her burger, then another. "This burger?" she says with her mouth full. "Is fucking amazing."

I laugh out loud. "It's good, right?"

She nods before setting the burger down and stuffing some fries in her mouth. "I'm so freaking hungry. I'm sorry."

"You shouldn't be. You need to eat more."

Her smile turns into a scowl. "Don't."

"Don't what?"

"Don't get all poor-Melanie on me, OK? Don't act like you need to take care of me. Because if that's all you feel for me, it's not enough."

I take a deep breath. "You fucking know that's not all I feel for you," I growl, and the smile she gives me, innocent and joyful, then suddenly sexy, makes my heart skip. I want to tell her more, but it's not the time or place for this conversation, and I don't want the mood to be too heavy. I want her to have fun.

When we're done eating, I grab Melanie's hand and we head out into the night. We still have time before the show, and I want to walk around with her. I want to show her this part of the city. I want to hold her hand where people can see. I want everyone to know that I'm here, tonight, with her.

CHAPTER TWELVE – MELANIE

We end up at a place called Velvet. It's a bar, and I look at Jake questioningly. He's a cop. And I'm not twenty-one.

"Don't mention your age," he says under his breath as a big bald guy approaches us and enfolds Jake in a hug.

"Jakey! Dude. So glad to see you, man."

"Melanie, this is my buddy Saul. Saul, this is Melanie."

Jake's friend sticks out his hand and I take it, expecting a handshake, but instead he brings it to his mouth and kisses it.

"How is it, Jake, that you're here with the most beautiful woman in the city?" he asks. "You're not that much of a catch, dude. How do you do it?"

Jake laughs and pats Saul on the back. "It's great to see you too."

"Come on. I reserved a table for you in the fucking VIP section, man." Saul leads us through the already crowded bar to a roped-off section with five small tables. He gestures at one. "I'll send over someone to take your drink orders. Enjoy the show."

"What show, Jake?" I lean over so he can hear me over the crowd.

He grins and shrugs mischievously.

"Just tell me! Please? I'm gonna ask someone else…" I push my chair out like I'm going to get up.

He grasps my hand. "Fine. I'll tell you."

I lean forward over the table.

"We're here to see a band."

"What band?"

He shrugs. "Station Gray."

My mouth falls open. "Wait. What? Are you serious?"

He nods.

"Holy crap, Jake! No. For real."

"I am for real! You know how they don't do big tours anymore and only play at local places? And it's kind of on the down low? Saul owns a few bars in Chicago, so he knows when they're going to be around sometimes."

"Oh my god. Oh my god. I've never been to any concert ever, Jake! And this is my favorite band."

"Yeah. I know."

I seriously don't believe it until the lights go down, and there's a spotlight on the small makeshift stage, and Saul announces the band. And there they are: Hipbone Junior, with his blond dreads and beat-up jeans, and Linnea, ethereal and gorgeous, like a hippie fairy, and Rugged L, his bald black head shining under the lights.

I've never heard live music before, and this is amazing. They play so many of my favorite songs, even "Needlepoint" (and I laugh with Jake about his grandma during it). They're this amazing mix of the Beastie Boys and Dido and Gorillaz, and I can't get over that we're *here* seeing them *live*.

"We have a new song tonight," says Hipbone Junior after a while. "We just wrote it, uh, yesterday. So forgive me if it's a little, uh… if we make some mistakes."

The audience cheers, and I grab Jake's hand. A new song, and we're here for it.

"So, it's called, uh, 'Rough Around the Soul.' It's about a girl. Here it is."

It's beautiful, the kind of song that I know immediately is going to be one of my favorites ever. It's got a strong beat, but a gorgeous melody on top of it, and the lyrics I remember are perfect.

126

Red lip cigarette
Eyes black coal
Delicate girl
So rough around the soul.

Jake surprises me by buying me a T-shirt. Apparently the band sells a small number of shirts at each venue, specific to that night only, so I have a new Station Gray shirt, with their usual old-fashioned station wagon logo on the front. On the back it's got the bar name—Velvet—and the date.

In the car on the way back to Bells Park, I'm sleepy and happy and curled up in the seat next to Jake, clutching my new shirt like a favorite stuffed animal.

"You know," he says. "I was wrong. At Baker's Square? When I said you were just a little rough around the edges?"

"Yeah?" My eyes are closed but I'm listening. "You kind of pissed me off when you said that."

He laughs. "You're not rough around the edges, though. You're rough around the soul."

I laugh, loving that he's comparing me to my new favorite song. "What does that even mean, Jake?"

"You've been through hard shit, Melanie. You're stronger for it. And you're beautiful not despite it, but because of it."

"I like that." My voice is quiet, and I'm fading off to sleep, and I'm happy, happier than I remember being in a long time. Maybe in forever.

CHAPTER THIRTEEN – JAKE

"Dude." James looks up as I enter the station a few mornings later. "You gotta go out with me tonight."

"It's too early for you to be asking me out," I grumble, heading to the kitchenette for some crappy coffee.

James follows me. "No. Check this out. So I met this girl on *Date & Fate*. And she's agreed to go out with me. But only on a double date with her friend. You know, in case I'm some weirdo or something."

"You are. And what the fuck's *Date & Fate?*"

"It's an online dating site. How is it possible you're single and don't know about *Date & Fate?*"

"Cause I don't need a fucking website to get laid." I pour some coffee into a World's Best Dad mug that's next to the sink and lean against the counter.

"What's going on?" My uncle plops himself into a chair next to the tiny table and looks at the two of us. "Who's getting laid?"

James speaks up. "Me, if Jake helps me out. Come on, man. The friend's pretty. My date sent me a photo."

"Eh, I don't know." I sip the watery coffee.

"What, you dating someone? He doesn't have a girlfriend, does he?" James looks at my uncle.

"No. He doesn't." My uncle gives me a sharp look.

128

My stomach clenches. Does he know something?

"I think it would be a good idea for him to go on that, uh, double date tonight. Right, Jake?" He's still staring at me like he knows way more than he's letting on.

"Whatever," I say. I have absolutely no interest in going, but I can't say *no* right here, right now. Not with Uncle Mike looking at me like that. "What time? Where we going?"

"Dude, thank you. You won't regret this. She said she wants to hang out local, so we're going to Lucy's tonight."

"That place is rank." I pour the remainder of my coffee into the sink, swish some water around in it, and set the mug in the drying rack.

"Yeah, but your date? She's blonde. And cute. You like blondes, right?"

"Sure." I head out of the break room and back to my desk without looking back at either James or my uncle. I have absolutely no interest in going on this stupid fucking double date. I have no interested in whatever girl James' date is setting me up with.

Panic overcomes me for a moment as I realize the only girl I want to be with is Melanie. Fucking eighteen-year-old *high school student* Melanie. *Jesus.* What the fuck is wrong with me? I can't stop thinking about how gorgeous she looked at the bar a few nights ago, and about how she fell asleep on the ride back. Her skin was pale in the moonlight, her breathing even and soft, and I wanted to keep going, just to let her rest.

At my desk, I wish I could call Melanie or text her. I have her number; I have files on all the kids in the drug class. But we've never officially exchanged numbers, which is kind of weird considering the relationship that's developed between us.

I want to know what she's doing, though. I want to know for sure that she's at school. I want to know what she's wearing, and whether or not she has anything to eat for lunch, or if she's working at the shit shop after school today. I imagine her wearing the T-shirt I got her at Velvet and smile to myself.

I pick up my phone and dial the Columbus High number. When the secretary picks up I ask for Principal Evans. She's not in, but I leave a message to have her call me back.

When I hang up, I jump when my uncle, right behind me, speaks.

"Principal Evans?" he asks.

Swearing inwardly, I turn to him. "Yeah."

"Checking up on the Cannon girl?"

"Yup."

"That better be all you're doing." He rubs his balding head and points a finger at me.

I glance to the side, making sure James isn't around to hear this conversation. "There's nothing for you to worry about."

"And still I'm worried."

I toss the pencil on the desk. "You don't need to be."

He shrugs. "I'm an old man. And I haven't been a fucking cop for thirty-five years without developing keen instincts. And my instincts, Jake, tell me you're on the verge of getting yourself in trouble. Don't."

"I'm not."

"Good." He stares at me for a few seconds longer before standing and heading out into the reception area to shoot the shit with the receptionist. "I love you, kid," he says, turning back to me.

"Love you too, man." And I do. But I don't love the way he knows what I've been up to. I don't like that at all.

"Hey." His voice is softer. "I talked to your mom last night. She misses you. Wonders when you're coming back."

"Oh yeah?"

"Yeah, Jake. Why haven't you called her?"

"I, uh, been busy." It's a shit excuse. But I don't have a real one.

"Bullshit." Mike always calls me out. "You're avoiding her. And she's been through enough. When your dad died, she was destroyed, Jake. You know that. You were around. So now, why are you begrudging her the opportunity to be happy?"

"I'm not." But the thought of her new *friend*, the guy she hasn't even officially called her *boyfriend* yet, makes me want to punch something. And the thought of my father, bleeding out on that dirty floor in that crumbling apartment building, makes me want to cry. It's my fault. Even if everyone else says it's not, I can't stop going back, replaying the scene over and over and over again, changing the details until we both walk out whole.

"Can't stay here forever." Mike looks at me with one eyebrow raised. "I love having you here, but you know you can't run away from shit. It'll always be there. You need to deal with it."

"What, you a fucking psychologist now too?" I force a grin at him.

"No. I'm your goddamn uncle. And I'm looking out for you." There's love in his eyes as he says it, but warning too. Warning I'm pretty positive I'm not going to fucking heed.

• • •

I head over to Lucy's, not at all excited about the night. I'm going for two reasons. One, so my uncle gets off my case. And two, to help out James. From what he says, it's been awhile since he's gotten some, and if going on this double date is the only way he can take a girl out, I can suffer a few hours for him.

I haven't been to Lucy's since the night I met Melanie. *Aria*. It occurs to me how different things would be if I hadn't gone there that night. If I hadn't taken her home, she'd just have been some random girl in the class I'm teaching. A random girl I'd probably have checked out—I'm a guy and she's hot—but never given a serious thought.

Like last time, the bar is dim and cloudy. Smoking's not allowed indoors, but for some reason there's still a thickness to the air. James and two women are already there, and I head to the table where they're sitting.

"Yo, Jake!" James gets up and gives me a man hug, hitting my back firmly a few times before turning back to the girls. They're both pretty, one a brunette and one a blonde, who's my date for the evening. She's got short hair cut into a sharp bob, and her face is narrow, giving her a mean look, but her smile is genuine.

James introduces us, and I sit down next to Mona, the blonde. James has already ordered a pitcher, so I fill my cheap plastic cup with slightly warm beer and drink some down.

"So," Mona says, "you two are cops?"

"Yup." James smiles, a proud look on his face. I need to let him know he's trying too hard already, but I guess I'll let him figure it out for himself.

"That's really cool." James' date smiles at him.

"And cops are pretty hot!" says Mona, laughing and nudging my arm with hers.

Jesus. Another time, another situation, I'd be all over this. All over her. I can tell already she wants to have fun, and normally I'd be up for that too. But ever since—well, ever since Melanie, if I'm being honest—I haven't so much as thought about other girls. And having one right next to me doesn't change that at all.

"What do you two do?" I ask, trying to move away from Mona as surreptitiously as possible.

"I'm an account manager at a bank. She's a teacher. Third grade. We've been best friends since high school." Mona downs her beer, then refills her cup.

I sip my drink, wincing at how warm and verging on flat it is. I smile as James and his date scoot their chairs back from the table a little to quietly talk together. It's good to see him having some luck. Of course, that leaves me to make small talk with Mona.

"You're single, right?" she asks, putting a hand on my leg.

"Uh, yeah."

"OK. It's just that…" She sighs and purses her lips, tilting her head and examining my face.

"Just that *what?*"

A shrug of her shoulders. "You don't *seem* single."

"What does that mean?" I swallow some more shitty beer and set my cup on the sticky table.

"You've got that, I don't know, preoccupied thing going on that guys who aren't really interested have."

"I don't know what you're talking about." I try to keep my tone light, but I'm annoyed by this conversation. Honestly, I'd probably be annoyed with any conversation tonight, but this one is especially irritating.

"Well, either guys are interested. Or they're taken. Or they wish they were taken, but not by me." She squeezes my quad, then lets go and smiles at me. "So which is it?"

"Are those the only options?" I force a laugh. "Look, I said I'm single. And I don't know yet if I'm interested. We just met."

She frowns. "I think you know. I think people know."

"Know what?" I run my hand though my hair and glance at the door, as if I could will Melanie to walk through it right now. Not that I could do anything if she did. James is here. And Melanie shouldn't set foot anywhere *near* this place ever again. Still…

"Know if you're interested. I think it takes only a second, and if there's an attraction, you'll feel it immediately." She snaps her fingers.

"So you've never met someone and after a while realized how attractive he was?" I ask. "It's either all or nothing the instant you see someone?"

"Pretty much. Like you." She scoots a little closer to me. "When you walked in and James said you were my date, I knew immediately."

Shit.

"I know," she continues, "that you're the kind of guy who I'd be very, very interested in spending time with. And I could tell that you'd be able to fuck me like I deserve to be fucked." Her fingers massage my knee, then travel up the inside of my thigh.

My hand lands on top of hers, stopping the progression. "Look, Mona," I begin. But she cuts me off.

"I'm attractive but you're not interested. Right?" She leans closer. "Or technically you're single, but you're kind of sort of seeing someone? Something like that?" Her hand is still on my thigh, and my hand is on top of hers.

"I don't... yeah. Something like that."

"You know what?" She leans closer, her face up against mine. Her breath smells like beer and mint. "It's your loss, Jake. I was thinking of getting my knees dirty tonight."

Seriously? Is she seriously saying these things to me? It's tempting. I won't lie. We could probably go in the bathroom right now and she'd get me off, and after that we could come back into the bar and order another pitcher. Maybe it would even be cold this time.

My cock's twitching, but not because of Mona. It's because I'm thinking of Melanie, kneeling on the floor of the library classroom, asking me if she was doing it right. *Jesus fucking Christ.*

"Yo, Beck. Let's get another pitcher." James gestures at me with his head, and gratefully I follow him up to the bar.

"How's it going with Mona, man?" he asks, raising an eyebrow and grinning at me.

"How's it going with, uh..." I can't remember the other girl's name.

"Fucking great, man. We've, you know, got a lot in common."

I pat him on the back. "That's good to hear."

"What about you?" he asks again after telling the grizzly bartender we need a refill.

I shrug. "She's... I don't know, dude. She's nice. I'm just not..."

"Don't fuck this up for me." James puts his hands on my shoulders and looks me squarely in the face. "Just pretend you're having a good time, all right? Cause if your date wants to leave, mine will go with her. Just give me another fucking hour. Can you do that for me?"

"Yeah. Fine. I can hang out for another hour." I don't want to, but James is so desperate. I glance over at our table, where the two girls are sitting close and talking. I wonder if Mona's telling her friend what an asshole I am. Except for messing things up for James, I honestly don't care. And I'm certain she can find any number of other guys who'd kill for a night with her. I'm just not one of them.

CHAPTER FOURTEEN – MELANIE

Molly scratches at the door of the antique shop, and I jump up to open the door for her. Light from inside the store illuminates the doorway, and immediately I can tell something's wrong with her. She's mewling at me like usual, but it sounds different. Like she's scared or hurt. Her eyes are wild, and as I move toward the door she backs up and hisses. And that's when I see it. Blood.

I can't tell where it's coming from, but I know she's hurt. "Hey, it's OK," I whisper, slowly opening the door so I don't spook her. I make gentle clucking sounds with my tongue, but as soon as the door opens she backs away even more.

"Shhhh. I'll help you. Don't run away."

But she does, and I catch a glimpse of her back leg, mangled and bloody.

Shit. I feel sick, my head dizzy and light, and I start after her but she disappears into the dark along the side of the building, sprinting fast despite her injury. She's gone. And I need to find her.

I lock up the shop and pull out my phone. I need someone to help me look, someone with a car. My mom's out of the question. And I don't have Jake's number. But I know where he lives, so I turn the corner and stand outside his three-flat, hoping he doesn't think I'm bothering him for something stupid when I tell him what I need.

He's not home. I knock for several minutes, but his apartment windows are dark and nobody responds.

Think, Melanie. Where else could he be? Anywhere, really. Maybe in another town having dinner at another Baker's Square or Denny's or something like that. If he's in town, there aren't that many options.

Maybe Lucky's? Lucy's. Whatever you want to call it.

I take off, jogging at a steady pace until the old garish sign, the "k" unlit, is in sight. Jake told me not to go there again, and I don't want to get Jones in trouble, but I'm only going to peek my head in, just for a second to check if Jake is there.

I grasp the worn wooden handle and pull the door open, the warmth and light, however dim, as well as the smell of stale beer from inside greeting me. I quickly scan the people at the bar—no Jake.

Just as I'm about to step all the way inside I see him. At a table with a woman. Their faces are close together and her hand is on his thigh, his hand on top of hers.

It's like a semi truck hit me, knocked me right over and kept going. My lungs have stopped working, or it feels like that at least. I need to leave before he sees me, before I have to look him in the eyes and know I was just a piece of ass and nothing more.

Like my feet are made of lead, I pick up my feet and turn. I force myself to walk as the door shuts behind me and I'm outside, alone, in the dark.

• • •

Through foggy eyes I bring up Stacey's number as I walk back to Main Street. I know she won't really understand, but hopefully she'll help me because we're friends. Or used to be at least. And I realize it's stupid; it's not like we'll be able to find a cat just by driving around. Cats are notoriously good at hiding, and in the back of my mind I know it's useless. But I can't just give up. Sometimes, even if you know something's a lost cause, you still have to try, at the very least to prove you're still human.

"What's up?" Stacey's talking loud, and I can hear music and voices in the background.

"Stacey? I need your help."

"You OK? Wait. Let me go to a quieter room." She's silent for a few moments, then I hear a door closing and she's talking once more. "Robby and Sam are being stupid loud. Ugh. What's going on, Mel?"

"This is going to sound dumb, but there's this cat? I've been feeding her outside the antique shop. And today when she came by she was hurt. Like, her leg is messed up and she was bleeding. She ran off, but I want to look for her. Is there any way you could, I don't know, drive me around?"

There's a long silence. "A cat? You want to go look for a cat?"

God. I knew she'd think it was stupid. It *is* ridiculous. Suddenly all I want is to be home and in bed with the covers up over my head.

But then anger flares up in my stomach. "Remember when you said you owed me?" My voice is hard. "You said you were sorry, and you'd have my back, and I need your help right now."

She hesitates. "I really can't, like, drive right now? I'm so stoned!" She giggles, then hiccups. "I could, like, get in trouble if I got pulled over driving like this."

"Stacey."

There's a longish pause, and she finally says, "You know what? I'll just send Sam. I mean, we were going to start a movie, but it's fine."

"No, forget it…"

"He really likes you, Melanie. Even though you've been ignoring his calls."

"It's really all right." I'm walking fast, hurrying to the antique shop, because maybe Molly's back now.

"Where are you? Meet him at the store, OK? I'll send him over. Anyway, Robby and I need some alone time."

She hangs up. When I reach the antique shop, I call quietly for Molly, but there's no sign of her except the few drops of drying blood on the pavement outside the store.

138

Where, exactly, are we going to drive? How do you even look for a cat? This is stupid. *I'm* stupid. But the one thing that keeps me going right now, that spurs me on to look for the cat is what I saw at the bar. I'll do almost anything to forget about that.

Sam pulls up in Stacey's Range Rover. "What's going on?" He gets out and comes over to me, enfolding me in a hug. He smells vaguely of beer—has he been drinking and driving?—but I'm glad someone's here to help me.

"Thanks for coming," I say, pulling out of his embrace. "There's this cat? I feed her sometimes at work. She's hurt. I tried to get her to come inside, but she ran off, and I'm worried she won't be OK out there all night."

"So she usually comes here?" He puts his hands like binoculars to his eyes and peers into the shop, right up against the glass.

"Yeah."

"All right. Let's put out some food and water. Just on the sidewalk. And then we'll walk around the area and see if we see anything. Sound good?"

"Yeah." I unlock the door and Sam follows me in, picking up items and setting them back down as I get the bowls and food.

"You've been ignoring me." He doesn't sound angry, just surprised. As though he's not used to being ignored.

"I've been busy." I hand him the bowl of water and we go back outside, setting the dishes down.

"I'm heading back to school soon. And I feel like we didn't really get a chance to hang out." He takes my hand and looks into my eyes, a half grin on his face. He's cute. Like, collegiate and smart and preppy cute. But he's leaving soon, and anyway, my heart was broken into a million tiny pieces no more than an hour ago, and I'm barely hanging on.

"Let's look for Molly, OK?" I pull my hand from his.

"Right."

For about twenty minutes we walk along Main Street and in the alley that runs behind it, quietly calling and listening for any sound, looking for any movement. But there's no sign of her. The food and water sits untouched in front of the shop.

"We could drive around," says Sam, "but honestly? I don't think it's going to help." His voice sounds sympathetic.

He's right. I know it. It was stupid for me to even call Stacey in the first place. "Thanks for trying," I say. "And, I don't know, have a good trip back to school."

"I'll drive you home. You can't walk alone this late."

Home. It doesn't feel like home. Just earlier, I was thinking about getting in bed and covering myself up, but suddenly I realize that home should also be where you have people who love you. Who look out for you. And maybe I don't have that. Maybe I don't have that anywhere.

"Or," he continues, "you could come over to Stacey's. Her parents are out of town, so Robby and I are hanging out there. You could sleep over there. I'm sure Stacey would let you borrow, like, clothes or whatever." He puts one hand closer to me, hovering near my thigh, just waiting for the all-clear. "Yeah?"

"Yeah. Yeah, OK." I don't want to lead him on, but I don't want to be by myself tonight. It's not like Stacey's any closer to *home* than my own house and mom, but at least we can drink and laugh and I won't be alone.

• • •

We're two episodes of *Supernatural* and one bottle of vodka in, hanging out in Stacey's rec room. I don't even know what time it is. Two, maybe? Three? It doesn't matter. I haven't been drinking, though the others have, but my head's spinning nonetheless, going over and over what I saw in the bar. Images of her face; his expression. Their bodies. I feel like vomiting.

Stacey's fallen asleep on the couch, and Robby's in the kitchen putting a frozen pizza in the oven after lamenting the fact that there's

140

nowhere around here to order from except Sausage Sausage, and their food sucks.

"Tired?" Sam's next to me on the couch not occupied by Stacey's sprawled figure, and he pulls me into a side hug. All night he's been making excuses to touch me; I've been carefully extricating myself.

"Exhausted. Yeah."

"Let's go upstairs. Find a bed to sleep in."

"Sam…"

"*Sleep*. All right?"

"Use the guest room," mutters Stacey, half-asleep. "Do not use my parents' room."

"Got it." Sam grabs my hand and pulls me to a standing position. "Come on."

The bed in the guest room is perfectly made. Like the rest of Stacey's home, it's decorated like something in a magazine. But I don't care about the décor right now—all I want to do is get under the covers and drift away, let my mind go blank for at least a few hours.

I crawl into the bed, fully clothed, and sigh.

Sam gets in bed next to me, the mattress shaking slightly with his weight. My body tenses, and I hope he plans to keep his promise that we're just going to sleep. Nothing else. Because I definitely don't want anything else from him. I don't want anything from anyone. Not even Jake. Not after what I saw.

For a few moments we lie in silence. And then he shifts his body closer to mine, draping an arm over me. His hand snakes across my chest, and he begins to massage my right boob.

I roll onto my stomach. "Stop," I whisper.

"Sorry."

Another couple of minutes pass, quiet again, but then he says, "Can we talk for a minute?"

I roll my eyes in the dark and turn over onto my back. "What, Sam? I'm tired."

"Me too," he murmurs, moving his body on top of mine. He kisses me, and for one second I kiss him back. Maybe I can do this. Maybe I can forget about Jake and the cat and everything else, even if it's just for a little while.

But I don't want to. "No. Stop," I mutter against his lips, which are hungry on mine.

"You're so hot, Melanie. Just a little…"

"No!" I push harder.

"I'm leaving tomorrow," he says, resisting my efforts to get him off of me. "Let's take advantage of an opportunity to have some fun." He shoves his hand up under my shirt.

"Get. The fuck. Off of me!" I push with all my might, and this time he sits back while I extract myself from under him and jump off the bed, standing next to it and glaring at him. "What the hell?"

"Yeah, what the hell?" His eyes are sparking with anger—I can see them even in the dark room.

"I fucking said no, asshole."

"Asshole?" He laughs, a dark and questioning chuckle.

"Yes. You're being a fucking dick right now."

"Shit." He rubs his face with both hands. "I'm sorry. You're right."

I look at him questioningly, not sure if he's being serious or sarcastic.

"No, for real," he affirms. "No means no. I'm, you know, a gentleman. And shit."

I can't help a half-laugh.

"Look, I can't drive you home. I'm kind of drunk? But if you want to sleep here, the room's yours. I'll go downstairs. I'm sorry about before."

Still hesitant, I sit back on the bed. "Thanks."

"Listen." He gazes at me, his eyes filled with genuine concern but bleary from the vodka. "You're, uh, nice. Smart. You deserve better friends than Stacey. I shouldn't say that, because she's my cousin's girlfriend. But just, you know, watch out around her."

"What do you mean?" My heart picks up, like my body knows he's going to tell me something I don't want to hear.

"Melanie, Stacey's not a very good friend. Supposedly the only reason she started hanging out with you again is so you wouldn't tell the truth about the drugs. She thought pretending to be your friend again and hooking you up with me would distract you."

"Oh." I bite my lip. I'm not really surprised, but I feel like all the energy's leaking out of me.

He puts his hand on my shoulder gently. "There's more."

I squeeze my eyes shut, then open them and look at him. "Tell me."

He actually looks sad as he speaks. "She's the one who told the scholarship foundation that you got caught in a drug-related offense."

"Jesus, Sam! What the hell?" Stacey comes around the corner. "What the hell are you doing? You weren't supposed to…" She turns to me. "Melanie. I'm sorry, OK? He's being stupid, and he's been drinking. Don't listen to him."

My stomach swirls with nausea, and I swallow, fighting down the urge to vomit. "Is it true? Just tell me the fucking truth, Stacey." My words are surprisingly steady.

"Get out, Sam." She turns to him, her face angry. "Just get the fuck out of here."

He mutters something under his breath and leaves, slamming the door behind him. Stacey plops down on the bed and glances up at me, a beseeching look in her eyes.

I shake my head. "Tell me, Stacey. Just tell me. Is it true?"

Her eyes leave mine, like she can't bear to look at me. "Which part?" she finally asks. "Which part do you want to know about?"

My body starts trembling, shaking so hard I can barely speak. "Is it true that you were the one who notified the scholarship organization that I got in trouble?"

Head down, she responds. "You're my best friend."

143

"That's not an answer, Stacey. Don't lie to me. I'm not your best friend, and you're not mine. We haven't been friends for a really long time. Longer than I even knew. The only reason you've been hanging out with me again is because you're scared I'll tell the truth, that the drugs in my locker were actually yours. Just tell me the rest of it, Stacey."

She looks up now, holding her head high and haughty, and I know it's over. Everything between us is over. The last nine years of friendship, gone, like a tiny scrap of paper in a gust of wind.

Sucking in a deep breath, she nods. The worst part is she looks almost proud. "Yes. OK, yes. I tried hard to be friends with you again because I was worried you'd come forward and tell the truth after you lost the scholarship. But it's not like we didn't have fun together again! You know it's true."

I shake my head. "And the scholarship? Are you the one who notified them? Principal Evans said they called her, told her they'd received an anonymous email and she was under obligation to tell the truth. Was the email from you?"

Stacey squeezes her eyes shut, and for a second I want to say, *Forget it. I don't really want to know.* But I need to be strong. The truth is, at the end of the day, the only thing we've got.

"Yes." Her voice is small.

"God, Stacey! Why would you *do* that? Like, seriously? Why?"

"I was jealous. Melanie, I was so freaking jealous of you. I couldn't stand it! You got into pretty much an Ivy League, and I didn't. Like, you've always been the smarter one. And I just… I was tired of it. I wanted to be the one doing something better this time."

"I don't… I can't… What the hell are you even talking about? U of I is an amazing school! And what does it matter that I was going somewhere else, somewhere supposedly better? Who cares? Why couldn't you let me have this? You know I have nothing, Stacey. *Nothing.* My dad is the fuck in prison. You *know* that. My mom? Do you have any idea how many bottles of wine she drinks a week? How she spends all her money on that instead of groceries or clothes? You know I wear whatever rejects I can find at the antique shop before they get donated. When people bring in bags of old clothes? That's how I *shop*. You've been my friend for, like, ever. You know these things. How could you? How the fuck *could* you?"

Her eyes are wide. Stunned. Slowly she shakes her head. "I don't know."

"And why didn't you just go ahead and notify the university while you were at it? Why stop at the scholarship foundation?"

She looks at me, her eyes meeting mine. "I'm not *that* awful. I'm not *that* much of a bitch. Besides." There's a beat, and she doesn't look at me. "I read a thing that they don't, uh, actually care about some misdemeanors all that much. Sometimes. So."

I burst out laughing, my body racked with hilarity.

"I *said* I was sorry. You're not going to tell people the drugs were mine, are you?"

"Maybe I will." I give her a defiant look. "What would you do, Stacey, if I did that?"

Her eyes widen. "I'll deny it. And you know my dad can hire the best lawyers, if we need to, right? And you can't? I just, like, want to save you the embarrassment of making some kind of ridiculous claim against me. Nobody would ever believe you over me." She licks her lips. "So you won't say anything, right?"

I gain control of my body and look at her hard, because I honestly don't get it. I don't get her. "Seriously? You seriously just asked me that?"

"Yeah. I mean, I don't want to get into trouble, Melanie. You already are, but that doesn't mean we both have to be, you know?"

It takes all my energy, every single bit of it, not to throw myself at her and claw her eyes out. Instead I stay calm, steady. "Stacey?" I say.

"Yeah?"

"Go fuck yourself." I walk right past her on my way to the door, so close she must feel the breeze of me leaving. And I don't look back. Because I no longer care. Fuck her. Fuck everyone.

I have no idea what time it is, and I don't have a plan. The gravel on the side of the road crunches under my feet as I make my way toward town. Stacey's subdivision is a few miles out, but the air is cool with an undertone of spring, and the moon is bright, and I'm not scared of being alone on a desolate road in the middle of nowhere. What's there left for me to be afraid of?

In the tall brush that separates the road from the fields beyond, unplanted and waiting for warmer weather, animals scurry away as I approach. Crickets chirp, and it's almost melodic. It almost feels *nice* out here, like I'm taking a leisurely walk to enjoy nature.

But that couldn't be farther from the truth. I half expect someone from Stacey's house to drive up and slow down in her Range Rover, urge me to get in so at least I don't have to walk the whole way back to town. But the road is silent and vacant, and I don't see a single vehicle until I get into town.

Pink and orange fight the blackness along the horizon, rising slowly and steadily before the sun, by the time I get to my house. I walk up the sagging front steps and open the front door, unlocked as usual.

The sweet and sour smell of wine greets me as I step inside, and I'm somewhat surprised to see my mom at her computer. Her hours are strange, though, and inconsistent. Sometimes she stays up all night, only to crash as I'm leaving for school. Sometimes she goes to bed early, exhausted and drunk after a day of cheap wine and wakes up before I do. I have no idea what's the case today; all I know is I don't want to talk to her. I don't want to talk to anyone.

"Where've you been?" She doesn't turn around as she asks the question.

"Out."

"Well, I figured you were *out*, honey, when I went to check on you and you weren't in your bed."

"I'm going there now." I start moving past her.

"Can I show you something?" she asks.

I take a deep breath. "Later, OK? I'm tired."

"Oh please? This one's my best yet!" She clicks away, then brings up YouTube and starts playing her video. This one is a slideshow of photographs of cats with scared looks on their faces while a dance beat plays in the background with a voice on repeat saying, "Toot, toot, kitty. Hello! Hello! Toot, toot, kitty. Hello! Hello!" The photographs aren't even switching in time to the beat.

I look away, because it's hard to understand how this is my life, how the one person I'm supposed to count on the most spends her life drinking wine and making absurd videos.

"Do you like it? It's kind of funny, right? And you won't believe how many views…"

"Stop."

"What?" She picks up her tumbler of wine and takes a big sip, then sets the glass down.

"Just stop, Mom, OK?"

"I don't understand…"

"And that's the problem!" I know I shouldn't start saying what I think, because if I do, I'll never stop. But it's too late now. It's like these things will keep building and building and explode inside me if I don't get them out.

She frowns. "What's the problem, Melanie?"

"The problem? The problem is that you're my mom. You're supposed to, I don't know, buy groceries once in a while…"

"I do!" she interrupts.

"And maybe make my lunch sometimes? Drive me to school? But wait. You can't! You can't drive me to school because you're too drunk all the time. It doesn't even matter what time of day it is. You're *always* drunk and you're *always* drinking."

"Melanie…"

"No. I don't want to hear it! I don't want to hear anything, and I don't want to see your videos anymore. You're wasting your time, and you know what else? They're stupid! Your videos are *horrible*. The photos are pixilated and the music is terrible, and most of it? You

147

don't even have the legal right to use! You're one of those people who thinks they know how to use Photoshop, but all you do is crop pictures and put them into a video. You don't know *anything*!"

She's quiet for a few moments. Then she starts clicking again, bringing Photoshop up onto her screen. "You think I don't know how to use Photoshop? Watch. Just watch, Melanie. I'll show you what I can do." Her words are low, quiet, but filled with something, a strange mixture of anger and desperation. I know that feeling all too well.

I want to leave the room. I want to go away from here. But I stand still, frozen in my spot, watching as she brings up a photo onto her screen. It's an old one that I've never seen, but I recognize the young version of my mom instantly. She's holding a baby—me—and we're standing on a beach. She's slim, her legs long and pretty, and her hand is on my head to keep the little white bonnet I'm wearing from flying away. Her hair blows back in the wind, and she's smiling broadly.

But when she clicks on something, a man appears next to us. My dad. He stands close to her but not touching, not quite. He's not smiling, and he looks like he doesn't want to be there with us.

She clicks him back in, then out of the photo once more. Where he was is ocean and sand, background that matches the rest of the photo. It's like magic, and I'm startled she can do something like that.

"See? Do you know how hard it is to cut out a person flawlessly like this? To leave the background perfect? See the water? The clouds? You'd never even know he was there."

"Mom…"

"You think I'm stupid. I know you do. Getting into University of Chicago, well, I'm proud of you, of course, but it doesn't mean you're smarter than I am, Melanie." Her eyes dart to mine, and she looks like she's scared.

"I never said I was smarter than you."

"Yeah, well, you didn't have to."

148

"I'm sorry if I made you feel that way," I stammer. How did this get turned around? Why am I suddenly the one apologizing? It's crazy; I feel like I'm in some weird alternate universe or dream where nothing makes sense.

"I make the videos because they're fun, Melanie. I enjoy it, all right? But don't for a second think that I have no real skills, because I do."

"Then why don't you use them? Why do you sit here all day long and drink and make those... videos? Why? Why don't you do something else? Something *real*?"

At first she doesn't answer. We stare at each other for a long time before her face loses its anger and she looks only sad and confused. "I don't know," she finally says. "I just don't know. I can't. I don't know."

"You could if you wanted. All these years you've been getting your disability checks, and the whole time you've had the skills to do something real, to make actually money instead of getting just enough to buy your stupid wine. Maybe you could, I don't know, help me pay for college? I just... I don't get it, Mom."

"I'm sorry." She shakes her head, then finishes the wine in her glass. At least she could have the decency to stop drinking while we're having this discussion.

I shake my head. "You're not, though. If you were really sorry, you'd do something about it."

"I can't," she says again.

"Whatever." As I head to my room, I hear the splash of liquid as she fills up her glass again.

Once I throw all the books from my backpack, I stuff it with a change of clothes, some basic toiletries, my phone and charger, and all the money I've saved from working at the antique shop. I know I should have opened up a bank account, but instead I've stashed it in a tampon box at the back of my underwear drawer. It's not a lot of money—$750 in total—but it's enough to last me a little while.

Where, exactly, I'm not sure. I have no idea where I'm going. But I know I can't stay here.

I strip out of my clothes; there's no time to shower, but I can put on clean stuff, at least. It's stupid, and I hate him now, but I can't help pulling on the Station Gray T Jake gave me. There's a mostly clean pair of jeans on the floor, and I put those on, along with warm socks and my Converse sneakers.

Then I head out into the living room.

"Oh, honey, isn't it too early to go to school?" She's still there, still drinking, still working on her videos. Like nothing happened between us just a few minutes ago.

"I'm fine." I continue past her to the front door. As I open it and step outside I hear her call after me, "Have a nice day!"

CHAPTER FIFTEEN – JAKE

My head throbs from drinking too much last night. I'm dying to know what happened with James and the two women; before leaving, I suggested to Mona that James would probably appreciate getting to know both of them. She smiled and winked.

But first, some coffee. I start a pot and stretch, looking out my front window at the grim street and know I've got to get out of here soon. I miss Chicago, and my uncle's got a lot accomplished in terms of building up the department while I've been here. He's not going to need me for much longer.

And I know, it's time for me to get back home. To talk to my mom. To somehow find peace with my dad's death.

The only thing stopping me is Melanie. I don't want to leave her. I haven't figured out my feelings yet, but thoughts of her stopped me from getting laid last night. I didn't want someone else. I don't want *anyone* else. It's fucked up, but there it is. She's the only one I want.

My cell rings, and the caller ID shows it's the high school.

"Hello?" I ask.

"Jake? It's Joan Evans." Her voice is fringed with worry.

"What's going on?" I've already put down my mug and am heading into the bedroom to get dressed. Something's up, and I need to hurry.

"It's Melanie Cannon. She didn't show up to school again. I called her mother, who said she left the house around four in the morning."

"What?" I toss a clean T-shirt from my drawer onto the bed, then open the next drawer, rifling through for a pair of clean jeans.

"That's what I said. I asked her why she let her obviously upset high school daughter leave at that time of the morning, or night, or whatever you want to call it. And she had no good answer."

"Is she worried? Does she have any idea where Melanie went?"

"She didn't seem worried," says the principal. "She said Melanie just probably needed to get some space. Or something like that. Jesus, that poor girl."

"Yeah. Look. I'm heading in to the station, and my partner and I will drive around, see what we can find out." One-handed, I'm trying to undress. I don't want to waste time.

"Her friend—or former friend—Stacey didn't show up today either, and nobody's answering at her house. I'm not worried about her, but she might know something. I don't know." She sighs. "Please call me if you find anything out. I'll do the same."

"Right." As soon as I hang up, I pull on my clothes as fast as I can, grab my badge and gun, and head to the station.

James is already at his desk with bloodshot eyes but a huge smile on his face. "Yo, Beck," he says with a proud nod.

"Busy night last night?"

"Not enough fucking Advil in the world for this headache." He gulps some coffee. "But yeah. Good fucking night last night. You'll never believe…"

I cut him off. "I want to hear all about it, man, but let's do it while we drive."

"Yeah. Sure." He gets up, just a little unsteady. "What's up?"

"The Cannon girl? Melanie? She's missing."

"Like, officially?"

152

"Nah. But she made a deal with the principal at the high school, and she left her house at four in the morning, so we're going to check out a few places, see if we see her around." I head to the door with James following.

"Saw her last night," he says.

"What?" I stop and turn to face him. "Where? What time?"

"At the fucking bar. Lucky's?"

"After I left?"

"Nah. She popped her head in. You were, uh, having a close conversation with Mona. I think Melanie saw us and skedaddled. Cops and underage kids in bars don't mix, you know?"

Shit.

"Yeah." I manage to stay calm on the outside, but inside I'm feeling absolutely fucked. She probably saw Mona and me talking and got the wrong idea. And I know I can explain it to her, and she'll most likely believe me. But with everything going on in her life, the last thing she needed was to be confronted with something like that.

"Where we headed first?" James gets in the driver seat and I buckle up in the passenger seat.

"The Grove. Her friend isn't in school either, so on the off chance that they're together we're going to check it out."

"Got it." James pulls out of the parking lot and drives down Main Street. "Dude," he says, "last night? Fucking epic, man. So I don't like to kiss and tell…"

"Whatever you say, man."

He laughs. "Yeah. You're right. I do." He begins a story about how both his date and Mona decided they should all hang out together, since I stood Mona up by leaving early. They ended up at Mona's place, and he's more than happy to share the details.

I'm having a hard time concentrating though. I'm worried about Melanie. My gut tells me something bad happened, worse, even, than her walking into the bar and seeing me talking to another woman.

Like usual, I'm surprised at the contrast between The Grove and the rest of Bells Park; it's like being in a completely different town. The houses stand tall and regal, spread out on large parcels of land, lit by the early morning spring sun. It's like a perfect, wealthy neighborhood out of a 1980s John Hughes film.

Stacey's house is impressive, with two huge white columns holding up a balcony from the second story of the house. We pull up to the front door via a circular driveway and park, leaving the car running.

It takes a few minutes after we ring for the door to be opened by Stacey, blonde and pretty but with bleary eyes and messy hair. She blinks at us a few times before speaking.

"Um, hi." She rubs one of her eyes with a fist, the puts her hands down at her side, pulling the sleeves over them. "Can I help you?"

"We're looking for Melanie Cannon. Is she here?" I glance past the girl, Stacey, into the house, where two guys are sprawled on the couch. I recognize one of them as Melanie's date from Baker's Square. The urge to march inside and punch him fills my chest, and I have to fight it down.

"Melanie? No." Stacey shifts from one foot to the other.

"Was she here last night?"

"Yeah. For a little while. What's going on? Is she OK?"

"Can we come in?" I ask.

"Uh, I guess?" It's obvious she wants to say no but isn't sure if that's all right. Instead, she pulls the door open and James and I enter.

The guys on the couch sit upright at the sight of two police officers in the house. The scent of liquor and stale pot lingers in the air. I'm familiar with this smell, the odor of next mornings and regret.

"We're looking for Melanie Cannon," I say to the guys on the couch. "What time did she leave here last night?"

The college kid, the one I fucking hate, shrugs and looks away.

154

"Maybe two?" Stacey rakes her hand through her hair, like she's trying to fix it up, but it's no use. She looks hung over and wrecked.

"Did she leave on foot? In a car?"

"Um, she walked," says Stacey.

"Do you know where she was headed? Did she say where she was going?"

"I don't know. She didn't say. Home, I guess?" Stacey sits on the couch next to the guy I guess is her boyfriend, and he puts his arm around her.

"What time did she get here last night?" I ask. This question, I admit, is more for my personal curiosity, so I can put together the timeline of what happened after she saw me at the bar.

Stacey looks at the asshole. "Sam? What time did you guys get here?"

He shrugs again. "I don't remember."

"But she came here with you?" I persist.

He nods. "Yeah. She was looking for some cat. Stacey asked me to help Melanie look. We didn't find it, but she wanted to hang out, so I brought her back here with me so she could party with us. I don't remember what time that was. Maybe midnight? I don't know."

"A cat?" asks James.

But I remember the cat, the gentleness that overcame Melanie, that softened out her hard edges when she took care of it and petted it.

"Yeah," the kid is saying. "It's some cat she feeds at the store or something. She said it was hurt. So she wanted help looking for it. Except we didn't find it."

I toss a few business cards on the table. "Call me right away if you hear from her. Got it?" I look at all three of them.

"Yeah," says Stacey. "Do you think she's all right?"

I don't answer. I nod at James, and we head out and back to the car.

"Nice kids," he says, rolling his eyes.

"They're fucking assholes."

"That's a little harsh, dude." James pulls out of the driveway. "What's up with you, anyway?"

"Nothing's up with me."

"Bullshit. Why are you so, I don't know, caught up in this?"

"In what?" I look out the window, afraid that if I meet his eyes he'll see the truth.

"This kid. She's in your drug class. And you talk about her with the principal. And you're worried cause she's missing and probably in trouble. But there's more, isn't there?"

"Fuck you."

"If I didn't know better, I'd think there's something going on." He stares straight ahead, and he's got this look on his face like he knows he shouldn't have said what he just said.

"Fuck you," I say again.

James pulls onto the field-lined road that leads back to the center of Bells Park. "Not judging, man. Just saying."

I grunt in response, and we don't talk all the way back to the station.

• • •

Something's wrong. Like, really fucking wrong. I feel it in my gut. I tell James I'm going to check out the antique shop, and head to the front door.

"Where you going, son?" My uncle's voice stops me. He's leaning against the receptionist's desk, chewing on a handful of Skittles from the bowl on the counter.

"Checking something out." I walk outside, knowing he'll follow, but not wanting to have this conversation in front of anyone else.

Outside, I wait for him to appear. He's still swallowing, and when he speaks, his tongue is colorful like the candy. "Where you going?" he asks again. He's not angry, exactly, but I can tell he doesn't want any bullshit.

156

"Heading to the antique shop." I nod my head in the direction of the shop, right there on the next block.

"What's going on?"

"The Cannon girl's missing."

"No official report filed, though?" He puts his hands on his hips, squinting at me in the early morning sunlight.

"Nope. But her mother says she left the house around four, and she never turned up at school."

He nods. "Probably just blowing off steam somewhere."

"Probably."

He stares at me for what feels like a fucking eternity. Finally, I break.

"What?" I ask. "What's the problem, Mike? We don't have any other calls right now. You want me to file shit or clean the office? Just tell me. But if not, I'm going to try to track down a troubled kid who could be in trouble."

"The operative word being *kid*, Jake."

"What's your point, huh? What are you getting at? If you've got something to say, just fucking say it." I've never spoken to my uncle like this, but I'm sick and tired of playing games. I don't have the time or patience for it anymore. I've had enough.

"Are you involved with her?" He stands still like a statue.

I try to match his posture, but inside I'm trembling, both with anger and fear. "No, man. That's crazy."

"If you've got something to say, just fucking say it," he says, using my exact words from just a moment ago. "Just tell me the fucking truth, Jake."

I sigh and look down at the ground before meeting his eyes. "The truth, Mike, is that I care about her. About her well-being. She's in my class and I want her to finish it. All right? That's it."

He turns his head and spits, then looks back at me. "You telling the truth?"

"I am." It hurts, to look him in the eyes and lie like this.

157

"I asked you to come here for two reasons, Jake. I needed your help. And you needed to get away. But don't be stupid. I trust you. Don't make me regret it." His eyes are boring into mine, like he can fucking see the lie in my heart.

"You can trust me." It's bullshit, but it's all I have right now.

• • •

The cat's there. I see it right away, lying next to two bowls. It breaks my heart to think of Melanie last night, putting out food and water and hoping to find it.

It's not moving, and I hope with everything I've got that it's not dead. Wherever Melanie is, she'll come back eventually. And what she doesn't need is another loss.

When I get closer and see the poor thing is breathing I sigh in relief. Thank fucking god.

Right away I see that one of its back legs is messed up bad. Bloody and mangled, it either got caught in a trap or chewed up by something bigger. I can't imagine the leg will survive and to be honest, the cat itself looks half dead already.

When I reach out to pick it up, it lets out a strange noise, a mixture between a meow and a hiss.

"Don't fucking bite me," I warn in a gentle tone.

It doesn't bite, but it scratches, a long swipe along my forearm. "Fucker," I whisper, but don't let go. After that initial attack, it's pretty limp, and I keep thinking it's dead, except for small movements, like it's trying to get comfortable in my arms, every few seconds.

Where the fuck can I take it? Bells Park definitely doesn't have animal control. And there are no shelters nearby, at least not that I've seen. If I take it back to the station, I know James will give me a hard time, and I don't want to face my uncle right now, but what choice is there?

I carry the animal back to the station and get into the undercover car, setting the cat on the passenger seat. Before pulling

158

out my phone to look up the nearest vet, I radio in to James to let him know I won't be back for a little while.

"Found the cat Melanie was looking for last night. It's half dead. I'm taking it to a vet, if I can find one. Any ideas?" I ask James.

He's quiet for a moment. "Yeah. Over in Bolster there's one. Good place too. My sister's dog had to have surgery, and... anyway, yeah. I'd go there."

"All right. Call me if you need me." For once I'm glad Bells Park is so slow and boring, because it means I have the opportunity to take off like this.

As I drive, I keep my eye out for Melanie, in the vain hope that I'll see her along the way, and I'll pick her up and we'll go to the vet together, and everything will be fine. It's fucking stupid. Nothing in life is that simple.

Bolster is much bigger than Bells Park, probably several times the size. The main strip off the highway features a giant Walmart, Home Depot, and plenty of restaurants. The veterinary office looks new and shiny, and I pull into the parking lot and grab the cat who, I'm relieved to discover, is still breathing. I've seen some shit, but I try not to look at the gruesome leg all the same. It makes me feel sick, as much as I hate to admit it.

As I head to the front door, I stroke the orange fur and tell the cat everything's going to be fine. It looks up at me and makes the saddest sound I've ever heard, a pained and desperate meow that seriously breaks my heart. Fucking cat.

"Can I help you?" The receptionist, a guy a few years younger than I am, nods at the cat in my arms.

"Yeah. I hope so. This cat is, uh, hurt. Pretty bad."

The guy comes out from around the counter and takes a quick look. "Wow. Yeah. That does *not* look good. Let me put you in a room and a vet will be in to see you in a few minutes, all right?"

He leaves me in a sterile, white exam room that smells like bleach and rubbing alcohol. There's a shiny steel exam table, and for a second I almost put the cat down on it, then think better of it and cradle it in my arms. The surface looks cold—too cold for an animal that's barely alive.

The door opens, and a woman in a white jacket enters. She's in her forties and attractive, her hair pulled back into a ponytail and her eyes kind but honest. "Hi," she says. "I'm Dr. Gellison."

"Jake Beck."

"Nice to meet you. Who've you got there?" She gestures at the cat.

"Oh. Um, it's a cat."

She nods at me like I'm a kindergartener.

"It's not mine," I say as an explanation, though that doesn't really explain things. "It's hurt. Here." Now I do set the cat on the table, as gently as possible.

She leans over to examine it, and I can tell by her face that she's not happy with what she sees. I grow restless as she opens the cat's mouth to look inside, then takes its temperature and listens to its heart. When she finally looks up, she's frowning.

"It's not good." I can see sadness in her eyes, but resignation too. I wonder how often she has to tell people their pets aren't going to make it. I wonder how many animals she's had to put down, knowing they're too sick or old or damaged to get well again.

"How not good are we talking?"

"Well…" She hesitates, stopping to pet the cat's side. "The leg can't be saved. And right now, her vital signs show her body's shutting down. She may have lost a lot of blood, and she's probably in shock. You say she's not your cat?"

I shake my head. "No. She's a stray. A friend of mine fed her sometimes. But it's not really her cat either."

She nods. "If there's no owner, there's nothing we can do."

"What do you mean?"

"I mean, taking care of this cat is going to require a lot of care. Expensive care. And even with that, there's no guarantee she'll survive. If we provided this kind of service to every stray out there, we'd go out of business."

160

"So what then? You'd just put it to sleep?"

She nods. "We can't afford the kind of surgery and IV and round-the-clock care an animal in this condition needs. Unless you're willing to pay?"

Fuck. "How much?" But even as I ask, I know I'm going to pay it. All of it. No matter what she says.

She shrugs. "Minimum, two thousand. That's just for the anesthesia and IV and amputation. Aftercare too. Prior to the surgery, though, we need to make sure she's stable, make sure she can handle the operation."

I close my eyes and breathe out hard. "Fine. Do it. Who do I pay?"

"They'll take care of you at the front desk. I'll take her back and get started. Does she have a name?"

"Um..." What did Melanie call her? "Molly. I think her name's Molly."

"All right." Dr. Gellison looks into my eyes. "And after the surgery, if Molly survives—I don't want to get your hopes up, Mr. Beck—I trust you have a home for her? We don't generally advise people to have outdoor cats. A cat belongs indoors. Especially as she's recovering. Is that something you can accommodate?"

"I'll figure it out."

"And I need to make it clear that there are no guarantees. She may not make it."

"I understand."

At the front desk, I give the receptionist all my information and, most important, my credit card number. I sign a bunch of forms and take off, with his word that he'll call me with any updates.

"Any time," I tell him. "I keep weird hours anyway."

When I leave the vet's office, I don't know where to go or what to do. All I know is Melanie's out there somewhere, but I have no idea where. I want to find her—I *need* to find her, but I don't even know where to start.

CHAPTER SIXTEEN – MELANIE

The bedspread on the motel bed is scratchy and probably dirty, but I don't want to look close enough to find out. I rest my head on the hard, flat pillow and watch Animal Planet, one of the only channels I can get on the small TV. It's better than C-SPAN or the channel where they're always doing makeovers on people's homes. That channel just depresses me.

Mostly, though, I'm worried about what to do next. When I left, I had no idea where I was going. Chicago sounded like a good plan at first, and I hitched a ride—something I'd never done before—with a woman in her fifties. She didn't ask any questions, and I didn't share any information, so we got along just fine. She said she could only take me part way to Chicago, and left me here in Waterville, about fifty miles from Bells Park.

It's a small town, but not as broken as mine. And fortunately The Sea Breeze, the motel just on the edge of town, doesn't require a credit card to reserve a room or for incidentals. The irony of the name, what with the nearest ocean being like a thousand miles away, amuses me. I've got a reservation for three nights. After that, I guess I'll go back home, but I can't be there now. I need a break. I need to be alone.

My phone lies on the desk across from the bed, and I stare at it, fighting the urge to grab it and see who's called. I turned it off a

162

few hours ago after leaving a message for my mom to let her know I'm OK. Not that she'd worry. She never does.

A knock on the door interrupts my thoughts—it must be the pizza I ordered. Here in Waterville there are actually two places that deliver, unheard of in my stupid small town.

My stomach, empty and hollow, growls. It's a splurge—an entire pizza and two-liter of soda just for me—but I can't even remember the last time I ate anything. I don't know what it was. I'm so hungry it seems like I could eat for hours and would never be full.

I pig out on pizza right there on the bed, not worrying about crumbs or grease or anything. Ravenous, I shove food into my mouth until I start to feel full. Then I eat two more pieces. Finally full, I lie back and watch a lion chase antelopes across the TV screen.

Life sucks. It fucking sucks. Or mine does, at least. Here I am, in a seedy motel, eating pizza and watching a shitty television set, and I have nowhere to go after this but back to my crappy hometown. My money will run out quickly, even at a cheap place like The Sea Breeze. Forget about staying in Chicago.

I don't want to go home ever again, even though I know I have to. I don't want to see my mom or Stacey.

Or Jake. I squeeze my eyes shut hard; I don't want to cry about him. He's not worth it. But I keep seeing him and that woman in the bar, heads close. My stupid, stupid mind insists on bringing up the image of her hand on his thigh.

The worst part is that I trusted him. We were nothing to each other—I get that, I do—but I *felt* like he was the one person I could really count on. The one person who, even though we really barely knew each other, wouldn't hurt me. How could I have been so wrong about him? How could my instincts about him have been so off?

Then again, I trusted Stacey, and look how *that* turned out.

I toss the almost empty pizza box onto the desk next to the unopened two-liter of soda and crawl under the covers, fully clothed and not even bothering to wash up or brush my teeth first.

There's a painting on the wall—it's one of those typical neutral sort of ones that you see in hotels and doctor's offices and places like that. Dark blue water meets lighter blue sky, and a bright red boat floats under puffy white clouds. You can't quite make out the figure in the boat. It could be a man. It could be a woman. It could be anyone, maybe even me. What would it be like to be on a boat, somewhere out on the water like that, surrounded by water and sky and clouds?

What if I could close my eyes and wish hard enough and send myself, by some impossible and mysterious process, to another place and be on that boat. Or in Chicago. Or with Jake, but a version of him that hadn't been with someone else.

I feel so stuck. And so alone. I don't want to see the stupid painting anymore. I don't want to see anything. I reach out and turn off the lamp on the nightstand. Then I close my eyes and hope to fall asleep quickly.

• • •

In the morning I feed dollar bills into the vending machine in the outdoor hallway, buying honey buns and pretzels and potato chips, enough to feed me for the entire day. I sit in my bed all day, napping and watching TV and snacking when I get hungry. At night I sleep hard, not waking up till morning, when I do it all over again.

• • •

Bang, bang, bang.

I sit up straight in bed, torn from sleep by someone at the door to my motel room. It's my third night in this room, and a quick glance at my phone tells me it's 3:30 a.m.; who the hell is knocking?

After slipping out from under the covers I walk, barefoot, to the door. "Who is it?" I ask, loudly enough so whoever it is on the other side can hear me.

"Your neighbor? In 214? Could you turn the TV down?" It's a man's voice.

"I'm not watching TV. I was sleeping."

"Huh. Must be someone else then."

"Yeah." I lean against the door, wondering if he's gone or still standing there.

"So, uh, since you're awake, you wanna hang out? Watch a movie or something? They got some, uh, pay per view shit here." He sounds like he's right up against the door.

"Oh. No. My boyfriend and I need to get up early in the morning." I feel my heartbeat pick up, both from the lie I just told and the fact that he's still out there, and I don't know who he is or if he's sane or not. Probably not, I guess, since he's fabricated a story about too much noise as an excuse to come over and ask if I'll hang out. And the fact that he's staying in this crappy motel in the first place.

"Oh yeah? I didn't see any guy go into your room, though."

I tremble, my limbs shaking from cold and fear. Has he been watching me? Does he know I'm alone? My pocket knife is in my backpack, but I don't know anything about this guy. He could outweigh me and outfight me and I'd be done.

"I'm out here trying not to be insulted that you're lying to me," he says when I don't respond. "You don't have a boyfriend, do you?" His voice is like hideous nails on a chalkboard, making me squirm.

Still, I say nothing.

"Fuck you," he hisses through the door. "You know what I mean?" He laughs, then I see his shadow through my motel window as he heads down the outdoor hallway. The door next to mine opens and slams shut.

The other door. There's another door that joins my room with his. I checked it earlier, and it was locked so even I couldn't open it. There must be some master key the clerk uses if people want to rent both rooms, but the thought that he's right *there* terrifies me.

And apparently he's figured it out too, because now he knocks on that door. "Good night," he calls out. "Sleep fucking tight, all right?"

I climb up onto the bed and pull my knees to my chest, burying my face in my arms and sobbing. I hate crying, but right now I can't help it. I want to call the clerk, but I'm worried the guy next door will hear me. I could go down to the front office, but he might follow me. Might grab me and force me into my room. I want to call the police, but then they'll ask why I'm here alone, and I'm not ready to go home yet.

Just in case, I turn on my cell phone, waiting while the provider name flashes on the screen and the app shortcuts start showing up. I've got seven new texts and a few new messages. Part of me wants to read the texts and listen to the messages. Part of me wants to see who, if anyone, has been worried about me. But I'm not ready to do that..

I almost jump when my phone rings. I don't recognize the number, but I'm scared of being alone, and if my neighbor is listening, he might be put off by hearing me speak to someone. He'll think I'm not as alone as I really am.

"Hello?" I ask.

"Melanie." It's only one word—my name—but I recognize Jake instantly. It's as though the tone and tenor and roughness of his speech have been programmed into my soul; I'd recognize his voice anywhere.

"Jake." I'm angry at him. Maybe I even hate him. But I'm terrified right now, and I don't know who else can help.

"Where are you?"

"I'm… I'm in a motel, and it's really gross, and the guy next door is trying to get me to hang out, and I'm scared because he keeps knocking on the door that separates our rooms?"

"Jesus. What motel? Tell me where you are and I'll come get you."

"It's The Sea Breeze Motel. In Waterville. I'm in Room 212."

"Dammit! Do you have any idea what kind of reputation that place has? Fuck. Stay there, Melanie, all right? And call me back

166

immediately if that asshole so much as tries to speak to you, do you understand? Do not open the door for him."

"OK." I'm weak with relief that someone's coming to get me, my body shaking from cold and fear. I grab my phone and my pocket knife and slip under the covers, lying as still as I can so I don't miss a single sound.

Barely half an hour passes when someone pounds on the door, but this time Jake's voice accompanies the knock. "Melanie? Are you there?"

I spring out of bed and peek out the window, relief pouring over me when I see him standing there in his usual jeans and T-shirt, gun holstered at his side.

When I open the door I can't help rushing into his arms; for a few minutes I want to enjoy being all right. I know it's over between us. I'll never forget the way he looked close-talking to that horrible woman in the bar. But relief overwhelms me and I let him crush me against him, his arms folding around me and holding on like he doesn't want to let go.

He steps back to look at me, hands on my shoulders as his gaze runs up and down my body. "Are you all right?" His eyes are dark and intense as they stare into mine.

I nod.

"Stay here."

He takes three huge steps so he's in front of my neighbor's door, and he knocks twice loudly.

After a few seconds, the door opens. I kind of think the neighbor thought I'd be standing there, and I imagine the surprise he feels to see Jake instead, a tough guy with a gun waiting for him.

I can't see the guy—he's still inside his room—but I watch as Jake puts his hand on the door so the man can't close it. "Have you been bothering the girl next door?" Jake asks.

"No, man. I don't know what you're talking about," the guy stammers.

"Listen to me, you prick. Right now? I want to pound your fucking face in. I'm not going to, though. But if you ever do something like this again, you better hope to fucking god that I'm not around, or you won't live to make the same mistake twice. Do you understand me?"

"Dude, sorry."

"Fuck off." Jake steps back and the door closes. His face is hard and angry, but when he turns to me it softens, his eyes widening as if asking me, once again, if I'm all right. "Let's go inside."

He follows me into the room. "This place is a fucking dump," he says, glancing at the ugly bedspread, the stained carpet, and the tiny television set.

"Yeah, well, I didn't have many choices." I sit on the bed. My relief at Jake arriving to help me out is quickly being replaced by awkwardness. He hurt me. And I don't want to be with him. I only needed him because there was nobody else to help.

"Listen, Melanie..."

I put up my hand to stop him. "No. I don't want to talk about it... about anything. Just, thanks, OK? I don't think that guy'll bother me again."

"Pack up your stuff." He picks up my backpack and looks around the room, as if he's going to get me ready to go on his own.

"Jake, no. I don't want to go with you. I don't want to be with you. I just... thanks for helping me, but I'm OK now."

"Yeah? How are you going to get home?"

"Bus, I guess."

"Is that how you got here?" His eyes are piercing.

"No. I got a ride." I'm embarrassed suddenly, because I realize how stupid it sounds, how stupid I was.

"You hitchhiked." He knows me so well.

"It was dumb. I was lucky not to get hurt." I'm being sincere. "And it was dumb to run away. It doesn't make your problems disappear. I was just overwhelmed." I sigh and stare out the window at the dirty parking lot. "I got in a fight with Stacey. Found out she was the one who notified the scholarship foundation I'd gotten in legal trouble. Then Molly—the cat?—got hurt. She's probably dead. And then I saw…" I can't say it.

"Please come with me, Melanie." I can sense him approaching me from behind.

"No, Jake. Please, just leave me alone."

"I can't."

I turn to face him. "Why? Why can't you leave me alone?" My voice is lower, all the energy leaving me suddenly.

He runs his hand through his hair, then rubs his strong and stubbly jaw. "I, uh…" His voice trails off, like he's trying to find the right words, or maybe like he knows the words but is scared to say them. "You're… I can't stop thinking about you, Melanie. Not because you're in that fucking class I teach. Not because I feel like I need to help you. I just…"

My heart pounds, and I take a step closer to him. There's maybe a foot of space between us, and even in this dim and grimy hotel room, I can see his eyes sparking as they gaze into mine. I hold my breath, waiting to see what he's going to say.

He shakes his head slightly. "I just need to take you back home," he finally says.

"No." I push past him and sit back on the bed, leaning against the flat pillows. "I'm not going with you, Jake. The night I left? I went to look for you at Lucy's. And I saw you there. With some girl."

"Fuck. Look. I know you saw me. My partner told me. We were there on a double date; James met this chick who would only go out with him if he set her friend up too. He brought me. It was a favor, and nothing happened."

"Whatever."

He sits on the edge of the bed. "No, not whatever. Melanie, I have no reason to lie to you. If I fucked her, I'd tell you. If I was interested in her, I'd say so. Between us? There's been no commitment or agreement, so I have nothing to hide."

Somehow I trust him, but it's not easy; I don't like to trust people. I don't like to make myself vulnerable. And the *no commitment or agreement* part stings.

"It's fine anyway," I tell him. "You're right that there's nothing between us. So it's none of my business. But thanks for coming to help me out here anyway."

"I hate when you say that." He puts his hands on his thighs, leaning over and looking down.

"Say what?"

"*It's fine.* You always say that, even when things are absolutely not fucking *fine* at all."

"Why do you care? It's just words." I scratch at the soft fabric of my worn jeans.

He sits upright, then shifts his body so he's facing me, still sitting on the edge of the bed. "Why do I care? I care because it fucking kills me to see you—so gorgeous and smart and wonderful—with so many shitty things happening to you. I care because you deserve so much better than anyone's given you. I care because somehow, despite your dad being in prison and your mom being an alcoholic, you've managed to get into one of the best universities in the entire fucking country, and even if you don't end up going there, you should be proud of yourself, Melanie."

He sighs, looking up at the ceiling for a moment before meeting my gaze, his eyes filled with more emotion than I've ever seen.

"And I care, Melanie, because I'm pretty fucking sure I'm in love with you."

"Some of us are trying to sleep over here!" The guy next door, obviously feeling confident with a locked door and wall between Jake and himself, bangs on the wall twice.

"Asshole," hisses Jake under his breath. "Come on. Let's get out of here."

Part of me wants to keep sitting on the bed, wants to make him repeat himself—because surely I didn't hear him correctly. But

170

he's right. We can't stay in this shitty motel with the stalker neighbor any longer. I throw my few belongings into my backpack and follow Jake out to the car.

• • •

We're mostly silent on the drive back to Bells Park. I watch the barren fields blur by as we get closer and closer. I have to fight the urge to ask him to turn the car around, to tell him to just drive me somewhere, anywhere, because I still don't want to go back.

But the truth is, I have nowhere else to go. If I run, I'm just running to another place, but I can never get rid of my problems. Deep down, I realize that if I don't stay here and finish high school—there are only a few weeks left—I'll just make everything worse.

The sun is rising, illuminating the dirty edges of downtown Bells Park: the cracked sidewalks, the patched streets, the rusted-out cars and sagging porches and crumbling bricks. I hate it here, but I guess I have to stay a little while longer.

"Hey. I have a surprise for you. I can't believe I forgot." Jake's voice, excited as a kid, interrupts my thoughts.

"I don't like surprises." But my heart feels a spark of joy, the same feeling I remember from Christmases years ago, when I was a kid and there were presents and lights, and I had no idea that my life was crumbling all around me because I was too young to notice.

"Yeah? You liked the last surprise I planned. And I think you'll like this one." Jake pulls up in front of his building, and I grab my backpack and follow him to the front door.

It occurs to me suddenly that he didn't even mention taking me home; I guess he knew I couldn't or wouldn't go there right now. It's like he knows me better than I imagined.

We enter the building and go up the stairs, where he gets out his key and starts to unlock his front door. "You ready?" His brown eyes are tired but sparkling, and I can't help jumping up and down.

"Yes! Just open the door. I want to see!" I don't even care that I sound like a fucking kid.

He unlocks the door and pushes it in, and there's Molly, limping but alive.

"Oh my god, Jake." I enter the apartment enough so he can close the door and sit on the floor. Molly meows and approaches me, rubbing her side against my knee. She's unsteady on her legs, and her back leg—the damaged one—is gone, a bandage wrapped around the stump.

I scoop her up as gently as I can and she settles into my lap, purring loudly as her eyes close.

"Jake, what even… How did you know? Where did you find her? Is she going to be OK?"

"It's a long story." He sits on the floor next to me. "I found her by the antique shop. I think she was looking for you. I brought her to the vet. They had to amputate the leg, and she stayed there on an IV for the past two nights, but they let me take her home today. She's medicated and unsteady, but they think she's going to be OK." His grin is beautiful. I swear I've never seen anything more gorgeous.

"Holy shit, Jake! I think you went a little overboard!" In the corner he's set up a cat bed, a scratching post—the big kind, with little ledges and caves for the cat to play in—and a big bin literally filled with cat toys. More toys than any cat could seriously ever use.

"Yeah." He rubs his jaw. "I guess I did."

"And the surgery and stuff? Did you pay for that?"

"Yup."

"Jake, how much was it? Wait. Don't tell me. I'll pay you back, OK? I still have…" I reach out to grab my backpack, trying not to disturb Molly, who's still sleeping on my lap. I pull out the wad of money and start to count it.

Jake encloses my hands in his, stopping the flurry of money counting. "No. Melanie, stop. You don't have to pay me back."

"I do! It must have been expensive. And you wouldn't have done this if it was any other cat. You only did it because she was, is, sort of *my* cat."

Jake takes the money from my hands and puts it back into the pocket of my backpack, zippering it up. "Stop. I won't take your money. I wanted to do this. I would do this a million times over if it would make you realize how worth it you are. How wonderful. If it made you see that you deserve people's help and love."

I look down, blushing. I don't deserve this. I know I don't. I've fucked up so many times in my life. I got caught with drugs in my locker, and I've skipped school, and I smoke and drink and sometimes even steal.

He tilts my head up, a finger under my chin. "I love you, Melanie. I'm too old for you. And it's wrong. But I need you to know that it's true."

I open my mouth, unsure what to say. I love him. I do. But I'm not sure I can form the words. I'm not sure he loves me enough for me to say it back.

He shakes his head. "Don't say anything. Here." He bends down and gently—oh so gently—scoops Molly out of my arms, settling her down into the plush bed in the corner. Then he reaches out his hand and when I take it, he pulls me so I'm standing.

He kisses me. At first it's gentle, just our lips barely touching and tasting, so lightly it could be a breeze or a butterfly. But our bodies can't stay apart. We step closer, finding warmth and friction, coming alive and on edge. Then the kiss is harder, filled with need and hope and desire. I touch his chest through his T-shirt, the hardness of his muscles comforting.

His hand covers mine, stopping its exploration, and he pulls back, ending the kiss. I glance up at him, question in my eyes.

"What would a visit to my apartment without you taking a shower be?" he laughs.

"Are you saying I stink? Again?"

"No." He grins down at me, his lips so perfect, his smile so warm. "But I want to take care of you, Melanie. I want you to feel warm and safe. So go take a shower, and I'll get some clean clothes ready and some food too—I'm positive you haven't eaten enough, because you never do. And then we'll, uh, hang out."

"Hang out?" I raise an eyebrow and run my hand up under his shirt, my fingers enjoying the hard ridges of his abs.

He growls and kisses my forehead, then grabs my hand and walks me to the bathroom.

"I can do that, you know," I say as he leans down and turns the water on, testing it until it's the perfect temperature. He gets a clean towel from the cabinet in the hall and hands it to me.

"I'll leave some clothes in here in a few minutes. Take your time, Melanie. I'll be there. OK?"

For some reason, I want to cry, but that's stupid, so I bite my lip and nod, then turn away before he can see the tears gathering in the corners of my eyes.

I stay in the shower for a long time, turning the water hotter and hotter and letting it wash over me. Jake's got this men's body wash, and it smells dark and spicy and I use lots of it, rubbing it all over my body in sudsy swirls. I shampoo my hair twice, just because it feels so good to be in the shower and I want an excuse to stay longer.

When I finally get out, the bathroom's so steamy I can barely see, and I dry myself off and wrap my hair up in the towel like I'm wearing a turban. Without me even noticing, Jake left a set of sweats, folded up on the tank of the toilet, and I pull on the big pants, tying the drawstring tight, then put on the long-sleeved T, a worn and soft 5K race shirt.

As soon as I open the bathroom door, I swear I almost faint from the kitchen smells. Coffee and bacon, and cinnamon. He's baking something. *Does he actually bake?* My stomach growls, and I remove the towel from my head, raking my fingers through my long hair.

In the kitchen, Jake's pulling a tray of cinnamon rolls out of the oven, and bacon and eggs wait to be eaten on the stove. The table's set, and I slip into one of the chairs.

"Did you *make* those?" I point at the cinnamon rolls that he's removing from the pan with a spatula and arranging on a plate on the table.

"Define *make*." He grins at me as he puts the baking tray away, then cuts open a little plastic pouch and drizzles the contents over the rolls.

"I don't know. Like, from scratch or something?"

"Nah. Pillsbury. You know, those tubes of cinnamon rolls that you open with a spoon?"

"Oh. Yeah. I've never had those before!"

"You've never had them? They're good. I mean, I'm sure cinnamon rolls from scratch would be better, but I wouldn't, you know…"

"Kick them out of bed?" I interrupt.

"You're fucking weird, Melanie." He laughs as he grabs my plate and fills it with scrambled eggs and bacon from the pans on the stove. He hands it to me and gestures at the cinnamon rolls. "Have as many as you want."

I put one on my plate.

"Coffee?" he asks. "Do you drink coffee?"

"What? You think I'm some kid who probably doesn't like it? I'm not a fucking child, Jake."

He rolls his eyes. "I didn't say you were. But not everyone likes coffee, all right?"

"Fine. And yes. Coffee. Please."

He hands me a mug, then gets a container of half and half from the fridge and a bowl of sugar and sets them in front of me.

I'm tempted to drink it black, just to prove to him how adult I am. But I hate black coffee. I try to ignore his grin as I shovel in sugar and then pour in cream until my coffee is light and really, really sweet.

He serves himself and sits across from me. "Eat," he says. "You're still too skinny."

"Still?"

175

He shrugs as he eats a slice of bacon. "Yeah. Still. I hoped you'd start eating more after the last time I told you you were too skinny."

"Oh, because I'm supposed to do everything you say?" I peel off the outer layer of a cinnamon roll and take a bite. It's fucking amazing. Or I'm really hungry. Maybe both. I have to resist the urge to shove the entire thing in my mouth all at once.

"Only the things you want to do." His smile is gone now, and his eyes are steady but filled with desire.

I lick the frosting off my lips, just to fuck with him, and he bites his lip.

"Later," he says, as if he can read my thoughts. "Eat first."

"I'm going to need that much energy?" I ask. "What exactly do you have planned?"

He takes a sip of his coffee, black, I notice, and sits back in his chair. "You did recently tell me you don't like surprises."

"Well," I admit, "the last two were pretty freaking incredible." I'm still blown away by the fact that he saved Molly. Found her. Paid for the surgery. And even though he said I don't need to pay him back, I swear I'll find a way.

We finish eating, and I start to clean up, but he stops me, standing behind me at the sink and wrapping his arms around me from behind. "Will you come to bed with me?" he asks, the words a deep whisper against the soft skin of my neck.

"Yes."

He sweeps me off my feet—literally—and carries me, giggling, into his bedroom where he deposits me on the bed. I lie back, my damp hair on the pillow, and my breath catches in my throat as he pulls his T-shirt off in one quick movement.

I don't think I'll ever get enough of that chest, muscular and lean, and that firm stomach. His lips curve up in a smile when he sees me staring.

"Like what you see?" he jokes, doing a stupid pose.

"You're... beautiful." And he is. I remember saying something similar to him the first night we were together, the night I lied about my age and my name. The night we were here in this same bed, but we didn't even know each other. And now, so much has happened and changed, but we're still here. Together.

His smile disappears, and he approaches me on the bed, crawling on top of me and looking down into my eyes. "Nobody is as beautiful as you are, Melanie." He kisses me gently on the lips. "I love you."

"I love you too." I've never said those words to a guy before. To tell the truth, I can't remember the last time I said them to anyone. Maybe my mom, years ago when I was still a little kid. I don't even remember that. Saying the words fills me with panic.

But when Jake kisses me again, I relax. After a few minutes he pulls up the hem of the shirt I'm wearing, and I arch my back so he can take it off.

The times before have been fast, furious, like we couldn't touch each other or fuck each other fast enough. This time, though, Jake's taking his time. For a long time we just kiss, his body on top of mine, pressing down. I can feel how hard he is, how badly he wants me, but still he takes it slow.

His lips caress my neck, biting gently, but his hands are still, braced on either side of my shoulders. I shiver as his mouth travels lower, sucking my right nipple until it's hard and I moan underneath him, squirming against him, trying to find friction for my aching body.

Next he moves to my left nipple, the tip of his tongue moving over the delicate skin, flicking back and forth and leaving me gasping for breath.

"Jake," I whisper, his name a plea on my lips.

He sucks my nipple, then releases it. "Shhh," he responds before licking the delicate skin of my stomach.

His tongue moves lower still, tracking an erotic line down my body. Now he finally touches me with his hand, gently moving it between my legs and pushing my thighs apart, and I melt down into the mattress.

His breath is warm between my thighs as he gently—oh so gently—touches me with his fingertips, skimming over my eager clit and traveling lower. One finger dips inside me, swirling in my wetness, then moves back to my clit, which he presses in agonizingly tight circles.

"Oh god," I whimper when his tongue finally takes the place of his finger. "That feels so good."

He stops to say, "Melanie, I want to make you feel like you've never felt before. I want to make you come harder than you thought possible. And by the way? You taste so fucking good."

My head falls back onto the pillow and my body relaxes all the way, more than I thought possible, as his tongue works its magic between my legs, his fingers inside my wetness.

I try to hold back. I try to make the moments last, to keep this feeling going as long as I can. But he's so *good*, and in only a few minutes I'm moaning hard, my pussy contracting with all the muscles of my thighs as the climax builds, stronger and stronger and higher and higher until I reach the peak and crash down, screaming his name over and over again.

There's nothing—no drink or drug or anything at all—that could ever be better than this. Nothing. Ever. There's Jake. And in this second I know I'll never need anything more.

I'm limp as he moves back up my body, kissing me with my taste on his lips.

"That was so good," I mumble against his mouth, hardly able to speak. "That was so, so good."

He responds by reaching down and gently touching me between the legs, lightly tracing over my still throbbing flesh. I jump, so sensitive there, and he smiles.

"That was just the beginning," he whispers. He's hard against my thigh, and I lightly rub my leg against him until he groans and whispers, "Fuck."

I push against him. "Get off."

He does, laughing. "Oh, I'm sorry. I just gave you the best orgasm of your life, and you're pushing me away?"

"You really think highly of yourself, don't you?"

He's on his back and I straddle him, smiling down into his grinning face.

"Well, wasn't it?" He raises an eyebrow and gives me a cocky look.

"Maybe."

"No maybe about it. You almost broke my eardrums with your screaming." His words are quieter, and his fingers skim over my thighs. "I like to make you feel good, Melanie," he murmurs.

"I like to make you feel good too." I slide down his body until my lips are *there*. The way his thigh muscles tense in anticipation turns me on, spurs me forward, and I lower my head, warming him with my breath.

He breathes out hard as I softly lick the head of his cock, then suck it gently into my mouth and releasing with a *pop*.

"Do you like that?" I whisper.

"Yes."

"Do you want me to do it some more?"

"Yes. Please." He lets out a strangled laugh.

I take him in my mouth again, massaging his balls at the same time. I roll my tongue all over his shaft, then grip the base of his cock with one hand while I take him as far as I can into my throat.

"Jesus." His eyes shut and his head moves back and forth on the pillow.

Finding a steady rhythm of sucking and moving my hand, I blow him until I feel him tensing under me and hear his breaths turn into moans.

And then I stop. "Am I doing it OK?" I ask, making sure he can hear the teasing in my voice.

He opens his eyes and looks at me, a half laugh, half growl emanating from his throat. "OK? That was fucking perfect."

"So, should I keep going?" Instead of waiting for a response, I bend down again, tickling the head of his cock with my tongue, licking away the pre-cum that's gathered there in one shiny drop. "You taste good."

"You're fucking killing me, Melanie."

I laugh, then take him all the way in my mouth again, pleasure coursing through me when I hear his moan of satisfaction. Again, I bring him to the brink, until he's breathing hard and his muscles are tensed and stop, popping off and grinning at him.

"Am I still doing all right?" I feign ignorance.

"*Melanie.*"

"I think," I whisper, moving up his body, "that I want to fuck you instead."

His cock is hard beneath me, and with one hand I guide him to my entrance, then slowly —really slowly—slide down onto him. We stare into each other's eyes, the moment intense physically but also emotionally. I've never watched someone like this during sex. I never wanted to, and I'd probably have been embarrassed. But with Jake, how we feel about each other is as important as how our bodies interact together.

I rock gently on top of him, and he reaches up to touch my hair delicately, like it's something beautiful and expensive. Like it's something he can't believe is his.

"I love you." His hands caress my thighs as I continue to ride him.

"I love you too, Jake." My movements quicken as my clit finds friction on his groin, and he begins to move in time to me, filling me deep and wide over and over again.

When I'm about to come, I close my eyes and throw back my head, falling forward and bracing myself up on my arms. My walls contract around his hardness, over and over again until he trembles and groans, driving up into me, slower but with more force than before.

Both our bodies still, and I climb off, lying next to him on the bed. Immediately his arms are around me, pulling me in close, my cheek against his chest as our breathing calms.

I could stay like this forever. I wish it were possible. I'd never have to worry about school, or my mom, or Stacey, or what I'm going to do next year. The pain of losing my dreams would be erased in this bliss right here.

But bliss is only bliss because it's temporary. Still, I cling to Jake as hard as I can for these few, wonderful minutes.

"You OK?" he asks after what feels like a long time.

"Yeah. You?"

"I'm great." I can hear the smile in his voice.

"Me too."

He shifts his body so he can look into my face. "I need to take you home soon, Melanie. Your mom probably wants to see you."

Probably not. I sigh. "I know. I let her know I was all right. I texted her every day I was gone."

"When she told your principal that you'd left the house at like four in the morning, Evans called me and I was fucking scared, Melanie."

"Why?"

"I thought something had happened to you. I don't know. And when I found out you'd seen me at the bar, I needed to tell you that you're the only one I want to be with."

"I'm sorry I worried you. I'm sorry I ran off. It was immature. I know it was. I was just so overwhelmed with everything."

Jake clears his throat. "Part of the reason I'm here now, in Bells Park, is because I kind of ran away from home too."

"What? Tell me about it."

He takes my face in his hands. "Later. We'll talk later. Let's just enjoy the next half hour together, OK? I'll go clean up and bring us some coffee and cinnamon rolls. Stay here." He points at me as he leaves, and I watch his naked, gorgeous ass as he heads to the bathroom.

I want to stay in bed. I want a second breakfast, and a second round of sex, but now that I'm thinking of all the things I need to face, it's impossible to relax. Sighing, I climb out of bed and pull on Jake's sweats and long-sleeved T.

"Hey," he says, coming into the room and handing me a fresh cup of coffee, pale and, I see as I taste it, sweet. Just the way I like it. "Where you going?"

"I can't stay. I need to, you know, face shit. I have to talk to my mom."

"Smart girl." He grabs a pair of underwear and pulls them on.

"Don't patronize me." I give him a warning look.

He puts up his hands in defense. "I'm not! I mean it. You're smart. And you're doing what you need to do. I respect that."

"I don't want to." I sip some more coffee. "I want to stay here all day. With you." Stepping closer to him, I run one hand over his still-bare stomach.

"I want that too." He takes the mug from my hand and sets it on the dresser before pulling me to him and kissing me, hard, on the mouth. He tastes like fresh toothpaste, and I taste like milky coffee, and the combination is exhilarating.

"Later. Can I come over tonight?" I look up into his eyes.

He stares back, eyes hot, lips turning up in a grin before he winks at me. "You better."

• • •

The front door is unlocked, and I take a deep breath before going inside. As soon as I close the door behind me, I hear Jake's car pull away, and a desperate sadness overtakes me for a moment. I hate the way it feels when he leaves. And I hate that I hate it. I don't want to need him. I don't want to need anyone.

"Hi, honey!" my mom calls out. Like usual, she's sitting at her computer, but I refuse to look at the screen. I don't want to see what random cat images she's working on today.

182

"Hi, Mom." I drop my backpack to the floor and wait for her to say something, anything, about me being gone for the past few days.

"Can I show you something?" she asks.

"Sure." Isn't she going to ask about where I was? Where I've been for the past few days? Why I left in the first place?

"You won't believe this!"

I force my eyes to her screen, where she's pulling up YouTube. That horrible video she made starts playing, the "Toot, toot, kitty. Hello! Hello!" one.

"Look." She points to the screen and I stand right behind her, trying to figure out what she's showing me. "Over eight hundred *thousand* views! Can you believe it?"

"Wow." I'm stunned. "How did you… why…"

"Some rapper, I think he must be famous? He *sampled* it in a video he made. I think that's the correct word. *Sampled.* Anyway, I guess he mentioned me in the comments, and all these people are watching my videos and subscribing. I signed up for ad revenue, and I think I can make some money, honey! Maybe for your college?" She gives me a timid smile.

"Oh, Mom." I back away from the computer and sit on the couch. "I'm really happy for you. But it still won't be enough for college. Unless you can make, like, $70,000."

"Is that how much it is?" She turns her chair so she's facing me. "What's that per year, then?"

"Mom, that *is* the cost per year."

"And that scholarship was going to pay your whole way?" She shakes her head. "I'm so sorry about that, honey. I wish that hadn't happened to you. I wish I could help." Her face looks sadder than I've ever seen it look.

I shrug. *It's fine,* I start to say. But it's not. Jake's right. I *do* always say that, even when it's not true.

"I wish you could too," I say instead. "I wish it hadn't happened. It sucks that I was so close to having something amazing like that and lost it all. For something that wasn't even my fault."

"I'm sorry."

"It's not your fault, Mom."

She shakes her head. "I don't mean about the scholarship, Melanie. I mean about everything." She gestures around the dim living room: at the sagging couch, the dirty walls, the snagged carpet, her own computer. "I'm sorry this is how we live. I'm sorry I'm, well, that I drink like this. I'm probably an alcoholic, to tell you the truth."

"You are." I cringe as I say those blunt words. But I'm tired of hiding things. I'm tired of lying.

She nods. "I wish I could tell you that I'll shape up. Join, I don't know, Alcoholics Anonymous or something and get better. But truthfully?" Her eyes are so filled with sadness I almost have to look away. "I probably won't. And I'm not going to make any promises I'm pretty sure I can't keep."

I don't know how to respond. She's being honest. And for that I'm glad. But deep down inside I wish I was enough to make her change.

"I'm glad you're back," she says.

"Did you wonder where I was? Were you worried? Did you even care?"

"Of *course* I did! But I knew you were OK. I know you. You're smart and responsible..."

"I smoke, Mom. Did you know that? I smoke cigarettes. And I drink. I've stolen liquor from the Save Lot like a million times! Sometimes I skip school. And I lost my college scholarship because I was caught with drugs in my locker. How is that being responsible?"

"You're a good kid. You always have been, Melanie." She's calm in the face of my outburst. It must be the wine. "And believe me, I know that it's despite me, not because of me. I could never take credit for who you've become. I can only thank God you turned out all right even though I'm a fuck-up."

"You're not a fuck-up," I say quietly. "You... I'm happy about your video, all right? That's really exciting." I still feel angry and antsy, but deflated too.

She'll never be the mom I want her to be, or even need her to be. So I'll have to learn to accept that and live with it. I can keep fucking up and keep blaming my shitty life. Or I can do the best I can and try to make something good out of everything I've been through.

"Thanks!" She perks up at the mention of her YouTube stuff, and turns back to her computer to work or check how many views she's gotten since a few minutes ago or something. "Oh hey," she adds. "There's a letter for you. It's on the coffee table."

"OK." I don't get a lot of mail, except for college-related stuff, and I don't really want to see any of that now. Still, I check and find a thin envelope from the University of Chicago. *Fuck.*

I'm positive it's a letter about how I haven't sent any money in to reserve my spot. The scholarship foundation would have taken care of all that. And I never followed up on postponing the start of school for a year; knowing my luck, it's too late for that too.

It hurts, that it's about to be final. All I want to do is rip this letter to pieces without even opening it, but I have to face the truth. About everything. It's time to grow the fuck up.

I grab my backpack and the letter and head to my room, the sound of my mom clacking away on her keyboard erased the second I shut the door. I sit on the edge of my bed and insert my index finger under the sealed flap of the envelope, then run it across the seal, opening it.

Dear Melanie, A payment to our office in the amount of $75,000 for the upcoming school year has been made by the Hart Foundation. As a result, your tuition is paid through the end of your freshman year. After tuition, living expenses, and fees, there is an additional $3,956.18 left over. Please contact our office regarding whether you would prefer a check in your name for this amount or the remainder to be carried over and applied to the following year's tuition.

I put my hand to my dizzy head. I kind of feel like I'm reading something in a foreign language. How is it possible that the school received that much money for my tuition? And what is the *Hart Foundation*? Could it have something to do with Mr. and Mrs. Hart from the antique shop? But they don't have money like that.

I'm sweating but freezing, and my body's shaking so hard I can't hold the letter still to read it again.

I double check the envelope, to make sure it's my name on it. It is, but I still don't understand.

"Mom?" I walk on weak legs back out into the living room and hold the letter out to her. "Do you know anything about this?"

"What is it, honey?" She takes it and reads it, then looks up at me. "Is this for real? What's the Hart Foundation?"

I shake my head. "I don't know. Do you think it could be Mr. and Mrs. Hart? From the shop?"

"They don't look like they have this kind of money." She hands the letter back to me. "But then again, you never know, right? People hide all sorts of things. Did you call the school to find out if this is legitimate? Maybe talk to someone in the, what's it called, registrar's office? Or financial department or whatever?"

"It's Sunday. All those offices will be closed."

"Then go ask the Harts."

"Yeah. I'm going now." In my room I strip off Jake's clothes, smelling them for a moment to inhale the scent of his detergent, to feel like he's here with me for a moment, and pull on some clean clothes of my own. Jeans, like usual. My red sneakers. A Station Gray T-shirt. Jake would approve.

Clutching the letter in my hand, I half walk, half jog the mile into town. I'm not sure if the Harts are even back from their trip yet, but I need to know. I need to find out if this is real or not, because I can't let myself get excited if there's a chance it's a joke. A setup. One more way for me to get burned.

The shop's open in the hopes that nonexistent Sunday shoppers will stop by, and before I enter I see Mrs. Hart at the counter, wiping it with a paper towel.

186

As I open the door, she sprays lemon-scented wood cleaner on the counter, and it smells fresh despite the dustiness in the shop.

"Hello, Melanie!" She looks up and smiles, then swipes at the counter some more before putting the can of cleaner on a shelf under the register and tossing the used paper towels into the trash. "You know you don't have to work today, right, dear?"

"Right. I know. I'm just stopping by." I feel silly suddenly. There's no way the money came from Mrs. Hart. This old store filled with mostly useless items is a stark reminder of that. But I have to know.

"Oh, that's nice. It's always nice to see you. Every night when you come in to work after school, I'm in such a hurry to get upstairs and start supper. I don't need to rush off this time."

I approach the counter and, with a shaking hand, slide the letter onto the newly cleaned surface. I take a deep breath. "Mrs. Hart, do you know anything about this? About the Hart Foundation?"

"Oh my, she works fast, our lawyer!" Mrs. Hart reads the letter, her pale pink lips smiling.

"What lawyer? What's going on, Mrs. Hart?"

She looks up at me. "Give me your hands, Melanie."

I do, and she grasps them in hers, soft the way only old people's skin is. Her eyes, blue and deep, meet mine. "It's a gift," she says. "For you. There are no strings attached. Nothing you need to do or say. Nothing you owe."

"I can't... It's too much..."

She shakes her head, scowling at me. "Stop. It's not *enough*. Your life... maybe you haven't told me the details, but living in this town we know everything about everyone. Things haven't been easy for you. And Mr. Hart and I, we love you, Melanie. You are honest. And good. We have no children or grandchildren, and we want to share what we have. With you."

"I'm not good, Mrs. Hart!" I pull my hands from hers and place them on the counter, the need to show her my ugly side, which

I'm positive she knows about but maybe doesn't, so she can make this decision with all the facts. "I've done a lot of things…"

"Stop." She puts her hands up. "I know. Everyone does things they regret."

"And it's too much money anyway."

"It's our money, and we'll decide what's too much. And what we do with it. We're old, the two of us. We run this store because it gives us something to do, but we made some very smart investments a long time ago, and then some more smart investments, and now we have money collecting dust. Well, not *literally*. We're not *that* old-fashioned that we'd have a box of cash under our bed!"

"Right." I'm stunned and dizzy, and I plop down on the armchair near the counter and stare at Mrs. Hart.

"Anyway, dear, we've paid for your first year through a foundation we set up specifically to continue giving money to your education. It's all worked out with a lawyer, and the foundation will pay for your tuition and room and board each year for four years. With a little extra for, you know, random expenses."

There are no words. I have no idea how to express to her how grateful I am, how life-changing this is. Her eyes tell me she knows, but I'm unable to speak.

"You know," she says, filling in the space where I should be talking, "when you told me you'd lost your scholarship, my heart broke for you. I knew I couldn't let that happen. And if I die tomorrow, I'll die knowing I helped you out."

"You saved my *life*," I exclaim. "I'll never be able to thank you and your husband for this."

"Just do well in college, dear. And I have a feeling you will. And maybe send a postcard once in a while."

"I'll send a postcard every single day! I'll send a thousand postcards!" I get up and hug her, my eyes prickling with tears.

Her arms fold around me. She smells floury and sweet, and she whispers into my ear, "I don't have any children or grandchildren. But I like to think of you as my granddaughter. I hope that's all right."

"It's more than all right."

The front door bell clangs as a rare customer comes in. "Now I need to work," says Mrs. Hart. "It's your day off. Go do something fun."

"I will. Thank you."

"You are more than welcome." She smiles at me fondly for a second before turning to the couple that just entered the store. "Hello!" she says. "If you have any questions about anything, please just let me know."

I fly—I seriously feel like my feet aren't touching the ground—out of the shop. Main Street is lit up by the sun, and I don't even care about the ugliness everywhere. Some things are beautiful despite it all. The maple tree on the corner, filling up with spring buds and getting ready to burst into life. The park bench in front of the hardware store that someone recently painted a bright and beautiful shade of shiny blue. A mom pushing a stroller, the kid gripping the string of a big, round pink balloon that hovers above them.

CHAPTER SEVENTEEN – JAKE

I know nothing good's going to happen when my uncle pounds on the front door yelling, "Let me the fuck in, Jake!"

It's my day off, and I just got back from dropping Melanie off at home. My plan for the day was a beer, maybe a nap, then I'd head to the cheap-ass gym at the station to work out if I felt like it. Now, though, Mike's at the door demanding entrance, and he sounds pissed.

"Hold on," I mutter, unlocking the door and opening it.

He pushes it hard, and I step out of the way just in time to avoid getting nailed by it.

"Jesus, Mike." I shut the door after he stalks in. "What the fuck's going on?"

"You tell me. You fucking tell me, Jakey." His face is a mixture of anger and sadness.

"Sit down." I gesture at the couch. "You want something to drink? Beer? Water?"

"No, nothing." He sits, and I occupy the chair across from him.

"What's going on?" I ask again.

"The Cannon girl."

Shit. "Yeah? I found her. Dropped her off at home. Just like I told you earlier."

"You fucking her?"

"Jesus, Mike. You need to be so crass?"

190

"Cut the shit." He sits forward, leaning toward me, his eyes on mine. "Tell me the goddamn truth this time. That's all I want. The truth."

I swallow hard and nod slowly. "We're, uh, involved. Yeah."

"Jesus fucking Christ. What the holy fuck is wrong with you?" He's standing in a heartbeat, walking back and forth in my living room. "I told you to stay the fuck away from her, and that meant out of her pants too."

"I didn't mean for it to happen. We met for the first time before she was in my class, before I knew who she was."

"Please tell me she wasn't a fucking *minor*." Mike's eyes open wide and he stares at me in disbelief. "She was eighteen, right?"

"Yes. She'd just had a birthday. I didn't mean for it to happen," I repeat. "And now..."

"Now? You're fired, Jake."

I stand up too. "Fired? You can't fire me! I'm your nephew, and I'm not even your employee! I'm on loan from the Chicago Police Department."

"Yeah? Then I'm fucking returning you. You've been here long enough. Too long." He stands behind the armchair, resting his hands on it and bending over like he's having a hard time breathing. "What were you *thinking*?"

"Look, I know I shouldn't have gotten involved. But I did before I knew who she was, how young she was. And now..."

"Don't say it." He points a finger at me. "Don't fucking say it."

"And now I think I'm in love with her." I can't hold it back. And it feels damn good to get it out there, to put it into the real world, out of the secret bubble we've been in for so long.

"I told you not to say it." The despair in his voice would almost be funny, if this situation wasn't so fucked up, if our entire relationship didn't suddenly feel like it was on the line.

"She's graduating in a few weeks anyway, and then who knows? College, maybe local. Maybe not. She's not sure. But she's not

191

a kid, all right? She's been pretty much taking care of herself for years since her mother…"

"Is a fucking alcoholic. I know, all right? I've been here a long time. Her dad is in prison. You know that too. You're messing with a delicate girl, Jake. She's needy, and when you leave her—when you leave *here*—it's going to hurt her. I thought you knew better than this. I thought you *were* better than this."

Jesus. "I'm sorry. I'm not going to hurt her. And she's not delicate. She's tough, Mike." But thinking about it makes me cold inside. I never set out to get into a relationship with her. It just sort of happened. I never thought about it or analyzed it or listened to the little voice in the back of my head telling me to stay away. To leave her alone.

And he's right that she's delicate. Because in some ways she's the strongest girl I've ever met. But in others, she's fragile as a glass thread. And I don't want to be the one who breaks her forever.

"You're a damn fool." He looks sad as he heads to the door. "Go back to Chicago, Jake. You got shit to take care of there anyway."

"I'm sorry." I take a few steps toward him, wanting his forgiveness, or at least his understanding.

But he shakes his head. "Save your apology for someone else." And he's gone, shutting the door behind him quietly. It'd have been better if he'd fucking slammed it instead.

I'm about to lock the door when there's another knock, much gentler than my uncle's.

"Jake?" Melanie's voice calls out, and my heart lurches. She must have run into my uncle in the hallway—did he say something to her? I can't imagine he would, and if he did, what would he have said anyway?

I open the door and she bounds into my arms, her body exuding joy I haven't seen in her yet. "I have the best news in the world!" Her face is radiant, her eyes glistening.

192

I can't help smiling back at her, despite the less than fucking stellar conversation I just had with my uncle. "What's going on?"

"Molly." She bends down, her news all but forgotten in her happiness to see the cat. After scooping the orange creature up, she sits on the couch, cat on her lap, and nods at the space next to her. "Sit. I want to tell you something amazing."

I sit close enough so our legs are touching—somehow, being next to her isn't good enough. I have to be in contact too. "So?" I ask.

"You aren't going to believe this. When I went home, there was a letter for me from the University of Chicago. It said that my entire first year had been paid for in full. Everything—tuition, and room and board, and expenses and fees and shit. And there was even some left over for whatever else I need it for."

"What?" I'm at least vaguely aware of how expensive University of Chicago is. "Did the scholarship committee change their minds?"

"No. You know Mrs. Hart? From the antique shop where I work?"

"She paid for it?" *How does that even make sense?*

"Yeah! She and her husband, like, made some good investments a long time ago and apparently have a shit ton of money. So they set up a foundation? Just for my college. And there's enough for all four years. I just… I can't…" She shakes her head in disbelief.

"Are you serious?"

"Yes!" she squeals. "I can't believe it. I just don't know what to think."

"That's… Jesus. That's amazing, Melanie." I put my arm around her and pull her close, so her head rests on my shoulder. "I'm so happy for you. You deserve this."

"You think so?" Her eyes are huge as they look up at me.

"I know so." I lightly kiss her lips.

"It's just… my whole life, or at least for as long as I can remember, I never expected things to work out. Like, I'd hope they

193

would. But I never let myself get excited because I just *knew* that something would eventually go wrong."

"Hope for the best but expect the worst?"

"Exactly." She nods. "So it doesn't seem real. It feels like a joke. Or a trick. You know?"

"But it's not. It's your turn, Melanie. Your turn for great things."

She scratches her cheek distractedly, then looks up at me. "It's kind of how I feel about you too." Her voice is quiet.

"What do you mean?" I ask.

"I don't know. Like I don't deserve you." She looks away and starts petting Molly, who's still cuddled up on her lap.

I close my eyes for a moment, then stroke her hair gently. "The truth, Melanie, is that I feel the same about you." It hurts me to say it, to acknowledge what I'm feeling and make it real by putting it into words. "You're headed to college, and you need to be free to experience everything without being tied down…"

"Stop! Oh my god, I love being with you, Jake! You're the best thing that's ever happened to me. Even better than getting the money for school."

"That's ridiculous." But my heart feels warm to hear her say it. "Come here." I sit back in the corner of the couch and pull her so she's leaning back on me. Her frame is so small—she's still too skinny—and she smells like shampoo. I close my eyes and enjoy the feeling of holding her like this.

Molly purrs gently, and everything feels really fucking *right*. I try to ignore what my uncle said, about breaking her. I try to ignore the gut feeling I have that maybe I need to let her go so I don't hold her back. But we have this moment, and I'm determined to enjoy it.

"Hey," she whispers after a few minutes, shifting in my arms slightly.

"Hey," I say back.

We stay like that, on my couch, for a long time. And I wish we could be frozen in that exact moment forever. I don't want to talk about how I need to move back to Chicago, and soon. I wish reality wouldn't insinuate its ugly self back into our lives, at least not for a very long time. With closed eyes, I listen to Melanie's breath, and the cat's purring, and the light sound of occasional traffic outside my apartment.

• • •

It's not till later that she asks me. Later, after I've made love to her twice, our bodies satiated and exhausted, clinging to each other in bed.

"Was that your uncle?" she asks.

"Who?" I run my finger gently up and down her back.

"When I was coming in, there was a guy leaving. He was, like, pissed."

I take a deep breath. "Yeah, that was my uncle."

"And he's your boss too, right?"

I laugh. "Yeah. Well, he was."

"*Was?*"

I think she knows. Her voice has a hesitance to it, like she doesn't want to ask but needs to hear it.

"He knows about us." I pull her closer to me, our naked bodies warm against each other.

"Oh." Her breath is warm on my chest. "I'm sorry," she adds.

"No, it's not your fault. You have nothing to be sorry for."

"Is that why you said *was*? As in he *was* your boss?"

"I, uh… he said he doesn't need me anymore." Saying he fired me is too hard.

"Wait. What? So what are you going to do?" She sits up and looks down at me, her eyes wary.

"I need to go back to Chicago. I need to go back to work there. And face the shit I left behind." I rub my face with a hand.

"You're leaving."

"Yeah." I sit up too, putting my arm around her. "Yeah, I have to. But you'll be coming to Chicago too, in just a few months, right?"

195

She nods, but I can already feel her pulling away. She breathes in. "Tell me about the shit you left behind. In Chicago. Before, you said you ran away too. I want to know about it."

"It's a long story, Melanie."

"I want to hear it. Come on. You know everything about me and my family and my fucked-up past. I know nothing about yours."

She's right. I sigh. "Yeah, so, my dad was a cop too."

"Was?"

I nod. "He died. About a year ago. I was there when it happened. I watched him bleed out after being shot in the gut. Couldn't get the paramedics there soon enough, and I did everything I could."

"Oh my god. I'm so sorry." She cuddles into me.

"Yeah. I mean. It was fucking horrible. And, you know, I keep going back over it. We were there together on call. And we both did everything right. But he got shot anyway. And it's hard not to keep seeing it, you know, in my head? Replaying it, but changing what happens, so there's a different ending. A different outcome. But it's not fucking like that, and I guess I need to man up and just get over it."

"Maybe. But I don't think people just get over things, you know? You can't make things un-happen."

"There's more," I sigh. I need to say these things out loud. "Back home. I was an only child, and I had a happy childhood. Like, the happiest. I feel guilty saying that, because you didn't have it great when you were a kid. But my mom and dad were so close. Always laughing and joking around. Even their fights ended up with them laughing hysterically together about something."

"That's nice," she whispers.

"Yeah. It was great. When my dad died, my mom was devastated. I mean, she didn't eat for days. She lost so much weight she had to start drinking those nutrition drinks, and we were all worried about her. I would have done anything to make her happy again, you know?"

Melanie nods against my chest.

"But I couldn't. Nothing I did helped her at all. And I was grieving too, so it was hard. It was really hard. Then she, uh, met someone." I'm struck with guilt suddenly, realizing what an asshole I've been by begrudging her happiness. "He's, well, a poet. And teaches poetry at the college level. It was really hard for me to see my mom with this guy after she'd been happy with my dad for my entire life. And they have a foster kid. This is actually their second one. The first went back to his home or something. I don't know the details. I should fucking know the details. But I never call her anymore."

"Because she has a boyfriend?"

I wince at the word. "Yeah. I guess. I feel guilty as hell because I still think I'm responsible for my dad's death. Or that I should have stopped it. And now she's starting all over. Brand new fucking life. She shouldn't have to do that."

"No." Melanie pulls away from me so she can look into my eyes. "See, it's *not* a brand new life at all. We never get a brand new life. We only have the same life, the one we've been given. And things happen. And time passes. And we can't travel back, but we can just keep going, you know? And try to make things better day by day. That's what I'm trying to do now. I think it's probably what your mom is trying to do too."

"You're too smart for your own good." I grin at her and push her down onto the bed.

She giggles, and I kiss her gently and think about her words, about trying to make things better day by day. I only wish I could be sure that I'm the best thing for her.

197

CHAPTER EIGHTEEN — MELANIE

The library's basement classroom is even more drab without Jake as the teacher. Some chubby cop has taken over, and he makes dumb jokes and *tries*, but it's painful to sit through class.

It's painful, too, to pass Jake's apartment, to know he's no longer there. He's back in Chicago. And even though we promised all sorts of things to each other—we'll talk every day, we'll text all the time—I feel like we're growing apart by the minute.

Graduation's coming up, and prom, which of course I'm skipping. Stacey's on the prom committee, and though we don't talk, I see her hanging up posters and giggling in the hallways about dresses and shopping and renting hotel rooms for after parties.

But I don't care. I'm almost done. Out of here. Chicago and college are so close I can touch them.

On prom night, I stay home. My mom goes to bed early, and I sit on the living room couch watching videos on my phone. All I can think about is how Jake showed up that one time with Thai food. Part of me believes he'll do that again, that he's driven back from Chicago because he knows it's my prom, and he'll knock on the door with a huge bag of food, and we'll go to his vacant apartment and eat out of the containers while we sit on the floor, like a picnic. And then he'll make love to me, over and over again, so I know he's mine and I'm his.

But he doesn't show up. I go to bed and lie awake for hours, listening to cars pass by every once in a while and wondering if things are over or just beginning.

We text a little bit.

Me: All the assholes are at prom tonight.

Jake: Why didn't you go??

Me: Not my thing.

Jake: You're probably not missing much.

Then nothing from him for the rest of the night. I wanted him to say: *If I was there I'd be your date.* Or: *I'll take you out to make up for it when you get to Chicago.* But he just gets silent, and I refuse to be the one always keeping the conversation going. I have too much pride for that.

Graduation comes and goes without Jake too. We talk sometimes, and I know he's busy getting back into his job in Chicago, and spending time with his mother. But I can't help feeling — knowing—that he's making excuses. That the distance I feel isn't just because we're not in close proximity. It's another kind of distance, the kind that can't be overcome by an hour drive to visit someone. And speaking of visits, so far he hasn't come back once to see me. There are a lot of reasons: I'm working this weekend. I'm helping my mom move.

But I can't shake the feeling that if he really *wanted* to see me, he would.

• • •

"Why don't you move to Chicago now?" Mrs. Hart is wiping down the knife display case when she turns to me with a smile.

It's a bright day in early June, the sun streaming through the front windows that I just cleaned. Molly is curled up in a cat bed by the front door sleeping. Since Jake moved, she's been living here. My mom's allergic so I couldn't take her home, and Mrs. Hart was glad to have her.

"Move now? School doesn't start till late August." I put the spray bottle of glass cleaner under the counter and sit on the stool.

"Honey, I can see it in your eyes." She stands in front of me, her own eyes kind and soft. "You're ready to go. There's extra money in the account. You could probably get into the dorms early. Or get an apartment, if that's what you'd rather do. I want you to be happy. You deserve it."

"I don't know." But inside, I'm shivering with excitement. The thought's crossed my mind, but I didn't think I could really *do* it. Maybe, though, I can.

Summer in Chicago. Bustling downtown. The busy and beautiful lakefront. Stores and shops and people and the chance to really *live*.

Mrs. Hart takes my hands in hers. "What's keeping you here, Melanie? Not this job, certainly!" She laughs. "You're done with school. Not that I'm trying to get rid of you, mind you! But I'm ready to see you make something of yourself. And I'm ready to see you happy."

"I'm ready to be happy," I say. It's true. I am.

• • •

Sight unseen, except for photos online, I rent a tiny apartment in a red brick three-flat near the university. I'm on the middle floor, with two students above me and one below me. The landlord says I can have a cat, so I'll bring Molly with me.

Mrs. Hart plans a small going-away party for me behind the antique shop, on a patch of brownish grass. It's a warm day, and I make lemonade from a powder mix that I buy at Save Lot. Mrs. Hart makes me a grocery list, including the lemonade powder and a package of iced oatmeal cookies, and some deli meat and crackers, and we set up a few plates of food.

Principal Evans comes, and my mom, and of course Mr. and Mrs. Hart, and even Mr. Tallman, my math teacher.

I didn't tell Jake about the party, but I still wish he'd show up, that somehow he'd found out about it and decided to surprise me. I'd be half-embarrassed and kind of horrified, since everyone would know our secret. But he doesn't come.

I haven't even told him I'm moving to Chicago early. It's a huge deal, but that's the problem. I don't want to put pressure on him, especially when he's being distant. I don't want him to think I'm moving now because of him, that I need him, that I'm trying to get his attention.

But maybe I should let him know. So when I'm packing up the leftover party food after everyone's gone home, I dial his number. But it goes to voicemail, and I don't bother leaving a message.

● ● ●

My mom helps me load a giant duffel bag that came through the antique shop into the trunk of her crappy old car. It's stuffed with my clothes and bedding. The apartment comes partially furnished—at least there will be a bed and couch and a small kitchen table with two chairs. Which is good because I don't have much to bring.

I have two boxes of books and odds and ends I don't want to leave behind. And Molly's stuff—litter box, bucket of fresh litter, cat bed, the giant scratching post treehouse that Jake bought. I actually think she's got more luggage than I do.

With Molly mewling in the cage in the backseat, my mom and I set off for Chicago. My heart beats hard with excitement the farther we get from Bells Park and the closer we get to my new home. Even the taped-up vinyl car seats don't bother me, scratching my bare leg. I've got on a tank top, and the window's rolled down—there's no AC in this car—and the breeze blowing back my hair is fresh and real and makes me feel so alive.

We hit traffic just outside Chicago, and I stare at the tall buildings and cars and people as we drive into the city.

"I'm going to miss you." My mom glances over at me before turning her eyes back to the road.

"I'll miss you too." I think I will. Not right away, but eventually. "You'll stay busy, right, Mom?"

She laughs. "That rapper, Kenlo, really got me noticed. I have so many followers on YouTube, you wouldn't even believe it!"

I wouldn't believe it if I hadn't seen it—she has hundreds of thousands of followers, enough people viewing her videos that she's making money off ad revenue. Who knows how long it will last, but for now, I'm happy for her. Thinking about her in the dark house drinking wine and clacking away at her keyboard is sad, but knowing she's enjoying herself makes it easier to think about.

The landlord's name is Simon Chooch, and he's a strange man with a whimsical lilt to his voice. He gives me the key to my apartment, sticks his fingers into Molly's cage (she hisses at him), and hands me a card with his number so I can call if anything breaks in the apartment.

New leaves are growing on vines that crawl over the bricks of the building, and the street it's on is both busy and homey. It's midafternoon, and there are people my age or a little older sitting on front porches and walking down the street, and it's hard to keep my heart from soaring. This is it. I'm *here*.

My mom helps me bring my stuff up to the apartment, and then she hugs me awkwardly and leaves, heading back to Bells Park. I guess I should feel scared or nervous at suddenly being alone in a new place. But I don't. My apartment is small, but the living room has huge windows looking out at the street, and the old wooden floors are scratched but shiny, and even the couch, though obviously old, is more comfortable than the one back home.

The bedroom is minuscule—just barely enough room for the twin bed and dresser that came with the place. And the kitchen has just enough space for one person to cook, then a tiny area by the back door with a table for two.

The floors creak, and the windows need to be propped up with a piece of two by four to stay open, and the paint on the doorframes is chipping, but there's so much natural light. And it's *mine*.

CHAPTER NINETEEN – JAKE

Lance, my mom's boyfriend, holds out two beers. "Your choice," he says. "I've got a Heineken and an olive-infused single batch craft beer from a local brewery."

"*Olive*-infused?"

"Oh, it's better than you'd think!"

"Nah. Give me the Heineken," I say. I flash back to that night at Lucy's in Bells Park, when the bartender told me craft beer is for pussies. I like craft beer, but even I have my limits, and olive-infused is one of them. I push from my mind the thoughts of what else happened that night, how it was the first time I met Melanie. How I haven't talked to her in a while, and that's fucked up. I'm not going to think about that right now.

I follow Lance into the living room of the spacious bungalow where he and my mom live. Lance is tall and thin, and he's wearing skinny jeans rolled up at the bottom with a tucked-in shirt and suspenders. His beard is long, and I'm pretty sure his glasses are for show, not prescription. In short: he's an aging hipster who teaches and writes poetry. And makes my mother happy.

She smiles as we enter the room, and I think she even blushes when Lance takes her hand and kisses it. I look away. It's strange. Different from the exuberant relationship she had with my dad, where they laughed, and he'd pick her up and swing her around. My dad, who would never have rolled up his jeans or worn glasses just for his image.

But Melanie was right when she said it's not a new life for my mom. She's not starting over. She's living her one life, and it's not up to me to decide how. The only thing that matters is that she's happy. And it's clear from the glow in her eyes that she is.

"I need some, uh, help with my homework." Jacey, the thirteen-year-old foster child who's been living with my mom and Lance, trudges into the room, her head down. I've met her a few times, and it hurts to see how broken she is, how much she's been through. My mom's told me Jacey's father isn't in the picture, and her mother is currently in rehab for a meth addiction. Presumably, Jacey will go back with her mom when she gets out; there's a sober-living facility that aims to reunite children with their parents. But this isn't the first time they've been through this.

Lance jumps up, too eager in his response. "Let's go sit down in the kitchen!"

Jacey rolls her eyes but follows, plodding behind him slowly.

"At least she's doing homework," I say softly.

My mom nods, pushing her brownish-graying hair behind one ear. "She actually does quite well in school. She's a bright child. Just in an unfortunate situation." I can see in the worry lines around her eyes how much she cares.

"It's great, what you're doing. You and Lance."

"We both just felt like we're at a place right now where we can help out. We're not planning to change anyone's life, but if we can provide even a small bit of hope or a glimmer of something different, we need to at least try. Jacey," she nods toward the kitchen, "is so smart, but her home life…"

I nod. "It's like… um…" I stammer, run my hand through my hair.

"Like what?" My mom, never missing a beat, looks at me attentively.

I shake my head. "Jesus. I don't know if I should tell you this."

She sits forward in her chair. "Honey, you can tell me anything. You know that."

"Yeah, well. This is kind of messed up. So messed up it's why Uncle Mike and I aren't talking right now."

"Hmm." She sits back again. "I thought something was going on. I talked to him two weeks or so ago, and when I asked about how things had gone with you out in Bells Park, he changed the subject. But I didn't pry."

I take a deep breath. "It's, uh... There's a girl, Mom."

"OK." Her tone is really matter-of-fact. But I know it won't be when I give her the details, all the ugly, sordid truths.

"She's young. Eighteen. And she was in high school when we started, um, seeing each other."

A muscle twitches in my mom's cheek, but she manages to keep her face even and nonjudgmental. I want to stop telling her about this, but I need to get it off my chest, and I need her advice about what to do. About whether or not I'd be totally fucking up Melanie's future by seeing her again.

"She comes from a messed-up family. Like Jacey. Her dad's in prison and pretty much nonexistent in her life. Her mom's a full-time alcoholic. Drinking all day and all night. Honestly? Melanie probably would have been better off in a foster home, but somehow she managed to survive and excel in school and do great. She got, uh, a scholarship to University of Chicago. She's smart."

I pause, and my mom nods for me to continue, her face still a mask of neutrality.

"Right. So. She got caught with drugs in her locker, but they weren't hers. She took the blame for her friend and had to participate in this drug program I was teaching out in Bells Park for Uncle Mike."

"Oh, Jake." Finally my mom speaks. "Why would you... How could you..."

I shake my head. "I don't know. I met her before I'd started teaching the class, and she lied about her age and who she was. From the moment I saw her, something… it's hard to explain. Something changed inside my heart. Or my soul. Like a shift. A continental shift of my soul. That sounds fucking stupid."

"No. It doesn't sound stupid. But what you did *was* stupid."

"I know. It's why Uncle Mike isn't speaking to me. He asked me to leave. I was ready to go anyway, but when he found out about me and Melanie…"

"Melanie." She says the name like she's trying it out. "Where is she now? Back in Bells Park?"

I nod. "Yeah. She'll be moving to Chicago soon for college."

"Are you two still together? Are you talking?"

I massage my jaw with one hand. "Not really. I, uh, I've been avoiding her."

"Is she too needy?"

"No. It's not that. Uncle Mike said something to me, about how she's fragile, even though she seems tough. About how I'll break her if I'm not careful, and I guess I don't know how to be careful."

She sighs, a smile gracing her lips. "You do, though. You remember all those strays you brought home when you were a kid? How you begged us to let you keep them? And then you volunteered all your time at the animal shelter in high school? The kind of person who does that knows how to be gentle. You're not going to break anyone, Jake. Do you love her?"

"Yes." My heart pounds at the thought, at the fact that I'm sitting here and talking about the girl I love, and that I can admit it out loud, to someone else.

"Then tell her."

"Am I going to fuck up her future by tying her down now? Shouldn't I let her be free to experience, I don't know, *life*?"

My mom laughs, her eyes sparkling as she does. "If a dad in prison and an alcoholic mom didn't fuck up her future, then neither

206

will a good man with a big heart. And she *is* free to experience life. This *is* her life, and you can choose to be in it or not."

I stand and pace, the next thing I want to say even harder for some reason. Finally I turn to my mom. "I need to apologize to you."

"For what?"

"For not letting you live *your* life. For wanting you to grieve for Dad longer. For not giving Lance a chance sooner because I thought I knew what was best for you, which makes no fucking sense. Sorry for swearing," I add.

She comes to me, taking my hands in hers. "Oh, Jake. I suppose I did take up with Lance sooner than anyone expected. It was definitely sooner than I expected. I thought I'd spend the rest of my life alone, and I was fine with that. My memories of your father are so wonderful that I could live on them forever. But, when you meet someone and, like you said, your soul changes, shifts, even a little bit, you can't walk away from that. I love you, honey."

"I love you too, Mom." I hug her tight, and when Lance comes back into the living room I hug him too, not tight—he gets a stiff man-hug and pat on the back—and he looks at me in surprise but smiles all the same.

"I'll see you guys," I say. "I've got somewhere to be."

• • •

Melanie's phone goes straight to voicemail, so I text her instead: *I need to see you. I'm so sorry I haven't been around lately. I'm an asshole, and I'm stupid, and I don't deserve you. But please let me know where we can meet.*

It's more than I've texted her over the past two weeks combined, I think, and what an asshole I've been hits me hard. It's one thing to need to take time or think about things. It's a whole other thing to send one-word responses to someone you supposedly love. *Do* love. I'm a goddamn asshole, and I hope she can forgive me.

There's not much traffic, and I make it to Bells Park in record time: forty-seven minutes exactly, when normally it take at least an hour.

I'm outside Melanie's house when my phone finally bings with a response from her. *You ARE an asshole. But I'll meet you. Wanna come to my place?*

The grin on my face is unstoppable, and my fingers, I swear, are fucking shaking as I type back, *Yeah. I'm outside right now.*

A few seconds later she responds: *Uh, no, you're not. Anyway, you don't even have my address. Do you?? (stalker)*

No way. She already fucking moved, and I wasn't there to help or be a part of it. Just like I didn't go to her graduation. Or anything else.

Maybe I'll hang out with your mom instead, I text. *Send me your address. I'll be there in less than an hour.*

She texts it to me, and I start to drive to the expressway, but turn around. I have one more stop to make.

• • •

James looks surprised but grins broadly when I enter the station. "Hey, man! Whatcha doing here? And thanks for leaving me to teach that fucking class, asshole."

"Just trying to keep you out of the house so you don't eat so much. Speaking of which, you look like you've lost a few pounds. Been working out?"

"Yeah. Gotta stay in shape so I can keep up with my *girlfriend.*" He raises an eyebrow and nods.

"The one I met at Lucy's that one night?"

"The very one."

"Are you dating both of them?"

"No, man. Just one. And we're exclusive, you know." He looks happy and proud, and I'm glad to see him doing so well.

"My uncle in?"

James nods, and I head back to my uncle's office. He's on his computer, and when he sees me, he freezes, then gestures me in.

"What are you doing here?" His voice isn't exactly cold, but it's not exactly welcoming either.

"I, uh, was in the neighborhood. Wanted to talk."

He nods slowly. "So talk."

"I was wrong. It was wrong, what I did. Getting involved. It was a mistake, professionally at least. I want to apologize to you."

"Yeah." He scratches at something on his desk, then looks up at me again. "Look, Jakey. I love you, kid. I always have, and I always will. You're a good kid. A good *man*. I don't want to see you fuck up. I want you to have all the best that life has to offer."

"Thanks."

"When your dad died, it was…" He pauses. "It fucking killed me. I lost my brother. But you lost your father. I need to look out for you and give you the best advice I can. But I don't want anything to come between us. We're family, Jake. And we always will be."

My eyes tear up, and I tense my face to keep from crying. "I love you, Mike."

"I love you too, Jake."

I shift from one foot to another. "So I'll, uh, see you…"

"You here to see her?"

Fuck. I was hoping he wouldn't ask, though I guess I knew it would come up. How could it not?

I clear my throat. "Yeah. I am."

"She's gone already."

"Yup. Just figured that out."

He nods and looks in my eyes. "You already know what I think. But I'm here for you no matter what. Got it?"

"Got it. Thanks."

He comes around the desk and hugs me, awkward and stiff at first, but then I feel the warmth and love he's always given me. We're family. And that will never change.

I say bye to James and tell him to visit me soon. "You can bring your girlfriend," I say with a wink.

Then I drive way the fuck faster than I should all the way back to Chicago.

CHAPTER TWENTY – MELANIE

He's scruffy. Like usual. And his jeans are fitted. Also like usual. His eyes are desperate, and his lips are gorgeous, and he's carrying a bag that smells like Thai food. I want to kiss him hard, now.

But I'm not that easy.

Molly is, though. She meows as she approaches Jake, purring louder than she ever has before.

"Hey. Looks like you're healing really well." His voice is gentle as he bends down to pet her.

"Come in." I step aside so he can enter, and I watch him take in the apartment, feeling proud of it. My very own first place.

"This is nice." His smile is warm. "Can I put this in the kitchen?" He's uncharacteristically shy, asking permission this way.

"Of course. Come on. It's not like it's hard to find. There's basically three rooms: living room, kitchen, bedroom. Oh, and a bathroom of course." I head to the kitchen, assuming he's following. I want to look at him, but I'm trying to play it cool. Like he did for the past few weeks.

He sets the food on the little table by the back door and stands, shifting his weight from foot to foot. He's staring at his boots, but finally he looks up at me.

"Hi." His voice is quiet.

I tilt my head and try to suppress the smile that's threatening to spread across my face. "Hi," I repeat.

"I'm sorry, Melanie. I, um, wasn't sure…"

"What?" Coldness seeps into my soul, all the warmth I'd been starting to feel chased out by the iciness of his doubt.

"I didn't want to hurt you."

"What a fucking line." I roll my eyes and turn, stalking into the living room.

"It's not a line." He's behind me, and when I sit on the couch, he paces in front of me.

"*It's not you, it's me.* Or, wait, maybe *You deserve better.* That's a good one."

"Melanie…"

But I'm not done. "I got one, and this one really applies. *I don't want to hold you back.* Is that the right one, Jake?" I cross my arms over my chest and look out the window.

"That last one. Yeah." He gives a half-laugh.

I look at him sharply. "Seriously? That's what you came here to tell me?"

"God, no, Melanie. I came to see if you'd take me back. I *thought* I was holding you back. I was worried about you living your life with nothing to stop you. I wanted you to be free, to make whatever choices were the best for you and your future."

"See, and that's the problem, isn't it? You've always thought you had to take care of me. I don't know how many times I need to tell you I'm not a kid."

"You're not. And I was wrong. I'm trying to tell you I was wrong." He sits on the couch, turning his body so he's facing me. "Look. How are you going to, I don't know, have illegal drinking parties with your college friends if you're dating a cop?" He lifts a corner of his mouth up in a grin.

This time I can't help smiling back, even though it's a tiny smile.

"You're supposed to be trying to sneak into bars with your buddies and staying up all night studying and, I don't know, doing typical college things." He takes one of my hands and holds it in both of his, rubbing his thumb over my palm gently.

"Except my life till now hasn't exactly been typical. And I don't think it ever will be," I whisper.

"No." His fingers gently lift my chin so we're looking into each other's eyes. "Your life isn't going to be typical, Melanie. It's going to be absolutely extraordinary. Like you."

His lips are so gentle on mine, like he's asking permission. I give it to him, biting his lower lip so he growls, a low and predatory sound.

"I love you." His throaty words vibrate against my skin. "I'm sorry I have been a total and complete asshole for the past few weeks. You deserve better."

"See. I *knew* it!" I joke. "That's a total breakup line."

He throws his head back and laughs. "Except I don't want to break up. I want us to be together, Melanie. I love you. I love you. I love you. I'll keep saying it until you take me back."

I roll my eyes. "Fine. I'll take you back."

"I have to warn you, though." His face gets serious, a frown dragging down his lips.

"What, Jake?" My pulse kicks up. I don't want bad news.

"My mom? She's going to think you're way too skinny. And she's going to be dropping food off for you *all the time*. And inviting you over for dinner, where she'll insist that you have second servings of everything, especially dessert. And her boyfriend? He's this old hipster who writes poetry and, after a glass of wine, likes to recite it as entertainment. Are you sure you're up for all that?" He's grinning, and his fingers whisper along my cheek.

His mother. His family. This is *real*. "Yeah," I say. "I'm up for all that. As long as I can meet your grandma, the one who listens to Station Gray."

"Definitely." He laughs. "What else are you up for?" His lips are on my neck, gently biting the delicate skin.

I gasp. "Um…" It's hard to speak with his tongue tracing its way down to my shoulder. I push him so he's sitting back on the couch and straddle him, feeling his hardness immediately. "I can tell what *you're* up for, though," I whisper, smiling as I kiss his lips.

He growls out a laugh. "I want you now, right here on the couch. And in your bedroom. Then in the shower would probably be a good idea. But maybe I should feed you first. I brought Thai food."

"Yes," I answer. "All of that. Let's do it all."

I can't speak anymore because his kisses leave me breathless. Sun is streaming in through the window, Jake is here with me, there's food in the kitchen, and I know, with a sudden and fierce certainty, that I can do whatever I want.

My world, which used to seem bleak and small and dark, is open wide in front of me.

• • •

Later, after we have sex on the couch, quietly because the curtains are sheer and it was daytime, and in bed then in the shower, we eat room-temperature take-out at the small kitchen table.

"Do you need to, like, go to work tonight or anything?" I ask.

"Day off," he says. "We'll figure it all out. Our schedules and everything."

"Yeah. So. You can stay for awhile, if you want. Or go home. Or whatever." I'm suddenly shy, unsure of how to navigate our new relationship in this new place.

"You think I'm going to fuck you, eat your food, and take off?" He raises an eyebrow at me and smirks.

I shrug, but I can't help smiling back.

"We have an entire city I need to show you," he says. "Let's start now."

"Yeah!" I can't wait to go new places with someone, to discover all the amazing things Chicago has to offer. "Where are you going to take me?"

"I don't know yet. Come on." He grabs my hand and pulls me up.

I grab my bag and keys and phone and we're out the door. We get in his car, and I don't ask where we're going. I don't need to. I trust him, and I can't remember the last time I really trusted someone.

He puts his hand, big and warm, on my leg while he drives, and I shut my eyes for a moment, relaxing in the bliss of everything that's happened today.

"Don't." His voice interrupts my thoughts.

"Don't what?"

"Don't close your eyes, Melanie. This city is yours now. You've got to see it. I'm going to take you down Lake Shore Drive."

We're driving, buildings on one side, the lake, so huge I can't see across, on the other. Boats dot the water, and though it's early evening bikers and joggers make their way along the lakefront path. The city sparkles, and my soul does too. I lower my window to feel the wind on my face, cool and alive and filled with promise.

THE END

A NOTE FROM THE AUTHOR

Thanks for reading Rough Around the Soul! If you liked it, please leave me a review on Amazon.com or Goodreads. Reviews help indie authors get noticed, so it would mean a lot to me if you shared your thoughts.

I've gotten a bunch of questions about the book, so I decided to include a short FAQ:

Why a taboo romance? I've been asked why I was motivated to write about an eighteen year old girl and an older guy. The answer is that I think taboo romance is really hot! And to be honest, when I was younger (well before I was happily married to the best guy in the world, of course!), I always had a thing for older guys. So this story was one I've wanted to write for some time.

Where did you come up with the title? I have lots of really awesome neighbors, and one night we were drinking and talking about romance novels and other wildly inappropriate things. This one guy, who's super burly and rugged, used the phrase "rough around the soul" to describe someone, and I thought it was so honest and beautiful and committed it to memory so I could use it someday.

Is Station Gray a real band? No, but it should be! I imagine the band to be a mixture of Gorillaz, the Beastie Boys, and Dido. I came up with the name using a random word generator until I found two words that sounded good together. My 13 year old came up with the idea for the logo (an old station wagon).

ABOUT THE AUTHOR

Maria Monroe is a contemporary romance author who lives just outside Chicago, where she was born and raised. The author of more than six novels, she attended the Writers' Workshop at the University of Iowa and is now part of the Published Author Network (PAN) of the Romance Writers of America.

Follow her here:
graffitifiction.com
facebook.com/mariamonroeauthor
twitter.com/authormaria

Find more of Maria's books:
amazon.com/author/mariamonroe

Enjoy this sample of the sexy college romance novel Julian & Lia by Maria Monroe!

Chapter One

"Oh my god. I'm so sorry." I put a hand over my face and turn to run out of the dorm bathroom.

"No, it's cool. We're almost done here," says a girl as she sits straddling the sink, her back against the mirror. I think I recognize her from down the hall.

"Almost done" apparently refers to her boyfriend shaving her *down there* while she smiles lazily at him. He dips the razor into the steaming water from the tap—how come it never gets that hot in the shower?—then runs it along her crotch before rinsing it off again.

He turns and grins at me. "You're next if you're interested," he says with a wink. "Just, you know, drop 'em and hop on up." He gestures at the sink next to the one where his girlfriend sits.

"Stop!" shrieks the girl, hitting him playfully. "Leave her alone. I think that's Greer's roommate," she adds in a whisper and tosses her hair back. How in the world her hair is so smooth and shiny is a total mystery to me, as are most things related to hair and makeup. Or fashion of any kind, to be honest. Their laughter bounces off the tiled bathroom walls.

I can't believe she's sitting there on display and doesn't even care that I'm here. Yet I'm strangely transfixed by the two of them. How is it possible to ever get to the point where you can be that comfortable with someone else? Jealousy swirls up inside me, and the loneliness that I've been feeling since starting college a few weeks ago intensifies. It's not lost on me that my identity here is defined by the fact that I room with Greer; I'm pretty sure nobody except my roommate even knows my name, and that's only because she was assigned to live with me.

"It's OK, I'll just . . . " I let the words trail off as I hurry out of the bathroom and back down the hall to my room. Once inside, I slam the door and throw myself on the bed. I realize that I'm being melodramatic, but I can't help it. Besides, there's nobody to witness my episode of self-pity; Greer spent last night in a friend's room. Down the hall. Because apparently it's so much more fun to be in someone else's room than stuck here with me.

For what has to be the millionth time I wonder why I decided to move into a coed dorm. It's three weeks into my freshman year at college, and I should be used to things by now. Everyone around me seems to be so comfortable, already moving around campus in little whispering groups, meeting each other outside the dining hall before heading upstairs into the mess of noise and smells that is, to say the least, overwhelming when you don't have anyone to sit with. Which I don't. People are already hooking up, couples already formed, and I'm not even comfortable peeing in the dorm bathroom.

There's no time to wallow in regret, though, because I have a class in ten minutes. I'll use the bathroom somewhere on the way to class, since I don't want to take the chance of walking in on the shaving couple again. Or the "mad crapper" from down the hall, who spends at least twenty minutes every day straining so loudly in the bathroom that the R.A. has written him up twice already. Apparently he's planning some sort of revenge on the R.A., and everyone on the floor seems to be in on it, except for me.

I pull on a jacket and head out to my Film Studies class, which I decided to take as an elective because the rest of my schedule is filled with boring requirements like math and English. The class is fun, and it's early, which, pathetically, makes me happy. My favorite time of the day is morning. I like campus best when there aren't many other students so my complete lack of friends isn't so conspicuous.

I use the bathroom and grab a coffee at the cafeteria, then pull the sleeves of my jacket over my hands and huddle into myself against the cold as I hurry down the sidewalk. I'm pretty sure I'm late, and I glance down at my watch for a second.

I run, hard, into someone. Hot coffee spills onto my hand and also onto the first thing I see, an arm covered in a gray sweatshirt. *Oh my god.*

"The *fuck*?" says a low masculine voice.

I stare at the coffee stain on that gray sweatshirt, not daring to look up. "I'm sorry. I'm so sorry," I stammer, my eyes still refusing to see whom I've assaulted. *Great. Making friends all over the place.*

There's no response after the initial harsh words, and finally I raise my gaze, right into the eyes of *him*, that guy from my Film Studies class. Julian. The one who always sits in the back corner, scruffy and slouchy and half asleep, but redeemed completely whenever he answers a question, which is seldom, and proves himself to be insanely smart. He's not a freshman—that much is obvious—and I'm not even sure why he's in the morning class when he can barely keep his eyes open. Now, he stands before me, a pissed off look on his face as he peers out from under the hood of a gray sweatshirt and looks at the coffee spilled on his arm.

"Oh. Hi," I say, blushing furiously and trying to talk my cheeks out of turning pink, but failing miserably.

He doesn't respond, just stares at me, a perfect mix of annoyance and amusement on his face. A corner of his mouth turns up in a sneer.

"We're in class together?" I continue. "Now. I mean, in a few minutes. Film Studies?" It feels like I'm physically unable to stop the stupid words cascading out of my mouth. I'm usually quiet, pathologically so, but when I get nervous, it's all I can do to keep myself from rambling on and on. "Anyway, I'm sorry. For, you know, crashing into you?"

Shut up, I will myself. *Just. Stop. Talking.*

His eyes are so green, surrounded by a ring of brown, and he looks so different from, and older than, the Abercrombie contingent that lives in my dorm. Instead of being clean-shaven and preppy, he has the distinct look of someone who doesn't give a fuck. Because he doesn't have to. Those eyes, and that stubble on his jaw, and that look like he's just gotten out of bed and thrown on whatever clothes he could grab is enough to make me feel tingly inside.

For a few seconds there is silence, and I have to use all my will power to stop myself from senselessly babbling again. When he speaks, his voice is low and with an edge to it, like he wants to laugh but is holding back, and also like he's a little bit pissed.

"As stimulating as this conversation is, I've got to get to class," he says. Then, to my horror, he mimics my tone and adds, "It starts in a few minutes? Film Studies? We have it together?"

With that he turns and saunters off, the frayed cuffs of his jeans almost scraping the ground. For a second I think—hope—he's going to turn around and smile or wink, something to let me know his joking was fun and not mean, but he doesn't.

"It starts in a few minutes? Film Studies? We have it together?" The words, his mocking tone, echo in my brain.

"Oh my god," I whisper to myself. "That was the worst *ever*."

I stand completely still, not wanting to seem like I'm following him or, God forbid, trying to catch up to him. Should I skip class? I could avoid him that way, but the one thing I've got going for me is my grades, and I'm not about to give that up. I'll just have to suck it up and admit, once again, that my reality never matches up to my fantasies. It never even comes close. The truth is, I've thought of Julian before. In my day dreams, it happens almost exactly like it just did, or at first it does. But in my imagination I'm collected and sexy, and Julian reveals his hidden kind side, and maybe we have lunch together, or coffee, or watch a movie, realizing we have tons in common besides one single shared class at nine in the morning. The actual encounter, though, was worse than awkward. I'm a dork, and he

221

is, sad to say, an asshole. And I wish, not for the first time, that I'm somebody else, somebody witty and sexy and able to turn a chance encounter into something more.

***

In class we're watching the old 1974 version of The Great Gatsby. I've read the book about a dozen times—it has just about the best last line of any novel I've ever read—but the movie is so boring. How people ever considered Robert Redford a heartthrob boggles my mind, or maybe I'm just attracted to dirtier, messier guys. Like Julian.

As usual, he's sitting in the back corner seat of the classroom, legs sprawled out in front of him like he doesn't quite fit into the desk. Also as usual, his jeans are rumpled, like he picked them up from the floor of his bedroom and put them on. He hasn't taken off his gray hoodie, but he's unzipped it slightly, and I can see a black T-shirt under it. For some reason I can't stop looking at his neck, and I keep thinking about touching it, running my finger along the top of his T-shirt. And then . . . I don't know what I'd do then. My innocence frustrates me, mostly because I never chose to be a prude. It just sort of worked out that way. I never had a boyfriend, so I never had any experience. Then I was afraid to find a boyfriend because I didn't know what I was doing, and so on: a vicious cycle of unwanted innocence.

I don't realize I'm staring until suddenly Julian catches my gaze, a grin spreading across his face, but it's a slightly menacing expression rather than a friendly one. When he lifts an eyebrow at me in recognition—of what? when I slammed into him this morning?—I blush, like usual, and look away.

The movie starts, and I scribble idly in my notebook. I want so badly to look back at him, but I'm sitting a few rows ahead, and it would be obvious; there's nothing to see back there except Julian. Class has never felt so long. I'm restless in my seat, unable to focus on anything but Julian. It's like I can *feel* him back there behind me. And in my mind, he's all I can see. That jaw, that neck, that chest, not quite visible under his sweatshirt. He looks so much older than any of the guys in my dorm, like a man as opposed to a teenager, and I feel a tingling begin, subtle but there, between my legs. I shift slightly to try to get rid of the feeling, and, as surreptitiously as possible, sneak a look back—I can't resist any longer.

He's looking at me, like he was waiting for me to turn around. There's that grin again, that cocky smile that leaves me both thrilled and inexplicably terrified. I whip my head back to the front of the room, hearing a low laugh from behind me, even though there was nothing funny happening in the movie. Or I don't think there was; it's not like I've been paying attention.

"Ms. Hudson." Professor Chooch's voice startles me into attention, and I cringe and slink down lower in my seat as he says, simply, "The movie's in the front of the room."

Oh god! My heart is pounding and my cheeks are flushed and hot. At least the room is dark so nobody can see.

Julian & Lia is available on Amazon.com.